SCRAPYARD SHIP

Mark Wayne McGinnis

Copyright

Edited by:
Lura Lee Genz
Mia Manns
Rachel Weaver

Avenstar Productions
14717 Vine Street
Thornton, Co. 80602
www.markwaynemcginnis.com

ISBN: 13: 978-1493526543
        10: 1493526545

Dedication

To the wonderful, inspirational women in my life:

My Mother, My Sister, My Loving Wife.

Prologue

"Captain, we'll intersect with the Banyan in… looks like two minutes," Ensign Smothers reported, looking almost as weary as the captain felt.

"What's the last count—now that the Malgos have turned tail on us and run?" Captain Larimer asked him, with contempt and disgust in his voice.

"We still have close to two thousand vessels, sir."

"That means little to me, Ensign, break it down."

"Twenty super carriers, one hundred heavy battle cruisers, seven hundred light battle cruisers, six hundred destroyers, and an assortment of smaller corvettes, private schooners, trawlers, supply tankers… anything that's space worthy and packs a punch is here, holding the line." The ensign got up and stretched. "Coffee, sir?"

"Yeah, three sugars," the captain said, looking up and realizing the bridge was nearly deserted. He'd sat straight through two shifts, getting up only for bathroom breaks and coffee. Their warship was the largest, most sophisticated vessel the United Planetary Alliance had constructed yet—a super carrier on a massive scale. At almost a mile long, the Prodigy was capable of launching hundreds of fighters in mere minutes. Two hundred rail guns and who the hell knew how many plasma pulse cannons were configured around the ship's hull. If twenty of these gargantuan vessels can't stop the Craing, then nothing would, he thought tiredly.

Captain Larimer wanted to put their heads on pikes, the whole damn species if he could. Two years previously, on a planet not so different from Earth, the Craing had leveled his home in a fiery blast, killing his wife and children. His story wasn't unique; the Craing had touched the lives of every crewmember onboard ship, as well as the thousands of others assembling today.

Finally, the moment was at hand; they'd pooled their forces. An alliance had been built—planets and star systems reaching hundreds of light years away—out to distant sectors. And now they waited. One last time. As expected, the Craing were arriving—one of their many massive fleets was ready to do battle. A warring fleet ready to obliterate anyone and anything that got in its way. But this time things would be different.

The captain looked at the primary display in front of him; they'd amassed their allied fleet into a cohesive, united military front—which in itself was nothing short of a miracle.

Morning shift had just begun and crewmembers were filling the empty seats at quiet consoles. Ensign Smothers handed the captain his coffee, and they stood together at the rear of the bridge, a bridge about the size of a small supermarket back home. Both men watched as a pretty crewmember, one with violet skin and amazingly long eyelashes, walked by with a virtual clipboard.

The captain smiled as his eyes followed her across the bridge. "...if I were just five years younger..."

"Five years?" the ensign quipped out of the side of his mouth, with a wry smile on his face.

"OK, maybe ten." The two men laughed briefly but quickly choked it off with the full realization of what the day would bring—the largest interstellar battle in recorded history. Captain Larimer mentally rehearsed their massive planned assault. Could they possibly be more or better prepared?

"Contacts!" one of the now on-duty crewmembers bellowed from his console. Eight large displays lit up with the current optics. The bridge went still—a momentary lapse in which comprehension hadn't quite caught up with what the brain had already figured out.

"We're not outnumbered, sir, but we may not have the advantage we were counting on," the ensign said, with an edge to his voice.

"Okay, bring us about to heading four six five—let's not give them such a big target to shoot at."

"They've got a lock on the Crescent Moon and the Bravo, sir. Incoming! Wide dispersal, looks like medium-yield conventional missiles."

The barrage had emanated from one of the

Craing Dreadnaughts. All eyes were on the main display as four yellow icons closed in on the Crescent Moon, and then another four on the Bravo. Fortunately, the Crescent Moon's attitude was perpendicular to the Dreadnaught—a poor target.

Two of the forward displays zoomed in on the balance of the approaching Craing fleet. Studying their vessel formation, the captain reckoned the Craing warship armada was not so different from that of the Alliance. He took it all in, analyzing their configuration; there were only four Dreadnaughts, though those Goliaths dwarfed even the Alliance's super carriers. The remaining vessels were an odd assortment of super carriers, light carriers, and destroyers. All had the same insect-like design. The destroyers appeared the most menacing, with their squat, beetle-like build. Recent reconnaissance provided had shown they were the newest addition to the Craing fleet, and by far the most dangerous. Until recently, the Craing preferred energy weapons, but these destroyers were also equipped with turret-mounted rail guns—not dissimilar to those used by the Alliance, but, he feared, more effective.

"Crescent Moon's shields held, but she can't withstand another barrage like that last one," said the ensign. Crewmembers watched as the remaining four icons approached the Bravo.

"Zoom in," the captain commanded. Time seemed to stand still as all four Craing missiles hit the battle cruiser broadside simultaneously.

In the vacuum of space, the explosions were minimal, but the damage was obviously catastrophic. The Bravo's hull breached at its four impact locations, causing the ship to first segment into four distinct pieces, and then each piece, subsequently, exploded separately.

"Let's move to shield the Crescent Moon's flank. With repairs, perhaps she's still in the fight," the captain said, now pacing up and down the length of the bridge.

Ensign Smothers listened to a hail and turned to the captain. "In from Command: the admiral wants each of the super carriers to actively join the party."

"Good—it's time to see how that invading swarm handles several thousand fighters and fusion-tipped missiles. Maybe that'll even the score some."

Even before he voiced it, the captain reminded himself it wasn't the Craing weapons they feared; it was their damn shields—almost impervious to energy or projectile weaponry assaults. More often than not, the Craing simply outlasted their adversaries. What he would give to capture one of those damn ships. Sure, they could be destroyed by nukes, but disabling one, actually capturing one, had not been done.

The captain stepped over to the helm pilot. At this point the entire fleet was engaged. While the Alliance maintained an orderly in-line configuration of ships, the Craing were willy-nilly all over space.

The helmsman looked up and said, "The

Alliance firing solutions are 4.6 times more effective than the Craing's, sir. I mean, we're unleashing a hell-storm on their ships, but they're not going down."

The captain realized before his crew, but eventually they would come to the same conclusion. His stomach sank. They were going to lose the battle today. After years of combat experience—most of that in command—he just knew. He turned and surveyed the bridge. An exceptional crew. They were all professionals, he thought to himself, battle worthy; they'd accepted the possibility of defeat when they first signed on. Even though they'd heard the awful stories—stories that bounced around the sector for years. They began with several captured crewmen, who'd somehow escaped from the Craing. They'd painted a clear picture: get captured in battle by the Craing and you'll end up becoming a part of their sick religious rituals—one that involved being sliced and diced and served up at meal time. Apparently, it was always worst directly following a battle. It had something to do with the Craing liking to consume their newly conquered.

"Incoming!" All eyes looked to the center display.

Chapter 1

Christ, he'd forgotten how hot San Bernardino got this time of year. Even without twenty or more windshields focused in his general direction, it would still be blistering. Jason looked out at a virtual sea of broken automobiles—acres and acres of chrome, plastic, and rusted steel. Lifeless headlights peered back at him. It was strange how the abandoned cars now seemed to be waiting for something. He wiped sweat from his stubbled chin. He needed a shave; he also needed a haircut. But why bother? Jason balanced his chair back on two legs and propped his feet up on the nearby table his Grandfather Gus had fashioned out of a welded stack of F-150 rims. It felt strange to be sitting on the porch Gus built by hand some twenty-odd years earlier. The property had been in his family for three generations, but Lord knows Jason hadn't expected to be back here again.

He reached for the last lukewarm bottle of beer from a now empty six-pack carton sitting at his feet—do they even make this brand anymore? He looked down at the water-stained cardboard with its big Blue Ribbon logo, now faded more into grey than blue... a telltale sign that Gus' refrigerator's contents had sat undisturbed for a long time.

Jason's father, Admiral Perry Reynolds, disappeared fifteen years earlier. Grandpa Gus had taken up the parental reins—assuming both father and mother roles to Jason and his older brother, Brian. Conflicting stories about the admiral's disappearance spanned from him being killed by a crazed interstate trucker to speculation that he had run off with a girlfriend, someone named Lilly.

When old Gus died, the property was on a fast track toward foreclosure. Jason stepped in at the last moment to pay the necessary back taxes. As Jason looked out at the yard, he let out a long, slow breath. My own little piece of Eden, he thought. Which was true. Because right now, he had nowhere else to go.

He noticed the black monitoring device snugly secured around his left ankle. It wasn't always like this, he thought. He was both husband and father and, like his own father, a U.S. Navy officer. He had reached the place where his life had seemed, well... fairly settled, and for the most part he was content. With that said, commanding a naval vessel was often arduous and required a high-degree of dedication. Something Jason's ex-wife complained about on a regular basis. But naval life fit him like a glove. His personality was well suited for weeks, even months at sea. Staring out at the hundreds, if not thousands, of scrapped vehicles, Jason was coming to terms with the bleak fact that his own military career was probably ending, along with his pension and the chance to reestablish family connections.

The last remaining rays of the sun bounced off an old Chevy Bel Air's bumper. Jason took a final swig of beer. He toasted the setting sun with his now empty bottle. "Here's to house arrest, day two!" He collected the empty beer bottles and headed back into the house.

The kitchen window, along with the porch and whole rear of Gus' house, enjoyed the same vista of the Central Valley Scrapyard. Jason hadn't always thought of the property merely as a scrapyard. As a kid it was more like a magical playground. A place where he'd spent countless hours investigating and discovering what their modern-day-waste pile could conjure up. Summer mornings were especially filled with new and exciting adventures. Looking back at his youth, Jason's embarrassment about where he lived occurred later, when he was well into his teens. That's when rival school kids and buddies alike started teasing him, and girls... well, they wanted nothing to do with a boy from the neighborhood scrapyard. About that time, Jason stopped telling people where he lived. Jason chugged the last drops from his beer, set it down and walked into the house.

He pulled out his cellphone. Three bars. It was only after trial and error, running from room to room, that he discovered the kitchen was the golden place to make and receive calls. He dialed and by the third ring, Mollie answered.

"Dad?"

"Hey, kiddo, what are you up to?" Jason

asked with enthusiasm.

"Just studying… well, MTV and studying. I got a Social Science test in the morning, and I can't seem to concentrate. Last day of school—half day tomorrow!"

"Why don't you turn off the TV? Maybe that will help."

"No, that only makes it worse. I need background noise. Maybe I'll put on a movie," she said, thinking out loud.

Mollie was a straight A student, which he never was, and so any advice from him would certainly be wasted. He changed the subject. "So what else is going on? Did you make up with your mother yet? You still grounded?"

Mollie paused. Then, annunciating each and every word separately, she said: "Don't–get-me-started, Dad. I'm-never–talking-to-that-woman-again!"

Jason barely held back laughing into the phone, just barely. At that moment he realized how much he'd missed the banter, the everyday problems, all the things that came with family. A lifestyle he no longer was a part of. "Well, don't be too hard on her," he said, with more conviction than he actually felt. "You'll get plenty of space away from each other this summer."

Beep. "Oops, I think I have a call waiting. You want to hold on, Dad?" But Jason could hear the call to greener pastures in her voice.

"No-no, sweetie, I'll see you tomorrow. I'm really looking forward to our spending some time together. Get that studying done, OK? I love you."

"Can't wait—and I love you too, Dad… bye-bye." She clicked off. Jason stood there, hovering over his grandfather's battered old sink for a long while—hanging onto the hollow silence of a disconnected line.

* * *

A slow, heavy scraping sound woke Jason up in the middle of the night. He'd taken to sleeping on the couch in the family room, which was situated directly off the kitchen.

He squinted into the near total darkness, just barely able to make out the soft blue glow of the digital clock on the microwave: 3:23 AM. Noises were common here—stray dogs running through the yard, cats on the hunt, and rodents scampering around. Most of those animals made their way into the yard at some point in time. Even after all these years, Jason still knew what sounds were what: the gentle scraping of a hubcap against chain-link fencing, or something munching on the last vestiges of upholstery.

But this was a different kind of sound. There was an intelligence associated with it, like a pattern of noises joined together—something that required conscious thought. Jason sat up and listened, straining to hear anything abnormal. A minute passed without another sound. It must have just been a critter, he decided. Yawning, he started to lie back down... Hummmm, Chickink, Hummmm. It was coming from outside, somewhere out back. He went to the window and peeked out through the mini-blinds. He surveyed the property—a collection of dark geometric shapes, dimly lit by low-voltage security lights, which cast long, distorted shadows into the near-darkness. Jason could hear shuffling sounds, like feet moving.

It was in the tool shed. Jason needed a weapon. He remembered Gus always kept an old Louisville Slugger within easy reach of the back door. Gus was never big on firearms around the house, not since Brian, Jason's older brother, was killed in a friendly-fire incident in Iraq. And there it was, right where Gus had left it, standing sentry by the sliding glass door. Jason snatched up the bat, slid open the door and tiptoed out onto the porch. The security lights didn't quite reach the back of the house, so he had some semblance of stealth. He only wished he'd pulled on a pair of pants—it's hard to play tough-guy when you're lurking outside in your boxers.

The shed, a patchwork of corrugated steel sheets and old pieces of plywood, was located about thirty yards behind the house. Like the hub of a big wagon wheel, multiple concrete pathways connected the shed to the rest of the scrapyard. Crouching down and trying to avoid the lights, Jason headed off in the direction of the strange noises. "Shit!" He swore as the soles of his bare feet crunched across a patch of broken headlight glass.

When he reached the back of the shed, he moved around to its side where there was a small blocked-off window and the shed's only door. The noises were louder here—something electric, a buzzing sound.

From under the door a bright band of light pierced the darkness. With the bat raised in one hand, he slowly reached out to open the door with the other, but his hand never made it to the doorknob. The door flew outward and smacked Jason square in the face—sending him sprawling to the ground, flat on his back. In a quick blur someone streaked past, off and running. "Damn!" His cheek throbbed.

Jason knew the smartest thing to do would be to just let him go. But with the kind of year he'd just had, nobody was sneaking onto his property, knocking him flat on his ass, and then dashing off freely into the night. Frustrated, Jason kicked out at the metal door—a loud clang reverberated into the night. He collected his wits and got back to his feet. Spinning around, he tried to determine which direction to go. Then he heard distant running, heading away—going deeper into the scrapyard. Jason ran off in that general direction. He quickly closed the gap.

"Stop!" he yelled, to no effect. Each side of the pathway was a blur of rusted metal—but now only five car lengths separated them. Squinting down the dimly-lit path, Jason noticed that whoever the guy was, his head barely reached above the level of a car hood.

He was wearing a blue LA Dodgers baseball cap, and he moved surprisingly quick for a little guy. He looked to be tiring, though. "I can do this all night," Jason hollered after him. The little trespasser darted from one side of the pathway to the other, his small head turning this way and that, looking for an escape route between the mountains of wheel rims, tall columns of tires, and three- and four-stacked-high car chassis. Good luck, dude, Jason thought to himself. This yard is packed tight. If nothing else, Old Gus had been organized—everything, every piece of scrap metal had its own specific allotted slice of real estate. No wasted space.

Jason could see the little guy was just about spent. His short arms flailed spastically up and down. Truth was, Jason was losing steam himself. They were quickly approaching the far end of the property and Jason was almost within reach. Jason made one more extended stride and, arms outstretched, dove for the little man.

Mid-air, his ankle bracelet started to vibrate, and then a "beep-beep-beep" sound followed. What the hell is that? Jason's fingertips had only grazed the man's shoes before he ran off into the night. Jason's bare legs hit the ground first, then his elbows, then his hands.

Sprawled on the cement, he looked down and saw the LED on his ankle monitor was flashing red, letting him know he was past the specified GPS limits of his confinement. The police had made it perfectly clear: "That device goes active—you're going to jail. Don't fuck with us on this, you understand?" Jason quickly got to his feet and ran back towards the house. Damn! Nervously he looked towards San Bernardino in the distance, and the soft glow from the city's lights in the sky. Jason wondered if a cruiser had already been dispatched. And there go any hopes of seeing Mollie again. Crap!

Halfway back to the house, the LED stopped flashing red and turned to green. Jason bent over, hands on his knees, and let out a long breath. He just might have caught a break. He turned and looked back down the pathway one more time. The short hoodlum was definitely gone—well good riddance. Jason hobbled back toward the house, following the trail of his own bloody footprints.

He made a quick detour to the shed to see what had attracted the odd visitor. The door was still wide open. Insects frantically darted around a 60-watt light fixture, its long cord swaying from the ceiling. Like walking into a time warp. Jason wondered when the last time was that he'd been in here? Five years, ten? He had spent much of his childhood in this shed, watching his grandfather tinker with old carburetors, starter solenoids, alternators, water pumps... but now the workbench held a different kind of machinery. Futuristic things Jason had never seen before. Things machined to tolerances far exceeding anything required by the auto industry. There were three separate cylindrically-shaped metallic components, each lying side by side atop the bench. Some kind of fiber-optic cable connected them together. All three components had a similar glowing blue light, pulsating behind a curved glass panel.

He bent over the bench, his face mere inches from the devices, his brow raised. He noticed several other toaster-sized pieces of equipment, similar to oscilloscopes, but much more advanced. These were lined up on the back of the bench, connected to the other glowing devices. He felt a slight vibration through the bench top. He shook his head and stood back. Probably best to leave everything as is. Jason found an old padlock and its key buried in one of the workbench drawers. He turned out the light and locked up the shed. Until he knew what those things were, he didn't want anyone going near the place.

Chapter 2

Jason awoke feeling a bit more optimistic—actually, more optimistic than he'd felt in two years. Mollie would be spending much of the summer with him here at Casa Scrapyard. That was something her mother, Nan, wasn't thrilled about—not with his recent problem with the Navy, but she'd recently acquiesced. The truth was, Jason was excited to see Nan again too. It had been a long time. Things hadn't ended well between them the last time they'd talked. He got up and scurried into the bathroom and assessed his looks in the mirror. After brushing his teeth, he tried to do something about his mop of bed-hair. Even after several attempts to wet it down, it just popped up again.

In the beginning they'd been happy. One of those rare, whirlwind love-at-first-sight stories you hear about but never fully believe is really possible. But it had been, at least for Jason.

It started with a simple blind date. Their physical attraction to each other was undeniable, but there was something else as well. They fit together—never wanting to be apart. Jason was finishing up at the Naval Academy and Nan had begun pre-law at George Washington University. Within several months, they decided to move in together, and six months later they were married. As far as Jason was concerned, their time together had been the happiest of his life. After close, stateside-duty assignments for their first years, his naval career as a sea-faring officer began in earnest. Extended tours, sometimes lasting for months on end, started to chip away at their marriage—a relationship still too new to endure the hardships posed by long absences and distance.

Even with Nan's busy school schedule, she was lonely. Jason's rare and fleeting shore leaves were never long enough to fully restore what was lost. Six years into the marriage, and Mollie just starting kindergarten, Nan filed for divorce. She had been the love of his life. Now, looking at himself in the mirror, Jason wondered why he hadn't tried harder to hold on to her.

His phone's ringing pulled Jason away from his thoughts. He answered on the second ring. "Hello?"

"We're at the gate, can you open this damn thing?" Nan barked, impatiently.

"Hi—oh, yeah sure, give me just one sec." He reached for his jeans and slipped on his shoes, "ouch, shit!"

The double-gates at the front of the house provided access to the entire property. It was kept locked. Primarily to keep kids and visitors, like the one Jason had the previous night, from getting into the scrapyard. Nan's minivan was idling at the gate. Jason could see by her expression she didn't want to be here.

Mollie was smiling and grabbing for her sweatshirt and backpack. At eight, she looked the same as Jason last remembered—a goofy, fun-loving kid. Over the past few months Jason had made it a point to call Mollie several times a week. He now hoped their relationship would be as good in person as it had become on the phone.

Jason unlocked the gate and swung it open. Nan drove through to park by the side of the house. Mollie was out and running before the van came to a stop. He hadn't seen her in months, and somewhere along the line she'd gotten braces. Her smile was still as radiant and contagious as ever. She jumped into his arms and squeezed. Mollie's feet twirled around as Jason hugged her tight. Several bobby pins held down her hair.

"So happy to see you, Dad," she said, her muffled voice buried in his shoulder.

"Me too, goofball, I'm EXTREMELY happy you're here!"

Mollie glanced back at her mother and whispered: "Mom's driving me absolutely crazy. Honestly, I'm not exaggerating... I couldn't have lasted a minute more in that house..."

Nan had gotten out of the van and was standing by the fence, looking around at nothing in particular. Jason could tell she felt awkward. They hadn't seen each other in nearly a year. If possible, Nan was even more stunning than he remembered, standing there wearing her favorite well-worn snug-fitting jeans—the ones she usually saved for weekends. Her chestnut hair was longer and tied in a loose ponytail. At thirty-six, she could easily pass for twenty-something. Jason caught himself staring. They made eye contact. "Hey, why don't you come in for a while?" Jason offered, trying not to sound too desperate.

Nan looked away, as if deciding. "I don't know, maybe I should just—"

Jason cut her off. "Oh, come on, a quick cup of coffee—"

After what seemed an eternity, she tentatively replied, "Um... okay, sure. Why not?"

* * *

Jason made a pot of coffee and they sat on the porch. Mollie was off investigating the house, deciding which bedroom she wanted to make her own for the weekend.

"So, how have you been, Nan?" Jason asked, filling her cup.

"Things are good." Avoiding his eyes at first, she then looked directly at him. "Jason, I have to be honest... this just feels weird, you know, talking like this after all this time. Like we're old buddies or something."

"Would that be so bad? Being friends?"

"What would be the point?" Nan spat back. Then, seeming to regret her outburst, she continued in a more controlled voice. "Why now? It's been years; don't you think it's best to just let things be?"

Nan sat back and smiled sympathetically.

"I'm sorry. This must be a difficult time for you." She furrowed her brow and went on: "But Christ, Jason, you're so damn impulsive! What the hell were you thinking, shooting those unarmed guys?"

Jason looked at Nan and saw her frustration with him. There was nothing she could say he hadn't already said to himself a thousand times.

It was over a year ago. Jason, a lieutenant commander on the U.S. gunship Tripoli, was on patrol off the coast of Somalia. He had just been informed that the Canadian super tanker, Christina, had been boarded by pirates. Recently, and all too frequently, Somalian pirates were brazenly attacking these big ships, demanding large ransom amounts from governments and corporations alike. In return, they promised a safe return of ship and crew. Fortunately, this time Jason's gunship was close by—less than a mile from the seized tanker.

It was a moonless, stormy night when four navy SEAL Zodiac rubberized crafts swept up to the besieged ship. The noise of their small but powerful outboard motors was barely audible above the sea's surging waves. Jason and fifteen others on his team had trained this same type of maneuver hundreds of times.

Their Zodiacs were soon positioned midship and aft on both sides of the tanker. At Jason's comms signal, the team silently climbed up long collapsible ladders and was onboard in less than two minutes. The Christina was completely dark. Dressed in black assault gear, each SEAL carried a standard issue SIG Sauer P226 sidearm, as well as an HK MP5N submachine gun, and was equipped with night-vision goggles. For assaults such as this, they would have access to a duffle bag filled with explosive breaching charges, bolt cutters, and a sledgehammer. The four SEAL teams moved forward with their weapons raised and ready. It became immediately apparent that this was not a typical pirate ransom situation. This had been a raid. A dead body lay sprawled on the deck before Jason. Eerily seen through green-hued optics, the crewmember's throat had been sliced from ear to ear. Blood pooled in a symmetrical circle around his head. Jason went on-comms to his team. "Stay dark and quiet everybody; team Zebra, I want you clearing the bridge—let's see if anyone is still in charge here."

Three more bodies, similarly killed, were found in the same proximity by his team. Right inside the forward bulkhead hatch, a woman crewmember had been bound. Trousers pulled down, she had obviously been raped prior to having her throat cut as well. Outside the hatch, Jason watched Billy, a mountain of a man and one of the toughest SEALs in the unit, walk over to the railing, throw up over the side, and then continue on to secure the ship. Jason heard noises and yelling coming from below deck. Laughing. Not English.

Jason, using hand signals, gestured for two of the assault team members to follow him down the stairs, and the other two teams to clear the top deck. The laughing became more pronounced as Jason and his team descended the stairs. A metallic clanging sound echoed off a bulkhead in the distance, followed by more laughter. More clanging, more laughter. Light poured out from an open hatchway just ahead, partially illuminating the dark hallway.

Jason signaled for his team to halt—he slung his assault rifle around to his back and used a small telescopic mirror to carefully peer inside and around the corner. He moved the mirror around, ensuring that he hadn't missed anything. He took in the scene in mere seconds. It looked to be the ship's mess. The tanker's captain was bound and secured to the far bulkhead, his legs and arms spread wide apart. Five Somalian pirates sat together at a large table on the far side of the room. Most of them were shirtless, their dark skins contrasted with the white florescent lights above. Machetes caked with dried blood lay strewn about the tabletop.

The obvious leader, a tall and emaciated-looking man, stood forward, closer to the bound captain, and held a woman crewmember around her neck. He held a knife up to her eye. Three of the captain's crew had been blindfolded. They each held a three-foot-long piece of pipe. Watching the events as they progressed, Jason felt bile rise in the back of his throat. In a sick and twisted form of 'pin the tail on the donkey,' the blindfolded crewmembers could only save the woman's life by taking shots at the captain.

From the looks of things, the captain had been hit numerous times. Blood seeped from an open gash on his forehead. His right ear was completely gone—an oozing dark red circle in its place. Terrified, the woman screamed—which produced another wave of laughter from the pirates. In Jason's ear-comm the other two SEAL teams were reporting in. A total of seventeen more casualties had been found, four of whom were rape victims. More laughter erupted from within the mess hall.

Jason instinctually took action. In fact, not reaching for his sidearm was never a question. With no thought, no hesitation, he pulled his SIG Sauer P226 from his holster, leveled it, and squeezed the trigger. The pirate leader, the one holding the woman, was dead before he hit the ground, a small bullet hole in the center of his forehead. The woman jumped back and screamed again. But Jason didn't stop there. He quickly followed up by squeezing the trigger five more times—also dead center shots to the forehead for each of the remaining pirates. They fell in near unison to the mess deck. Later, there would be conflicting reports from his SEAL team. Something about the other pirates reaching for their weapons, but Jason doubted that that was true.

As events happened, the story was leaked to the press and immediately sensationalized to mega-proportions. International media and other news organizations had a field day. Before Jason knew it, he had been elevated to quasi-hero status: Lieutenant Commander Jason Reynolds inflicts sweet revenge on merciless pirates. But then it was up to a special U.S. Navy Tribunal to decide his fate. Would Jason face charges for second-degree murder and spend years of his life locked up somewhere in a brig, or would he be found innocent due to mitigating circumstances? Still at the tribunal stage, set up by the Judge Advocate General's Corps, a non-judicial proceeding which comes before any kind of court martial, Jason thought his life was over. He'd been fortunate... not being required to wait out the decision process in a cell. He wasn't sure if this was due to his favorable past service record or, more likely, his father being the famed Admiral Perry Reynolds.

Now, looking over at Nan's delicate profile, Jason wondered if she too thought of him as a cold-blooded murderer. Mollie laughed at something in the house. When she burst outside, she wore her deceased uncle's catcher's outfit from high school. Brian, shorter, stockier than Jason, was perfect behind home base. The hat was a little big for her and the catcher's mask flopped around on her face. She tossed a baseball up in the air a few times—then back and forth into an oversized mitt. Giggling, she crouched down and outstretched the mitt in front of her chest, "You ready to play, Dad? Come on... let's play ball, sports fans!"

Nan just shook her head. "Was that yours?" she asked, now smiling at Mollie's antics.

"No, Brian was the baseball player in the

family—I was the football jock," he replied, picking Mollie up and twirling her around, her laugh contagious. Jason set her down, and she dizzily scampered back into the house, the sounds of laughter following her.

"Actually, I'm surprised that stuff's still around," Jason said, sitting back down across from Nan.

"For goodness sakes, haven't you explored the house since you've been back?"

"Not really, too many ghosts around here. What with Dad taking off, Brian never coming home and now Gus gone... I'm fine just hanging around the kitchen and family room."

"Oh, don't be such a pussy," she said, with a wry smile. "Anyway, how do you know old Admiral Perry hasn't returned? Maybe he's sprawled out in a bathtub back in there somewhere?"

"Well, I've wandered around enough to know he's not here. To be honest, it's kinda creepy here; everything looks the same as it did fifteen years ago, when I went off to Annapolis. Brian's room hasn't been changed since he went into the service."

Nan's attention was interrupted by something out in the scrapyard. With a furrowed brow she pointed. "You have someone working here, in the yard?" she inquired.

"No, why?" Following Nan's gaze, Jason saw who she was referring to. The short man was back. He was halfway down the same path Jason had chased him on last night—now pulling a flatbed cart that carried the same three metallic objects Jason had locked up in the shed.

Jason stood up and went to the edge of the porch. "Hey! Get the hell off my property, you little shit. And don't come back here again!" The little man paid no attention to Jason's verbal onslaught and continued on his way. Tempted to give chase again, Jason remembered his tender feet.

Nan looked at him for a second before commenting, "That's a bit hostile, don't you think?"

"Absolutely not… I chased that same guy out of here last night. He's been sneaking into the yard, going into the shed… doing experiments." Even before he had finished saying it, he realized how stupid that sounded.

"Experiments? Huh! What kind of experiments?" Nan asked teasingly, without trying to hide her smile. "You mean he's like some kind of reclusive scrapyard scientist?"

"Ha ha, I don't know what he is," Jason replied, acting overly indignant, "but I'm thinking I should call the local cops; have an APB put out on the guy."

"Sure, if you think you need the help," she said, now seeming to lose interest in the subject altogether. "Anyway, I should go. You guys have fun. Maybe between the two of you you'll catch your man. Just be careful. Try not to put Mollie in harm's way, okay?"

"Yeah, well I'm sure he's harmless. By the looks of him, even Mollie could beat the stuffing out of him."

Nan's cell phone started ringing to the song lyrics Boom Boom Pow. She fumbled with the phone, sending the caller to voice mail. "Mollie thinks it's funny to sneak different ringtones onto my phone. But, hey—you got to love The Black Eyed Peas." Nan got up and walked back into the house. Once in the kitchen she made a detour over to the fridge and took a peek inside. "Good God, Jason—what were you planning on feeding Mollie while she's here?"

Crap! Jason had forgotten to order groceries. It was on his list of things to do. Not being able to leave the property was inconvenient—not something he'd gotten used to yet. "I'm already on it," he fibbed. "I'll have groceries delivered later today. Um… what does Mollie like to eat these days?"

Rolling her eyes, Nan shook her head in disbelief. "If you can wait a few hours I'll try to drop some food by later on today. But you're going to have to work out your food and supply needs—long-term."

Jason walked Nan out to her car. She yelled goodbye to Mollie and climbed in behind the wheel, giving him a quick smile as she backed down the driveway. Closing the gate, Jason felt more optimistic than he had any right to. At least Nan was talking to him again and that was a start. Back in the house, Mollie was sprawled out on the couch waiting for him.

"Mom's gone?"

"Yep, it's just you and me, amigo."

"What are we going to do now, Dad?" she said, scanning the family room. "You don't have a TV or even a stereo?"

"We're going on a safari," he said, in as serious a voice as he could muster.

"Safari? Like a wild African safari? What are we hunting for?"

"A hoodlum," he said. "A wild scrapyard hoodlum."

* * *

Jason brought along a small backpack, outfitted with a few necessities, including two water bottles, binoculars, a small tool kit, a knife, and his cellphone. They also brought along some makeshift walking sticks... ready to set off for the great unknown. Mollie was, as usual, a good sport and willing to make it a fun adventure. The scrapyard itself was massive, spreading hundreds of yards in every direction. Vehicles of all shapes and sizes had been dumped here since the early 1930s—long before Jason was born. Even before old Gus was born. How Gus originally acquired the property, Jason had no idea. Mollie hadn't visited the scrapyard since she was a small child, but just like him as a kid, she became captivated by this great accumulation of junk.

"It's kind of sad," Mollie said, poking her walking stick at a '63 Rambler's broken taillight. "I mean, all these cars... they each have a story. You know what I mean? Like, look over there, that white car..." Jason followed her glance.

"Yeah, that '68 Buick... it was in an accident. You can see the whole front end is all bashed in. Someone might have died in that car, Dad. A whole family might have died in that car. It seems all the cars here have a sad story. Their car lives ended in this yard—their final resting place."

"I guess that's true... but there's another way to look at it, Mollie," Jason replied. "Many of these old cars and vans once brought people real happiness—some for a very long time. And then they just conked out—no accidents, no drama, too old to be driven, so they gave up the ghost." Jason picked up a rusted drum brake assembly and threw it back onto a pile of scrap. A frightened cottontail jumped out of the heap and ran into Mollie's foot before skittering off.

"Woo-oh little rabbit! You scared the crap out of me!" Mollie screamed, watching its fluffy tail disappear beneath a pile of chrome bumpers. "Hey, are we following these?" She gestured toward a trail of dark brown footprints on the path.

"Kinda—we're at least going in that general direction." Jason pulled out his binoculars and scanned the seemingly endless field of derelict vehicles. Memories flooded back to his childhood when he'd played here. He once knew every inch of the place.

"What are you looking at?" Mollie asked, while climbing up onto several tire rims to get a better view.

"I'm looking at a red 1960 Cadillac."

"Yeah, so what's so interesting about an old red 1960 Cadillac?" Mollie questioned back.

"I played in that car-spot a hundred times, and that's not the same car. For one thing, it's the wrong color. The car I played in was sea-green... and it was a convertible."

"Maybe Grandpa Gus moved it," Mollie said, not understanding his over-preoccupation with the old car.

"Maybe. But let's check it out anyway. Come on." They crossed over onto a perpendicular pathway that led them in the direction of the big red Caddy. Yeah, this was definitely a different car. And something else was strange. The undercarriage axles and wheels were gone; the car was sitting flat on a concrete pad, making it impossible to see beneath it. Recalling how Gus stretched a dollar, it didn't seem like something he'd do. As they got closer, the monitor on Jason's ankle restraint beeped twice, letting him know he was at the limit of his house-arrest parameters. Mollie looked down at his ankle and smiled.

"Mom told me you had that thing on your leg. She said you had to wear it instead of going to jail. She said you killed some bad men and that's part of your punishment."

"She told you all that, huh?" Jason asked.

"Yep, that's what she said."

Jason saw movement up ahead. The driver's side door on the Cadillac flew open and the little man in the baseball cap climbed out. He was holding some kind of rifle, which was loosely pointed toward the ground. Jason was familiar with most weaponry, but not this one. It was a small rifle of sorts, well suited for the little man. But less mechanical—futuristic. Perhaps an energy-type weapon? Why on earth would he need a weapon? Also, there was something strange about the way he moved, something Jason couldn't put his finger on. The little man stood there for a moment, taking in his surroundings. His head suddenly jerked up towards the sky, giving extra attention to a commercial passenger jet. With the door wide open, Jason could see into the interior of the car; it had been completely gutted—seats, steering wheel, dashboard—everything had been removed.

"Hide," he whispered to Mollie, crouching down behind a rusted old Chevy school bus. She crouched down next to him and they watched as the little man proceeded to shut the car door and head in their direction. It was then, once he had gotten closer, that Jason realized the little fellow wasn't quite human.

Up until then Jason hadn't actually seen his face. He'd been walking or running away from Jason and the baseball cap had obscured his misshapen head. He looked like the character in the popular Spielberg movie, ET: oversized-almond-shaped eyes, a rounded triangular-shaped head, little stubby arms. All that but with a unique, defining difference: this alien was also part machine. From ten yards out, Jason could clearly see he was more mechanical than organic; strange, too, since he was whistling a tune and acting anything but machine-like. Jason flattened himself closer against the old bus, hoping the now-armed robot-man-thing would pass by them without noticing their presence. He pulled Mollie closer to him and motioned for her to do the same.

His ankle monitor chose that particular instant to make a single 'beep' sound. Jason cringed and stole a quick glance at Mollie, who was scowling and shaking her head at him. The robot creature, clearly on edge, spun to see what the noise was. Startled, a knee-jerk reaction caused him to pull the trigger—sending a bright blue bolt of energy in their direction. The mechanical man stood there transfixed, his weapon's muzzle pointing in their direction.

Somehow Jason knew, even before he turned to Mollie, that she'd been hit. Turning to look at her, his eyes were drawn to a small, still smoldering burn hole in the middle of her chest, ruining her Hello Kitty T-shirt. She looked up at him, wide-eyed, a mixture of astonishment and fear. Only one word escaped her lips, "Daddy?" before she crumpled to the ground.

Jason grabbed for her. Took her in his arms—hoped that if he held her tight enough, long enough, the truth of what had just happened would somehow change—that his little girl would come back to him. He'd seen death on a regular basis: the vacant gaze when spirit has left the body—when a person's life is over. Jason fell to his knees and cried out, "Mollie, Mollie, Oh God, Mollie…" He continued rocking her lifeless body—there in that grimy graveyard of rusted-out old cars, buses, and scrap metal. He set her body gently down on the ground and closed her eyes, then moved several wayward strands of hair off her face. The dread now rushed in at him from all directions. Why now, after all their years of being apart? Away at sea, then the divorce. Why now when they were just getting to know each other again? Jason looked down at Mollie.

The only person who had loved him unconditionally was now dead. He felt the rage build from his core. He wanted blood.

Jason spun around, arms outstretched, and leaped onto the small robot creature who had not moved. As with the bullets he'd fired into those pirates' heads, there was no thinking, just raw primal action. His fingers wrapped around its thick metal-like neck and he squeezed with every bit of strength he possessed. He squeezed until his arms shook. But this metal didn't react the same way as human flesh. Not to be deterred, Jason began banging its head against the concrete path. He did this repeatedly, over and over again, until its baseball hat flew off and he heard the satisfying crack of metal striking concrete.

A shrieking shrill emanated from the robot's distorted mechanical-looking mouth. It was trying to say something, but Jason had little interest in what it had to say. It screamed even louder, just a single, choking, string of words.

"I… can… save… her…."

Jason stopped and looked into the robot's two glowing amber orbs. There was concern there, pleading, which was surprising to see in a mechanized being. "What do you mean you can save her? Can't you see? You've killed her!" he screamed, ready to resume his assault on this mechanical abomination.

"The ship," the robot croaked, "we need to get her to the ship within five minutes." The robot squirmed out from under him and rushed towards Mollie's body.

"Don't you touch her, don't you go near her!" Jason yelled. The robot stopped and looked back at him. In a calm and deliberate voice it said: "There are many things you don't comprehend yet, but believe me when I tell you, not all hope is lost. You need to pick her up and come with me… hurry, do it now!"

Jason had nothing to lose and somewhere in the back of his mind it occurred to him that he was talking to some kind of creature that shouldn't even exist. Maybe it, he, whatever it was, could do something for her. The alternative was too devastating to imagine. He picked up Mollie's limp body and felt her head roll loosely to the crook of his arm. He felt incapacitated with dread. The robot, which seemed no worse for wear, darted off towards the Cadillac. Jason quickly followed behind.

He swung open the heavy car door. "Hurry,

get in, get in!" the robot barked, prodding Jason to move faster.

"Where? In there? What the hell are you talking about?" Jason yelled back, but stooped down anyway and scurried into the Cadillac. The robot closed the door and pressed a small button. As the three of them tightly huddled together, the floor started to lower. It was an elevator of sorts and they were descending. The walls of the makeshift shaft were a patchwork of things pilfered from the scrapyard: automobile hoods, car doors, and even the side panel from an old ambulance.

"It's already been a minute and thirty seconds," Jason barked. "Come on, God damn it! How long are we going to be stuck in this thing?"

The mechanical man didn't move and continued to stare forward. They dropped several hundred meters before the elevator slowed and came to a complete stop. It was an opening to a large tunnel. The robot, wasting no time, jumped out and signaled Jason to follow.

Jason's mind raced, three minutes and counting. They ran through a large tunnel; sporadically-placed light fixtures flew by in a blur. Jason and the robot ran another full minute before the tunnel opened up into a massive underground chamber. Still at a dead run, Jason noticed the mechanical man was tiring. "Don't you dare stop now!" Jason barked, passing him and looking back over his shoulder. Jason stole a glance down at Mollie's face. Her lips had turned blue, her mouth agape.

Workers in dark blue uniforms worked at consoles and workbenches; they looked up with surprised expressions. More strange electrical devices, much like those in the shed, were strewn about, being worked on. But as astonishing as everything seemed to Jason, they paled in comparison to the odd-looking spaceship parked in the center of the chamber. The ship was huge, over a football field in length and almost half of that in width.

Jason looked down at Mollie, lying lifeless in his arms, hoping that his running hadn't disturbed her in some way.

"Come on! We're over four minutes, where do I go. Where?" Jason screamed.

The robot ran past him and quickly scurried up a long ramp, disappearing into the back of the ship. Jason ran after him. Oh God, would they make it in time? Time for what? Would the robotic-creature really have some magical formula to bring her back to life? Then Jason noticed someone had hand-painted the words The Lilly in bright yellow lettering directly over the open hatch. Jason ran into the ship.

They continued running down a narrow, brightly-lit corridor. Hatchways and divergent corridors flew by as they progressed deeper into the bowels of the ship. The robot abruptly stopped. "Hurry, through the DeckPort," he prompted, pointing toward another open hatch. The little man-thing took hold of Jason's wrists and they scurried across the threshold together.

From the top of his head down to his toes, he felt a slight tingle run through his body. They were somehow transported to another deck—another corridor. The robot ran ahead and made an abrupt turn up ahead. Jason followed.

Eventually, Jason caught up, ending up in a circular, medical-looking room. There were several long clamshell-type enclosures and what looked like monitoring devices—with connecting display units—mounted to a bulkhead. The robot pressed a button and one of the clamshells started to open. Showing his own desperation, the robot repeatedly hit the button over-and-over again. With it only halfway open, he gestured for Jason to set Mollie's lifeless body inside. "In here, put her inside."

Jason was quickly hustled out of the way, and the robot started entering a series of commands onto a small touchpad device. The top portion of the clamshell began to close, culminating in a sucking thump sound. Several colorful displays became active; one display had a rotating virtual 3D representation of Mollie's body.

"That's it? That's all your going to do?" Jason asked, fuming. He looked for an indication that it wasn't just a ruse by the robot to avoid another beating.

"Now… we wait," the robot said, turning away and quickly walking out of the room. Jason surveyed the space around him. Like the contours of the ship itself, the room was a mixture of fluid lines and gentle angles.

Functional and purpose-oriented as this space was, it seemed almost artful in its architecture. Soft, indirect lighting highlighted cushioned wall panels. And super clean—no scrapes, no dings on the bulkheads. Jason stood still, his hand still rested on top of the clamshell-device capsule. Never one to pray or really contemplate on anything more than present-time physicality, the here and now, he prayed. He prayed for Mollie, he prayed for himself, and he prayed for second chances.

Jason could see Mollie's illuminated face through a small rectangular window. He thought he noticed an eye-flutter. Was it merely his imagination? Then the 3D full-body representation changed slightly, showing the faintest indication of a beating heart. He must have stood there over an hour before he realized the robot was back in the room, checking the displays and making additional adjustments.

"Now she must rest; it will be a while longer. Please, you will come with me."

"I'm not going anywhere, robot," Jason snapped back. "I'm certainly not leaving Mollie alone in this place."

"Do not worry, we'll be close by. And you may refer to me as Ricket. That's what your father called me."

"What?"

"Please. Mollie will be fine here," Ricket softly replied. The robot headed out into the corridor and gestured he should follow. Jason stole one more glance at Mollie and reluctantly left the room. He realized the mechanical man, Ricket, was talking to him again.

"What? What did you say?" Jason asked, following him as they passed by several large equipment-filled compartments. Jason noticed that Ricket, at some point, had retrieved his baseball cap from up above. With it, the robot almost looked human again. They made their way to what seemed to be the ship's bridge or command center. Slightly oblong, the surrounding bulkhead was more like a massive curved virtual display, completely encircling the room 360 degrees. Consoles were configured around the perimeter, as well as in several middle rows. "I think it's time you tell me what the hell is going on here, robot."

"Please, refer to me as Ricket..."

"Whatever," Jason interrupted. "Ricket, Robot, I really don't give a shit what you're called. Tell me, what is this place and who the hell are you people?"

Ricket moved to one of the console chairs and sat down. "Please, sit anywhere you like. Up top, I was already on my way to bring you here when—"

"When you shot and killed my daughter?"

Ricket was quiet for a moment, then said, "Your father will explain everything."

"Really? That would be some trick, since he's been missing more than fifteen years."

Ricket started typing something at the console before looking up toward the large virtual display that encircled the room.

"Hello, Jason," his father said, his smiling face filling the screen. "How are you, son?"

"What the hell is this? And who the hell are you?" Jason asked, looking first at Ricket and then at the man on the screen.

"I can't even imagine what a shock this must be for you. So before I say anything else, let me begin by saying I'm truly sorry." The man on the screen looked weary. He had salt and pepper hair—more salt than pepper. Wearing a dark grey uniform and what appeared to be admiral's insignias on his collar, he continued, "I have very little time to talk, Jason. I'm asking you to put everything aside—all your questions, even your anger, and just listen to what I have to say. Can you do that for me?"

Jason was losing his patience. He turned to leave… he had a daughter to tend to.

"Wait," his father pleaded. "Please."

Jason hesitated and then turned back to face the screen. He nodded, almost imperceptibly, for his father to continue.

"Sixteen years ago, your Grandfather Gus discovered the ship you're standing in now, The Lilly. A sinkhole had opened up at the back of his property after an extended rainstorm. Ol' Gus spent weeks investigating. The sinkhole connected to an underground aquifer. Probably dried up for millennia. Gus eventually discovered The Lilly, the name I gave the ship you're now standing in. Anyway, your grandfather never really trusted the government—so he called me. It took me several months before I could schedule leave. Truth is, I thought he'd lost his marbles and I'd be spending my time looking for a retirement home for him. Wrong! How that old codger managed to descend down hundreds of feet, and then dig a few hundred yards deeper into the aquifer—well, it's pretty amazing. A spacecraft half buried and beat to hell. He showed me The Lilly, and that's when everything—and I mean everything—changed!"

"So you're telling me Grandpa Gus knew you were alive for the past fifteen years?" Jason spat, exasperated. "It nearly destroyed our family; Brian took it the hardest. What was so damn important that you couldn't let us know you were still alive?"

"I couldn't tell you, or anyone else, because I had discovered something that could literally alter the course of humanity."

"Oh for God's sake, don't you think that's a little melodramatic? Come on, Dad... your own family? Who would we tell? And why..." His father cut him off.

"Listen to me, Jason. Right now, I'm twenty thousand light-years from where you're standing—on another planet—in another solar system. What I'm doing now, and what I've been doing for the past fifteen years, is protecting Earth. I learned after breaching the vessel and reviving Ricket that Earth had been visited thousands of times by numerous alien species. For the most part, we were simply watched, investigated... but all that changed in

1947, with what's known as the Roswell Area 51 incident. Some of those alien life-forms we found? They're actually called the Craing, and they were not here for auspicious reasons. Thirty-two Craing scout ships stayed in higher Earth orbit for twenty-eight days—all for the sole purpose of cataloguing, mapping and germinating our planet for future, large-scale human harvesting."

"Do you know how ridiculous that sounds? Why should I believe anything you say? How do I even know you're really my father?"

Admiral Reynolds hesitated, a sardonic smile levied on his worn face. "Can you really ask me that, Jason, as you stand there on a buried spaceship with a talking robot—two things that don't exist in the 21st century?"

"Okay…" Jason paused, considering his father's words. "You knew about this but didn't involve the government or our military, for God's sake. Why not?"

"When I said germinate, I meant exactly that. Jason, thousands, no, multi-thousands of human-like beings have been introduced into Earth's populous. Each one strategically placed in government, military, and large corporate positions… Jason, we're the goose being fattened up for the proverbial Christmas feast. And by the way, that day… is today."

"Today, like we're being attacked by aliens today—why today? That's ridiculous."

"It doesn't matter why it's today, the Craing think in terms of hundreds, sometimes thousands of years. Their return date was probably established back in 1947. Our only hope was to stop them en route. That's what I've been doing out here, along with a confederation of other at-risk planets. We were hopeful—in fact, fairly sure—our plan would work: hundreds of warships converging for an interstellar ambush to stop the Craing in their tracks. But Jason, it didn't work. We didn't win." Admiral Perry stopped talking and took a long look at his son, trying to come to some kind of decision. Eventually he continued. "It's taken me several days to configure this FTL connection. Weeks ago I sent The Lilly back, just in case things didn't work out here—which obviously, they haven't. Jason, there is no one I can trust on Earth with the information I have shared with you. The Craing and their human-like inhabitants are ruthless and will stop at nothing to ensure a smooth incursion. Now, this is important. When they come, you will not, I repeat, will not stay and fight. I'm putting The Lilly in your charge, Jason. But there are other stellar allies still in this fight—their people's existence, as well as our own, depends on us building new, stronger alliances and eventually beating back the Craing. But that time is not today. This is not the time to play hero; get your family onboard, and do it now. It's important they talk to no one. Listen. This is important. The Craing are looking for The Lilly. It has technology they are desperate to get ahold of. There's a probable chance they tracked her entry back into Earth orbit... maybe even to your general location."

"Here? Are you serious?"

His father held up his hand. "Shut up and listen," the admiral barked. "Ricket has been instructed to teach you what you need to know—what will be necessary over the coming months and years. If I could do this myself, be there like a real father should be, I would. I'm proud of you, Jason." The camera shook; a blast thundered somewhere in the background twenty thousand light-years from Earth, the transmission obscured with blocky digital artifacts. "One more thing," Admiral Perry said. "Come to the Altar system, we need your help—I need your help, Jason..." The feed went dead.

"Hey, isn't that Grandpa?"

Jason spun around to see Mollie standing in the open hatch. A uniformed crewmember stood next to her. Looking as though she had just awoken from a nap, with the exception of the small burn hole on her shirt, Mollie, inexplicably, looked alive and fine.

"So, Dad, where are we?" she inquired, wide-eyed, looking around the bridge.

Jason jumped to his feet and swept her up in his arms until he heard her muffled cry, "Dad, I can't breathe, let me down!"

Jason put her down. Right then and there he decided not to mention anything to her about being shot or, God forbid, her dying. At only eight years of age, why complicate her life like that? Ricket moved forward and took her by the hand, leading her to a nearby chair.

"Mollie, I would like to apologize for shooting you earlier today."

"Terrific," Jason barked at Ricket. "I wasn't going to mention that to her... at least not yet." He glared at the robot, speechless. Studying Ricket up close, Jason noticed the strange and complex intricacies of the small face—a true mixture of both biological and mechanical layers of transparent skin, covering organic tissue connected to whirling gears, moving pistons and actuators, all of which worked together, causing his jaw to open and close as he spoke. Mollie, too, with her brow furrowed, was closely inspecting Ricket's face.

"You can call me Ricket; that is the name the admiral, your grandfather, gave me. A good name, yes?"

Ricket didn't seem to be the least bit self-conscious about their combined close scrutiny. "Hi, Ricket, it's nice to meet you. So why did you shoot me? What was that thing you put me in? And what are you? Are you like a robot? Was I really dead?" Excited, the rapid-fire questions shot out of her, one after another, leaving Ricket no opportunity to respond.

"Mollie," Jason interrupted, putting a hand on her shoulder, "I need to go up top for a while. I want you to stay here with Ricket."

"I don't want to stay here. I want to come with you."

"It may not be safe right now up top and I

need to get your mom. Just stay here—I'll be right back, OK?" Jason turned to Ricket. "You, robot—Ricket, nothing can happen to her—you will ensure she is safe and happy, you got that?"

"There is still much to discuss, Jason, we should…"

"No," Jason interjected, "maybe later, but now I need to leave."

"We'll walk you out," said Ricket, gesturing for Mollie to follow.

"So was that Grandpa?"

* * *

Leaving the ship and halfway down the ramp, Jason noticed there were other small robots and drones milling around, some even floating at workbenches, or attending to the various computer systems. Surprised, he heard a familiar voice.

"JASON! OH MY GOD! Jason, it's me… I'm at the gate. Are you there?" Frantic, Nan's voice echoed and bounced off the rock walls.

"What the hell?" Jason looked over to Ricket, "What is that?"

Calmly, Ricket pointed to one of the hanging loudspeakers above them.

"I suspect that is your ex-wife at the front gate. We're tied into the gate's intercom system." Seeing the confused look on Jason's face, Ricket went on: "We get many deliveries here: UPS, FedEx, DHL… they let us know when there's a package left at the gate." Ricket pointed to a small rusted box affixed to the wall. "You can talk to her; just push the button."

Jason scrambled over to the intercom and pushed the button, "Nan, hi! Um… just hold tight. I'll be right there."

"Jason! There's been some sort of an attack—where are you? There are ships… They're landing, Jason." Her voice cut off— sounds of energy weapons echoed in the background. Jason looked up from the intercom. The cavern shook—he felt explosions above.

"Ricket, now you're with me. And you, what's your name?" Jason asked a young crewmember.

"McBride, sir." Wide-eyed, he came to attention.

"Anything happens to that little girl—" Jason barked, "—and you're toast."

"Nothing will happen to her," McBride replied, meeting Jason's unwavering glare.

The alarm and relentless vibration from Jason's leg bracelet began as soon as they entered the cramped elevator. The navy—hell, all military services—would be recalling and reactivating their personnel back to base.

"Any way to make this thing go faster?" Jason snapped. He forced himself to take a long, deep breath—thinking of Nan in trouble above, he swallowed back the lump in his throat.

"No, just one speed," Ricket replied, bending over and eyeing the device strapped to Jason's leg. Lifting his pant leg, he tapped at it—once—twice—three times. The alarm stopped and the iron bracelet was released from his leg, falling to the floor. Jason studied this strange creature. He'd have to keep a close eye on Ricket.

Chapter 3

The sky was ablaze. Thick black contrails crisscrossed the sky. Mere yards from where they had emerged from the Cadillac, flames leapt from a charred and mangled F-22 fighter lying upside down—canopy and pilot crushed. Its two Pratt and Whitney turbofan engines continued to whirl while thick black smoke billowed. Above, like a swarm of bees, Craing fighters circled in unison. Whatever battle had ensued seemed to have ended as quickly as it had begun. The ground shook as the last F-22 crashed—this one closer to the house. Jason heard an ominous low-frequency sound blaring shrilly in the distance. An alarm or a warning—its effect caused an almost overwhelming sense of impending dread and doom.

"We need to get to the gate," Jason yelled over the thunderous noise. Ricket followed him with weapon held high—ready to fire. Debris covered much of the yard. Although hard to see through the heavy smoke-filled air, Jason spotted something in the near distance. Crossing over to an adjacent, more direct path, they could now clearly discern an alien ship. It had landed several hundred yards from where they stood. The pale green Craing ship appeared crouched and menacing and was the cause of the incessant blaring sound. Six long landing-gear supports, insect-like, angled down from a bulky rectangular-shaped hull. It looked like what it was—a cargo vessel.

Ricket nodded towards the ship. "That's a Craing light cruiser—used for ground assaults, but mostly for procuring indigenous species."

"Like hostages... they're taking hostages?"

"No, they have no need for hostages, more likely captives or slaves. They'll be transported off-planet and brought to one of their many mining operations around the sector."

Jason and Ricket arrived at the gate. Fortunately, the house was still intact. Noticing the driveway, Jason sucked in a breath. Nan's minivan, or what was left of it, was a smoldering, blackened metal frame.

Jason stood there. His white-knuckled hands gripped the chain-link fence. "Nan... they've killed her. Those fuckers killed her."

"I'm not reading things that way," Ricket said, looking up at Jason.

"What the hell does that mean... reading things that way?"

"My internal sensors would have detected if a biological mass was present," Ricket replied. "Nan was not in that vehicle when it was destroyed."

Relieved, Jason searched for any sign of her. Visibility had started to clear. "There, off to the left—what is that?" Jason pointed as he opened his backpack to retrieve his binoculars.

Ricket looked off towards the nearby foothills where Jason had pointed. About a quarter-mile away, a dozen people were walking single file toward the alien ship. Small, heavily armed aliens pointed weapons towards their head. Jason's brow furrowed. "Those are my neighbors and they're being herded like sheep." Then he spotted her. Nan was helping an elderly man—his walker not suited for the rough desert terrain. A nearby alien jabbed a rifle muzzle into the elderly man's back, bringing him to his knees—even at this distance, the old man's pain was evident.

"We have to do something. There's only eight aliens—"

"Yes—eight armed aliens," Ricket interjected, "and the captives are already being ushered onboard. We can't possibly get to them in time," Ricket said.

Ignoring him, Jason fumbled for his keys and unlocked the gate. Jason grabbed the rifle out of Ricket's hands and sprinted toward the alien vessel. He felt his heart was going to beat right out of his chest. Nan was now at the vessel's ramp. I need to get her attention. Jason stopped and began jumping up and down, waving the rifle over his head. He cupped his hands around his mouth and yelled, "Nan! Nan!" Half way up the ramp she stopped and turned in their direction. "I think she can hear me," Jason said aloud. He yelled again at the top of his lungs. "I'll come for you! I'll find you, Nan… I'll find you!" She disappeared into the strange, bug-like ship. Jason pointed the strange rifle towards the alien ship. "Where's the fucking trigger on this thing?" he yelled, frantically inspecting the rifle only to have it pulled from his own hands. Ricket brought the rifle up and fired continuously as bright bolts of energy impacted near the back of the ship.

Jason retrieved his binoculars, taking in every detail. "There are markings, like symbols, on the ship's hull."

Ricket nodded. "That would be the ship's unique fleet and sector designation."

Within moments, and seemingly unaffected by Ricket's gunfire, the Craing ship lifted off— accelerating up through the atmosphere at tremendous speed. Jason continued to stare into the sky long after it had disappeared.

"Ricket, the admiral will get my help just as soon as I track that ship and get my wife back. Understood?" Jason didn't wait for an answer. He simply turned away and headed back towards the ship below. "And you don't mention any of this to Mollie."

* * *

It was a quiet ride as they descended back down the elevator shaft. Jason stared straight ahead, his face stone-like, emotionless— although his clenched, white-knuckled fists conveyed his true inner turmoil. A uniformed officer was waiting for them when they walked out of the elevator. Jason noticed two brass bars on his collar. Nervously, the officer wiped his sandy blond hair off his forehead. Shorter than Jason by several inches, he came to attention and saluted.

"Lieutenant," Jason said, addressing the young officer. "Look, I'm an inactive Navy officer. So, no need for..." The younger man interrupted Jason mid-sentence.

"Sir, I'm Lieutenant Perkins—I apologize for any misunderstanding."

"What misunderstanding? And as you were... relax, Lieutenant."

Jason continued to walk fast down the cavern in the direction of the ship. The dire situation above was still fresh in his mind. Perkins and Ricket scrambled to keep up.

"Sir, before we set off for Earth, the admiral provided clear orders. I'd like to review them with you now, or at the earliest possible time."

Jason paused, and looked at Perkins. "Well, what is it...? Get it off your chest, Lieutenant Perkins."

"Lieutenant Commander, I was instructed upon meeting with you to deliver this—first thing." Perkins handed Jason a large white envelope. He flipped it over and read the text written in big block letters:

EYES ONLY — LIEUTENANT COMMANDER JASON REYNOLDS

Jason tore off the top of the envelope and emptied the contents into his other hand. A folded letter and two small brass eagle collar pins lay in his open palm. He opened the letter and read the contents.

Jason,

I'm hoping you and I had the opportunity to talk prior to you receiving this letter. If not, Ricket can bring you up to speed.

Shipboard life is not as formal on The Lilly as you are undoubtedly used to on a U.S. Navy vessel. But I've tried to carry, as much as possible, the traditions, and even some of the formality associated with the U.S. Navy into our own young, interstellar military force, which is called the United Planetary Alliance, or simply Alliance.

I've actually been back to Earth numerous times—right there at the small aquifer base beneath the scrapyard. I've watched your career, stayed connected as best I could, albeit from a distance. You're a fine officer, Jason. Even with the outcome of that Somalian pirate situation. I wasn't there but doubt I'd have handled things any differently. The two captain's clusters are no mistake. This, as informal as it may be, provides official notice of not only your promotion to the rank of captain, but induction into the United Alliance.

If you're feeling overwhelmed and totally unqualified, well, you are absolutely correct. In fact, you have no idea how little prepared you are. But what has taken me fifteen years to discover, exploring one end of the galaxy to the other, you will learn in mere weeks. The technology on the ship is beyond comprehension—some of which I only recently discovered. The Lilly is one of a kind, from an alien race most probably long extinct. Whatever her origin, whoever her designers, or her original crew, remains a mystery. The ship's technology is hundreds, if not thousands of years in advance of anything I've come across. Without Ricket's help it wouldn't have been possible to get her back into space, let alone traversing the universe. But there is far more that we don't know about this vessel than what we do know.

Until now, I've never let her out of my sight. If she were to fall into the hands of the Craing... The implications are staggering. Imagine Adolph Hitler, mid-way through World War II, being offered advanced weapons technology hundreds, if not thousands, of years in advance of the Allied forces. There would have been no stopping him. For some reason, the Alliance has chosen me to lead our forces against the hostile aggression by the Craing. And subsequently we've pooled our forces from planets in multiple sectors, even those thousands of light-years from Earth. We are a force of approximately two thousand warships.

I fear my days here are numbered. My location is no longer a secret. It seems we have a mole in our midst, either here on this planet among our ranks, or there on The Lilly. That's something you'll need to deal with. Moving forward, I only hope what we have planned will be enough. We'll find out soon enough. If the Craing make it through our lines, no doubt Earth will be taken. Get off the planet and come to the Altar system. One more thing—the crew is inexperienced. I'm sorry, but we just could not afford to leave our best there, while the Craing are here knocking at our door.

Properly manned, The Lilly would have

a crew of about 200. You have a ragtag
crew of about 30. Not necessarily all
misfits, but we had to pull from where we
could: A civilian doctor from Jhardon, a
planet here in the Altar system, from
Planetary University; ground forces
officers; several men released from the
brig; even an athletic sports personality. By
the time you come onboard, they will have
undergone HyperLearning, which will help.
Both Lieutenant Perkins and Ricket will
bring you up to speed on everything else.
Good luck, son.
Dad
Admiral Perry Reynolds
United Planetary Alliance

Jason replaced the captain's clusters as well
as the letter back into its envelope.

"Thanks for delivering this to me,
Lieutenant Perkins. We obviously have a lot to
talk about." Together, the three of them hustled
back down the rocky tunnel. Jason looked back
at Ricket and the lieutenant. "Right now I need
more information," Jason said. "Do you have
access to any of the TV news feeds from
above?"

"Yes, of course, we've been monitoring
events as they've unfolded. It's apparent that
this isn't a planet-wide invasion—at least not
yet. We believe they are right here, specifically
in this part of North America, looking for The
Lilly."

"The Craing followed her here?"

"No, that would not be possible," Ricket
chimed in. "As your father explained, there is a

mole, someone aligned with the Craing opposition forces. The Craing were tipped off and subsequently were waiting above Earth in high orbit. We believe the Craing detected the ship just prior to our going underground. Their incursion has been limited to a fifty-mile radius above."

Lieutenant Perkins then continued: "Four Craing light cruisers were deployed—seems they are either killing off local populace or, in some cases, bringing them onboard their ships—most likely to be interrogated. Right now, San Bernardino is center-stage news around the world."

"What the hell is the military doing while all this is happening?" Jason asked, even more agitated.

"The military was fast to react. Ground forces have been deployed and hundreds of fighters were scrambled from Vandenberg, Edwards, as well as Los Angeles. They were all quickly destroyed with little damage, if any, to the small contingent of Craing fighters." Jason stopped running and looked at Perkins, momentarily speechless.

Scowling, Jason felt like he wanted to punch someone. "So, what's the latest you've heard?"

Ricket continued on towards the ship. The lieutenant shook his head. "They've gone. All four Craing ships lifted off and all but one have left orbit."

As they rounded the final corner into the

main cavern, Jason was surprised to see the crew had assembled into three rows of ten—all standing at attention in front of the ship. Unsure what was expected, Jason brought himself to attention and acknowledged their salute in return. He looked at each one. The crew was a disheveled lot. They were giving it a good try, but it was obvious they lacked any real discipline—several wore a smirk—several others looked generally pissed off. Observing their behavior, Jason wondered what he'd gotten himself into.

"I'm Lieutenant Commander Jason Reynolds. I'm assuming most of you, if not all of you, know my father, Admiral Perry Reynolds. It seems we've been thrown together—and an odd lot we are, yes?" Smiling, Jason looked to his new crew, feeling unsure if a smile was appropriate or not.

"Everyone, please stand at ease," Jason said. "The truth is I probably wouldn't have joined this fight. I had my own battle to contend with. But now the fight is personal. Our planet has been attacked and someone I care about is locked up in the hull of a Craing cruiser. Truth is, all I can think about is getting this thing up in space and chasing them down. So bear with me." Jason had a fleeting image of Nan being ushered up the gangway of the Craing ship, causing his heart to skip a beat. "From what I understand, we're safe here underground. Though the Craing know we're near. Let me get situated and then I want to meet with each of you. I'll come to you, where you are stationed, and you can tell me what you do and a little about yourself." Jason took one more look through the ranks. "Dismissed." The group disbanded and went back to their previous duties. Ricket headed off towards the supercomputer-type machines against the wall. Lieutenant Perkins stood with Jason.

"Sir, may I show you the ship?" the lieutenant asked, with obvious pride.

"What are we doing here? What's it going to take to get this ship up in space?" Jason asked, frustrated. The ground shook, and muffled explosions reverberated from above off in the distance. Rocks and dirt fell from the cavern walls.

"As you can tell, the Craing want this ship. But we've never fired her weapons, didn't even know how to access them until recently. We're not ready. And frankly, neither are you. We go up there now—go up against that warship—The Lilly will be destroyed."

Jason took a breath and acknowledged Perkins's points with a nod. "All right. So a tour it is. Lead on, Lieutenant," Jason said.

Lieutenant Perkins looked to the ship and held his arms out wide as a used-car salesman would when making a pitch. "The Lilly is 125 meters long, in earth measurements, with a width of 75 meters. She has five distinct decks. Her outer hull is coated with a hardened self-repairing substance—it's similar to other nanotized materials utilized throughout the ship.

And there, close to the two primary drive units, are the two fighter bay doors—although all openings, hatches and seams are virtually invisible when closed." Lieutenant Perkins shrugged. "Something to do with that same nanotized material. The ship has a complement of six one-man fighters available—although one is out of commission."

"Being repaired?" Jason asked.

"Trying to… like with everything else on the ship. There's no repair manual—figuring out the operation, maintenance and repair of things has been pretty much a crap shoot," Lieutenant Perkins said, shrugging.

"Shall we move inside and continue?"

"One question, what is that circular thing at the top forward area of the hull?" Jason asked, pointing to a curved section near the top front of the ship. It appeared to have a slightly different composition, and an almost dome-like appearance.

"That's the observatory—if time permits, we'll see more of that from inside," the lieutenant answered, pointing to the gangway leading into the rear of the ship.

Once back inside, Lieutenant Perkins was ready to continue the tour. "And here we have the—"

"Excuse me, Lieutenant, would it be possible to continue this tour a bit later? I need to check on my daughter," Jason said, showing concern.

"Yes, I'm sorry. Thoughtless of me. Let me

show you to your cabins." The young officer led the way, looking back over his shoulder to ensure Jason followed. "We'll be moving between decks, sir. I need to warn you in advance that our doing so involves a phase-shift process—and the only way to explain it is to show you. But leave it to say, there are no elevators or stairs on this vessel." Lieutenant Perkins turned towards an adjacent corridor and paused in front of a wider hatchway—which, under closer scrutiny, wasn't really a hatchway at all. Outlined in a frame of light blue, the opening itself was translucent—almost like looking through water.

"You're at mid-Deck Level 1 right now, sir. We'll be moving to Deck 4 above. Before entering here, what is called a DeckPort, hold up four fingers—like this—before entering."

Lieutenant Perkins held up four fingers, stepped forward, and disappeared out of sight. Jason remembered this process from earlier with Ricket, when first bringing Mollie into the ship. He stepped into the DeckPort and felt the same, not unpleasant, tingle. Jason emerged on what he assumed was Deck 4 to find the lieutenant waiting for him, with a smile on his face. Jason looked around and nodded his head in appreciation.

"And if two people enter the port at the same time—but are going to different decks?"

"It's not a mechanical process, sir. You'd go to the floor you indicated and they, in turn, would go to theirs." Jason nodded again, while trying to keep the bewilderment from his expression.

"The truth is, the hand gestures are not actually needed. There are 32 separate and individual DeckPorts on this ship. The Lilly's AI is highly intuitive and can take you between decks as well as to any ports automatically, once you have been nano-configured—like the rest of the crew have been. We can discuss it later, if you wish." Jason nodded. He was quickly feeling in over his head. The corridors were somewhat wider on this level. He noticed again the cleanliness of the ship and the fluid-artistic lines of the padded walls, which on this level were a soft tan color. They walked for what seemed a long time before coming to several arched doorways.

"We are at the officers' quarters section of the ship and, specifically, the captain's suite," Lieutenant Perkins said, gesturing towards the widest of the three doorways. "Mollie is already inside." Lieutenant Perkins stepped forward— just as with the DeckPort—but this time what appeared to be a solid door disappeared before him, allowing access to the captain's suite beyond.

"Dad! Where have you been?" Mollie asked, admonishing Jason in a motherly tone. She got up from the floor where she had been playing some kind of 3D virtual game—which hung suspended in the air—seemingly waiting for her next move. She ran over and hugged her father, giving a disapproving scowl as she looked up at him. He hugged her back and smiled. Taking in the surroundings, Jason was again taken aback by the ship.

Lieutenant Perkins said, "This is the captain's ready room." To the left was a hallway, which Jason guessed led to the rest of the suite. The room was divided into two sections: the first was a conference room with an oval table. configured with multiple large display units placed high up on the curved bulkhead. The adjoining room, more like an office, held a large desk with a stone or marble-type surface. Four comfortably padded chairs and a matching couch completed the furnishings in the cabin. The lieutenant continued to speak as they proceeded down the hallway.

"Here you have a kitchenette and a small eating area." Jason noticed a small alcove and virtual workstation across the hall from the kitchenette.

"What's this?" Jason asked.

"Oh, that's similar to the food replicator in the kitchenette; it's your garment replicator. This is used for things like your daily spacer and officer jumpsuits as well as any other casual attire—everything here is recyclable. Of course, garments are custom-sized and fitted to each crewmember's unique body. Similarly, any replication of combat-type gear is handled through the Gunny's station on Deck 2." The thought of needing combat gear had thrown Jason, but in lieu of recent events it made sense.

"Moving down the hall, you have two

bedrooms—here on the right is Mollie's room, with her own wash facilities, and here on the left is your bedroom, also with its own wash facilities." Jason took it all in. Both of their cabins seemed relatively large and well appointed for a military vessel. Again, Jason needed to cut the tour short.

"Would it be possible, Lieutenant, for you to give my daughter and me some privacy? We really need to have some time right now."

"Of course; I'll be on the bridge, one level down at the forward end of the ship."

"Thank you—I've been there and will find you shortly," Jason said, quickly ushering the lieutenant out of the suite. Turning back to Mollie, he was more concerned how to best explain everything that had occurred up top— the attack by the Craing, her mother's abduction...

"Come on, kiddo, sit down for a sec," Jason said, gesturing for her to sit on the couch. "None of this is going to be easy for you, Mollie. And I'm very, very sorry. Things are happening beyond our control. Unbelievable things. There's a war of sorts occurring above our planet and we are now involved in it."

"Yeah, I know all this already, Dad," she said, rolling her eyes. "Remember, I saw you and Grandpa talking?"

"Oh, that's right... wasn't sure how much of that you actually understood. But Mollie, there's more to it than that. The Craing, the aliens that Grandpa was talking about... Well, they're above us right now, attacking our home, our planet. And worst of all, they've taken your mother and others onto their ships. But I'm going to get her back—I promise you, we'll somehow get her back." Mollie's eyes brimmed with tears, comprehension of what her father said now taking hold. Looking down at his daughter, Jason wondered how she was going to handle what was coming.

"Dad?"

"Yeah, Mollie?"

"When are we going after her; when are we getting Mom back?"

"Very soon."

Chapter 4

Jason arrived at the bridge four hours later. Tired, but he had needed to spend some quality time with Mollie before putting her to bed. Earlier, they had played several virtual games—all of which she'd easily won. She was a natural at thinking in terms of 3D space. Her favorite, a virtual Hide and Seek game, with AI-generated avatars—so real-looking even Mollie's Hello Kitty T-shirt was perfectly depicted. Looking down at the quasi-transparent, perfectly scaled representation of The Lilly, Jason realized it was just as much a learning tool as it was a game. He'd watched her getting totally enveloped in the game. Then, at other times, the reality of their situation would sober her mood. Sometimes for only moments, sometimes longer, the tears would come. Then, just as quickly, they were gone.

"Oh, Dad, watch this—it's so cool," she said, excitedly. She jumped up off the floor and pushed several of the chairs back against the wall, giving them more room for the game. Using her hands, she pulled and stretched the corners of the virtual ship, making it almost fill the room. Then, using a finger, she tapped at the side of the now-floating representation of The Lilly—it gently spun around on its axis.

By the time they finished playing, they both had an excellent idea of the ship's basic layout, including the bridge, mess hall, observatory, gymnasium, engineering and communications sections, and something called the Zoo—which had Mollie more than a little interested. Jason also noticed there were numerous inaccessible greyed-out areas.

Lieutenant Perkins didn't immediately notice Jason standing mere feet outside the entrance to the bridge, giving Jason time to take a better look around the ship's command center. The room was oblong, with gently curved and padded bulkheads narrowing slightly towards the front of the room. As he'd noticed before, the most impressive aspect of the bridge was the massive curved virtual display that completely encircled the top of the room 360 degrees. Both sides of the room were lined with consoles and a myriad of complex instruments; each had an integrated small monitor. Additionally, there were three two-seater consoles, each one at a different level, facing forward. A command chair and two smaller officer's chairs placed slightly behind it were located on the top level at the back of the bridge. The room easily held ten crewmembers, but only four were present. Two men sat with their feet up on their consoles—laughing and cavorting about something. Lieutenant Perkins sat in the command chair reviewing his tablet—although Jason noticed the tablet was completely virtual and there was no actual hardware present. The lieutenant looked up when Jason entered the bridge. A boson's whistle sounded from somewhere followed by "Captain on deck!" announced in a pleasant female voice.

"Good evening, Captain," greeted Lieutenant Perkins, as he stood and came to attention. Jason, not comfortable in the least with having the captain moniker, let alone full responsibility for the vessel, smiled and took a seat at a nearby console.

"As you were, Lieutenant, please sit." Jason gazed around the command center again before looking at the junior officer. "Can we have the room for a moment, gentlemen?" Jason requested, and then waited while the other three crewmembers shuffled out. "You and I both know I'm ill-prepared to captain this ship, Lieutenant. It seems fairly insurmountable, my learning what will be necessary to—" Jason looked around again, defeated. Lieutenant Perkins smiled and sat down next to Jason.

"Basically, sir, you just don't know what you don't know yet."

"There has to be someone onboard more qualified to command this ship than myself," Jason said flatly.

"I'm from a small town in Iowa, one of the few crewmembers also from Earth. Three years ago I was pulled into this war, similar to you, and brought before the admiral on a day when my life changed forever. I was clueless, totally out of my element here. Hell, I was a junior officer—just off my first tour in Afghanistan. I flew a helicopter, for God's sake."

Jason smiled at the younger officer's

candor. "OK, so how do I get up to speed with all this?"

"Both Ricket and The Lilly have amazing technological capabilities—and the ability to infuse you with the necessary technical knowledge for you to move forward, all fairly quickly. It's more of a medical procedure than anything else. What they cannot do is make you into a natural leader. Or someone the crew will willingly follow into battle. You already have those unique qualities, and that's why we need your help. The admiral has faith in you, and to be honest, so do I."

Jason noticed the top of a baseball cap moving behind one of the consoles, and then Ricket appeared to the left of the lieutenant. Like a small child, he climbed up on a chair, turned, and sat facing forward. "We must proceed with your HyperLearning process as soon as possible," Ricket said, looking from one to the other. "That is, if you have decided to join the crew, and commit to this endeavor."

"So what kind of procedure will this be? Is it dangerous? Nothing can happen to me; I may be all Mollie has left."

"Not so dangerous—but quite painful," Ricket replied evenly. The lieutenant squirmed in his seat and nodded his head.

"Truth is, it hurts like a son of a bitch—it's no fun. There's a different HyperLearning procedure for every rank. I can't even imagine what it'll feel like for a captain," the lieutenant said, eyebrows raised.

"My father went through this?"

"Yes," Ricket replied, "for both the captaincy level, and then again later for the admiral's."

Jason looked from one to the other—deciding what to do. "I really don't have a choice, do I?"

Both Ricket and Lieutenant Perkins replied simultaneously: "Not really."

Jason couldn't think of a reason to put off the inevitable. He was like a ship without a rudder right now—unable to properly lead the crew and frustrated that more and more time was elapsing without a rescue attempt plan for Nan, or even some semblance of a plan.

* * *

From what Ricket had conveyed, the procedure would take several hours, and his recovery time would be a day or two after that. Jason was anxious to get into space and on track to find Nan. He would do whatever was necessary to make that happen. But seeing the state of the crew, their limited experience and total lack of discipline, well, it didn't give him much confidence.

Once in Medical, Dira, a female med-tech or perhaps a doctor of alien origin, was helping Jason prepare for the procedure. She had instructed him to empty his bladder and bowels, and then change into a special outer garment. Dira helped Jason into the same clamshell capsule Mollie had been placed in earlier. Jason lay back and tried to relax. He saw Dira looking over Ricket's shoulder as he rapidly entered information into the terminal pad. Ricket was explaining to her how to configure a captain-rank level HyperLearning module for Jason's particular physiology. Jason saw Dira nod her head as Ricket went through a list of screen prompts and configuration settings. It seemed Dira was being trained on the use of this equipment. Ricket's calm monotone voice was starting to make Jason sleepy. But then he heard the tension in Dira's voice as she pointed to a listing on the screen.

"So he'll be getting the full spacer prep material, including astrophysics basics, applied quantum theory, the latest FTL design material, the biological as well as nano-sciences package, and the complete operation and maintenance of space-bearing vessels material? That seems like a lot, Ricket, at one time."

"Actually," Ricket said, "the admiral has ordered up the complete HyperLearning panel for Jason, everything The Lilly has to offer, including the admiralty-level strategic capsule." Ricket paused and looked over at Jason.

Dira, shaking her head, said, "That's the same procedure your father undertook, and substantially more to boot." She took a step back and put her hands on her hips—an indignant expression on her face. "Personally, I think that's too much, and why are you doing the nano-implants procedure simultaneously,

Ricket?" Ricket and Dira held each other's stare, and then both looked at Jason, eyebrows raised.

Jason was pretty sure he was hearing a bit more information than he should be. He definitely felt uncomfortable with a technician questioning an officer in front of him. Or was Ricket really an officer? Jason couldn't imagine this sort of disrespect occurring onboard a naval vessel—insubordination was a serious infraction. But then again, maybe Dira was right to question Ricket—especially if what Ricket was configuring was considered dangerous? But why not hold the conversation off line, in private? Jason realized his mind was quickly reeling out of control. He'd deal with the crew and what was proper military conduct over time. For now, though, he needed to sleep and get the procedure over with. He noticed the two of them looking at him for a response.

"Yes, load it up. I won't have time to undergo this procedure again, and I'll need all the intelligence data you've got to be at my disposal. Please, finish up and get things moving along." Both nodded. Dira, attempting a smile, clearly looked worried. After a few more taps at the screen, the clamshell began to close. Jason abruptly leaned forward and turned toward Ricket.

"So, don't forget Mollie is up early," Jason reminded. "She'll be looking for me. You'll be there, right? You'll explain where I'm at, right?"

Calmly, Ricket replied, "I'll be there, yes;

I'll explain where you're at. Lie back and stop squirming around, please."

Jason's last thoughts before he drifted off to sleep were of Mollie, then of Nan being forced onto the Craing ship.

He had never experienced anything close to this. The pain was unrelenting. But it was the invasion of his mind, his thoughts—a complete disregard for his inner sanctity—the total loss of self that was the worst. He'd become conscious several times during the night. At one point, he looked out and saw Dira watching him. Her pale violet skin contrasted with her short black hair and, something possibly unique to her species, eyelashes extending several inches. She gave him an assuring nod, checked his vitals again, and left Medical. By the time the clamshell was open again, Jason felt like he'd been thrown off the side of a building. Dira was there, using a wet cloth on his forehead, concern in her eyes.

"So, I guess I survived," Jason said, attempting a smile.

"Actually, it was touch and go. Around 2:00AM I checked in on you. Your vitals registered higher than they should. Then you alarmed two more times in the night, showing tearing had occurred in your cerebral cortex. Ricket had assured me that the nano-implants would repair any damage. He was right. Once they were introduced, no more problems."

* * *

Jason was back in his own cabin the following afternoon. He needed another full day before he felt steady enough on his feet to move about the ship. Mollie had mothered him to distraction. In his absence, she had figured out how to use the food replicator located in the captain's kitchenette. Chicken soup seemed to stay down the best. Both Ricket and Dira had come by to check on his progress, as well as Lieutenant Perkins, who was now sitting in a chair at his bunk side. Over the past few hours, Jason had come up with a basic plan, and he needed to bring the lieutenant up to speed.

"First off, I need to understand Ricket's role aboard this ship—does he have some kind of rank or position?"

"We all just refer to him as the Science Officer. Perhaps a better description is caretaker. He's pretty much the only one who knows how things work."

"How's that possible?" Jason said, exasperated. "I take it we have a qualified engineer onboard?"

"Yes, that would be Horris Latimer. From what I understand, he's amazing with FTL fusion drive mechanics."

"So, what's the problem?"

"Although Horris would never admit it, he's utterly confused by the propulsion system on The Lilly. It uses a totally different technology than he, or anyone else here, is familiar with."

"How about Ricket? How much does he understand?"

"Quite a bit—at least enough to keep things running."

Jason shook his head, not sure his questions were fully being answered.

"I've made a list of the section heads I'd like to meet with first thing—starting with Chief Engineer Horris, then the head of Security, followed by all the officers."

Jason was quickly getting accustomed to his enhanced cognitive abilities. Amazed, it was as if overnight he'd acquired encyclopedic knowledge and advanced technical experience that normally would take years or even decades to possess. Now he could draw upon it at will— whatever information was required was right there, available for the asking.

First stop was engineering, situated on Deck Two. Jason left Mollie in the care of Dira, who had volunteered to show her the Zoo.

Fully nanotized, and just as Lieutenant Perkins had promised, the DeckPorts were now intuitive, or personally attuned to which floor and location Jason wished to visit.

Stepping through to Level Two, Jason easily found the section marked Engineering. He had showered, shaved and dressed in the provided captain's everyday spacer's jumpsuit— similar to those worn by the other officers. On his collar were the new captain's pins from his father. The Engineering door dematerialized as Jason entered. Engineering was a large section; some areas were open to the two decks above and below. Black gangways of some kind of composite material crisscrossed the bulkheads at various levels. Several crewmembers above him had stopped to look over the railing. Apparently visitors were uncommon in Engineering. Two men were having a heated discussion ahead of Jason. They looked up at the same time—both came to attention.

"As you were, gentlemen," Jason said, smiling, with his hand out to shake. "I'm Captain Reynolds." Jason immediately thought how strange it was that several days ago he had found it difficult to own that title, but things were different now. The men shook hands.

"I'm Chief Horris, but everyone just calls me Chief. This is Seaman Bristol." Bristol nodded, but quickly excused himself. Jason eyed the chief, who was a big man—his overalls tight across his large belly.

"Nice to meet you, Chief—hope I'm not interrupting anything important?" Jason queried, gesturing towards Bristol's rapid departure.

"Not at all, sir… just not in agreement with one of the rank and file—nothing I can't handle."

"I don't mean to step on your command style, Chief, but it's not the crews' place to argue with their superiors. That's flat out insubordination."

"Well… I don't think it's as much insubordination, as it is young stubbornness. You know how it is…"

"No, Chief, I'm sorry, but I don't. And you're not doing Seaman Bristol, or anyone else on this ship, any favors by encouraging lax conduct. When the time comes, and it will, you'll want crewmembers who take orders, not argue with them."

"Aye, sir—and yes, I agree. Guess we've let things run amuck too long around here." Chief looked a bit sheepish. "How 'bout I show you around Engineering. This is an incredible ship, and boy is she fast. Of course FTL is nothing new; all the Alliance vessels travel beyond the speed of light, but The Lilly comes at it differently—not bending space around the ship, but bending space around projected multiverse versions of the ship. The admiral never fully tested the ship's capabilities in that regard."

Jason spent the next hour on a tour of Engineering. Chief Horris did a good job pointing out the various systems that drove the ship. Jason found he not only understood the mechanical aspects of the two large drive units, but much of the theoretical properties behind them as well. Unfortunately, his recent HyperLearning curriculum had not included anything relating to one aspect of The Lilly—specifically, her exotic drive antimatter configuration.

"I'd like to tell you we have everything figured out, but we don't. Ricket seems to have the best theoretical mind onboard, but even he has yet to figure out some of its technology. We have two antimatter drive units that don't use standard antiprotons. The technology on The

Lilly is in undiscovered territory. Fortunately, systems in Engineering don't seem to need much in the way of maintenance. As far as I know, they've never gone down."

"What if they were damaged in battle? How will you repair them?"

"That was a major concern of the admiral as well. In fact, that's the primary reason the ship has been kept well back from space confrontations. The speed of the ship, and her phase-shift capability, have made her invaluable to the Alliance."

"Phase-shift capabilities?" Jason asked, now totally confused.

The chief smiled, "Ah, so the HyperLearning module didn't quite cover everything, did it? Let me put it to you this way. Did you see an exit out of this massive underground aquifer? Did you see any way to fly this ship in or out of here?"

"Um, actually no," Jason replied, trying to remember if he saw another egress or tunnel or any other way in or out. "How the hell did you get it in here?"

Chief Horris smiled, enjoying the confused look on the captain's face. "We never flew in or out of this damn cave—The Lilly can phase-shift through solid matter. Once you come to terms with how this ship utilizes the multiverse—actually piggybacking into parallel universe realities, it starts to make more sense. You'll see these same principles used in other on-board systems as well... like the DeckPorts, drive propulsion, medical, just to name a few."

"OK, but back to my original question. How do we repair the systems on this ship when damaged?"

"First of all, the outer hull is another exotic composite material—it's infused with self-repairing nanites. As you've probably noticed, everything inside and outside of this ship looks brand new. Those little buggers are constantly at work—they live to conform to their pre-programmed configuration. I don't know what it would take to put a hole in the hull, but it would have to be something in the nature of a fusion-tipped missile. I don't think energy weapons would have much effect on her. But again, we haven't actually brought her into battle."

"OK, what's the second point? What aren't you telling me?" Jason felt he was pulling teeth for information, that the chief had a sense for the dramatic. He obviously was proud of the ship he served on but come on man—get to the point.

"We've been held underground for close to three weeks now. Truth is, we're all going a bit stir crazy. But Ricket, who's never idle, has been exploring areas of The Lilly we didn't even know were here. In fact, there's a whole fifth level, a sub-level in-between the Fourth and Fifth Levels. We call it sub-Deck 4B. Anyway, we didn't see it hidden above the two drive units. The level is close to thirty feet high. Within this area is one more phase-shift system—more like a phase synthesizer, of sorts.

If you're wondering where Ricket disappears to lately, it's there—he's trying to figure out how the hell to use this thing."

"Well, what is it? Why would you need a phase synthesizer?" Jason asked, confused.

"To make something that does not exist on this plane of existence. We think, or Ricket thinks, that the phase synthesizer can manufacture new ship components on demand as well. So to answer your question, sir, if something gets damaged in battle, there may be the capability to replace parts instead of repairing them."

"Thank you for your time, Chief. I'm sure I'll have a lot more questions—but this has been very helpful. Oh, one more thing. What can you tell me about the onboard armaments?"

"Well, two things." Jason prepared himself for more of Chief's grandstanding. "She does indeed have weaponry, and no, they've never been battle tested. You'll want to connect with our gunnery chief—Gunny Orion. She's situated on Deck 2, forward near the bow."

"She? A woman's the gunny, huh?"

"Oh yeah, and I suggest, sir, you keep any 'it's a male-dominated-world' inference out of your tone when you meet with her. She's a Marine and not one who's accepted gender-based limitations. Although she looks human, she's actually from Tarkin—a planet situated close to where the admiral is now. She was quite famous there—some sort of sports figure, from what I've heard."

Chapter 5

En route to see Gunny Orion, and near the far end of the ship, Jason was pinged; a soft, almost melodic sound indicated there was an incoming message from Lieutenant Perkins. Only the message was via his recently acquired nano-implants. Jason's brow furrowed. Why hadn't he been informed on how these damn implants work? Then, answering his own question, he realized he already knew the answer. It was another skill given him via his strenuous HyperLearning treatment.

"Go for Captain," he said aloud.

"Captain, sorry to disturb you, but we have a situation. Um, well…"

"What is it, Lieutenant? It can't be that bad. Tell me." Jason was feeling more at ease in his new role as commander. But somehow he needed the ship's crew to act like a competent military contingent, not old granny's knitting circle.

"It's your daughter, sir. Can you port over to Deck 3, designation E25? She seems to have—well, there's an emergency situation. Can you come right away, sir?"

"Absolutely. Is she OK? What's going on, Perkins? Has she been injured again?" Jason was already running toward the closest DeckPort. He knew exactly where Deck 3, E25 was located; not from the HyperLearning ordeal as much as from Mollie's virtual game. That was the ship's designation for the Zoo—which he still wasn't clear on.

* * *

Jason sped out of the DeckPort at a full run, nearly toppling over another crewmember in the hallway. He felt guilty he hadn't spent enough time with Mollie as it was. She'd already had a near fatal, actually totally fatal, mishap. What kind of danger was she in? Jason's mind raced. Perhaps he'd have to talk to someone in Security about getting a sidearm. Apparently things were more dangerous here than he'd realized. He sprinted down two more corridors and made a sharp right toward the entrance of the Zoo.

The door dematerialized—Jason rushed in and quickly surveyed his surroundings. The room was huge; in fact, it didn't make sense. The area seemed bigger, more expansive than the ship itself. Jason's first impression was that it was some kind of optical illusion. But that didn't translate to what he was seeing. There were numerous large enclosures—each one a separate natural environment. Some were desolate and rocky with high-up cliff protrusions that jutted out at near horizontal angles. Others were lush, forest-like areas, and another was totally aquatic, with light green steam billowing into the air—the water seemingly suspended—nothing there, no glass, nothing to contain its liquid contents. As phenomenal as these observations were, they paled in comparison to what Jason was now seeing.

Each enclosure held one or more large animal—if animal was even the right terminology. Strange species, alien species, as they moved about here and there within their confined spaces. Suddenly, a man-sized worm organism jumped from the aquatic liquid into the air—then, at the apex of its jump, it seemed to hover and then spin its body 180 degrees— revealing two eyes, a nose and a mouth. A mouth that was smiling. As quickly as it appeared, it was back below the surface. Jason's heart nearly leapt from his chest as a loud trumpet-like sound blared right behind him. Startled, he lost his balance and fell on his backside. Ready to run if necessary, he spun around on his butt and saw a full-grown, 11-foot-tall Indian elephant.

"Hi, Dad!" Mollie yelled down from her perch near the animal's massive head. "This is Raja. Raja, this is Dad." Mollie gave Raja a loving pat and giggled. Then Jason noticed Dira, a wide smile across her face, standing to the right of the elephant's thick front legs. Lieutenant Perkins, also smiling, was leaning against the bulkhead by the Zoo entrance.

"What the hell! You scared the living daylights out of me. Whose idea was this, anyway?" Jason blurted out, having a hard time keeping the smile off his own face.

"It was Dira's," Mollie said, with unabashed laughter. "She said you're too serious all the time and it would be good for you."

"Did she now?" Jason retorted, seeing Dira with a hand over her mouth, laughing uncontrollably. Jason looked up at his daughter—beaming and obviously proud of herself. He spun around on his heels and took in his incredible surroundings. Strange sounds and smells filled the air. Nearby, what looked to be a saber-toothed tiger emerged from a cave; its expression seemed bored by all the commotion.

"How on earth is all this possible?" Jason inquired, looking over at the lieutenant.

Lieutenant Perkins walked over and extended a hand to help him off the ground, which Jason accepted. "More phase-shift technology. Very little of this compartment is actually onboard the ship itself. The combined Zoo enclosures are many square miles in circumference. Like DeckPorts, when you enter the various habitats, you're actually moving across to a separate, albeit connected, piggybacked reality of the multiverse. That's according to Ricket, anyway. I don't pretend to understand it all. Here, watch this." Perkins walked to a nearby control panel, looked back at Jason and then pressed a key. The thirty or so habitat enclosures all rotated around like a large carousel until they were replaced by a new, completely different set of environments and animals. "There are multiple different sets—

cool, huh?" Perkins said, resetting the enclosures to the original configuration. Just then, an older man with a long grey beard and dirty green overalls walked up. He carried an old wooden stepladder over his shoulder and was now positioning it near the front of the elephant.

"Time for Raja's dinner, little one," the man said, gesturing for Mollie to come down. Dira climbed halfway up the ladder to assist Mollie, who now seemed a little more nervous of the height. Mollie slid down on her belly and Dira caught her and led her down to the floor. Mollie gave Dira a hug and then one to Jason. Dira crossed her arms under her breasts and looked over to Jason. "Mollie would like to ask you a question, but I think she's afraid to ask."

Embarrassed, Mollie blushed, and for once was tongue-tied.

"Well, what is it, kiddo? What do you want to ask me?" Jason queried, crouching down to Mollie's height.

Mollie smiled and then quickly glanced at Dira and the older man. "I want a job, Dad. I want to work in the Zoo, helping Jack take care of the animals." She gestured to the man with the step ladder.

Jason sobered a bit. "I don't know Mollie— the animals here are dangerous. That's a saber-toothed tiger standing fifty feet from us, for God's sake!"

"The animals do not cross over into the ship itself. Raja here is an exception. She's a good old girl and needs human contact." Jack scratched his beard and shrugged. "Even I don't cross over into the habitats—we have droids do the heavy lifting in that regard. Pen maintenance, feeding, medical support—it's all automated."

"That's all fine and good, but I can't help thinking of that movie Jurassic Park—yes, all good intentions, but what about when the chaos theory raises its ugly head?" Jason saw Mollie's face fall, then tears welled-up in her eyes. It had been wonderful seeing Mollie so happy sitting up there on the elephant—a nice diversion from the stress over her mother's abduction.

"How about I give it some more thought?" Jason said with a smile. "Dira, Jack and I, and uh... maybe Ricket, will meet tomorrow and go over all the details; what you would and wouldn't be doing at the Zoo. How's that sound?" Jason looked over at Dira and Jack, who nodded their heads in unison. Mollie, tears turning into a wide smile, squealed with delight and hugged her father. Leaving Jack to his duties, they walked out of the Zoo.

Jason wondered why he hadn't already known about this area of the ship. Had his HyperLearning session been incomplete? He realized there was a growing list of things pertaining to The Lilly that he needed to ask Ricket about. He also needed to talk to the gunny and whoever was in charge of ship security—there was nothing in his memory about that. Mollie and Dira disappeared into a nearby DeckPort. Jason turned to Perkins.

"Who maintains ship security, Lieutenant?"

"I guess I do, for the interim," the lieutenant replied. "One of those positions we weren't able to fill prior to leaving the Altar system."

"Let's talk about that later. I have some ideas."

* * *

Jason found the Gunnery section of the ship, but it was secured and didn't allow access. Jason used his NanoCom to locate Orion and discovered she was on her way back from the gymnasium. Jason heard her coming before he actually saw her. Twenty yards down the corridor she was running and dressed similarly to what athletes on earth wore—some kind of form-fitting Lycra outfit, white athletic shoes, and a matching headband. She was humanoid as far as Jason could tell, with a complex and somewhat confusing mixture of both feminine and masculine characteristics.

"Sorry, boss... didn't know you'd be stopping by today," Orion said, slowing and coming to a stop in front of Jason. Up close he noticed her dark skin was actually an intricate pattern of geometric tattooed symbols. She pulled a small towel from around her neck, emphasizing her protruding large biceps, which any male body builder would surely envy.

"I'm just making my rounds, getting to

know everyone as best I can," Jason said, following her into the Gunnery. He figured she had unlocked the entrance through her own NanoCom—and then was aware he could have done the same thing himself. "I'd like to spend some time with you discussing the ship's armaments and defenses." Jason noticed several racks of weapons, including an assortment of energy-type sidearms and rifles. Like the garment replicator in his suite, there was a similar device here, yet on a much larger scale. Orion gestured toward the device.

"We'll need to get you a combat suit fabricated. The AI has already taken your body measurements, so I'll put that into the works."

As Orion settled in behind a desk, similar to his own but smaller, she quickly logged into her computer system. Not unlike the lieutenant's tablet, everything here was virtual. A light blue and glowing outline of a large display console hovered above the surface of her desk. She tapped at it and it spun several degrees on its axis, allowing them both to better see the display. She typed several keystrokes onto a virtual keyboard and a 3D representation of The Lilly appeared. Jason thought it looked similar to Mollie's game.

"OK. Here we have a representation of the ship, yes?"

Jason nodded, and waited for her to continue.

"Not sure how aware you are on our progression at bringing various dormant systems online. When the ship was first discovered, some fifteen years ago, her AI was basically wiped clean; pretty much everything still worked, but anything specific to her previous or original crew had been stripped out. Probably why there are still significant holes in what we know and don't know concerning the ship's operation. Ricket has had to painstakingly recode much of her access parameters. I think Ricket and the Lilly Artificial Intelligence have a love-hate relationship, but that's just me. The last three weeks have been remarkable in regards to what we've—mostly Ricket— uncovered. Not only the discovery of sub-Deck 4B and that phase synthesizer contraption, but some kind of JIT utilization for ordinances."

"JIT?" Jason repeated.

"Yeah, like companies or manufacturers, they have a Just In Time process where they only build what they need and avoid having to stockpile massive quantities. As you'll see in a moment, this vessel has a full complement of energy weapons, including four powerful plasma cannons. The problem's with our non-energy weaponry. I couldn't find any ammunition stores on the ship. A gun without bullets is pretty much useless, yes?"

"Seems to me the phase synthesizer would have to churn out ordnances at incredible speed. Missiles and such are complex multi-faceted devices," Jason said. "How close is Ricket to bringing this online?"

"Hmm, well, let's find out," Orion said,

biting her lip. "Lilly, connect an audible com request to Ricket, please."

"Hold one moment while I see if he can join your conversation," Lilly AI replied in a definitive, matter of fact tone. Orion rolled her eyes, much the same as Mollie would do. Jason smiled, but it was yet another example of his crew in serious need of less personality and more discipline.

"Go for Ricket," the mechanical voice replied.

"I'm here with the captain in Gunnery, Ricket. He has a few questions for you."

"Good afternoon, Captain, how may I assist you?"

"Orion's the second person who's informed me about the phase synthesizer device. What can you tell me about it? What's your progress in getting it to work? Is that even the right terminology?"

"Apparently it was never not working. An amazing device. Virtually every system on the ship is tied into the phase synthesizer. What I hadn't discovered until recently, is that it utilizes hundreds of micro-ports, which are similar to DeckPorts. Why Lilly wouldn't automatically inform me of their connection, I'm not quite sure—but I suppose she has her reasons."

Jason realized that Ricket, like others on the ship, had a cautiously respectful relationship with the AI. Almost as if the AI had loyalties elsewhere.

"Have you been able to configure the phase synthesizer for weapon ordnances?"

"Have not tried, Captain, but now that I have coded the missing interface, I see all ship systems have come online." Ricket sounded more excited than Jason had previously heard. Seemingly, getting the phase synthesizer to work must have been quite an accomplishment—the missing puzzle piece that would allow The Lilly, fifteen years later, to become fully operational again.

"Thank you, Ricket. Orion out."

"Lilly, please run through your weaponry. Both offense and defense capabilities for the captain."

"Of course, and good afternoon, Captain Reynolds." Jason recognized the voice as the one he'd heard on the bridge.

"Good afternoon to you as well, Lilly," Jason said. He'd never had to consider the social and operational dynamics of a virtual crewmember. The virtual 3-dimensional representation of the ship came alive on the display. Lilly's voice, distinctly feminine, slightly authoritarian, perhaps even bossy, proceeded to describe her defensive as well as offensive systems. Jason watched as the various hidden weaponry, highlighted in shades of red, could be deployed from virtually every section of the ship. Then, when each of the two massive rail-gun assemblies snapped down, one forward and one aft, Jason noticed Orion's concentration had become even more intense.

"This part's all new, Captain," Orion said, excitedly. "Whatever Ricket did with his coding efforts, the ship is now capable of so much more. Look how the rail gun systems can now access needed munitions automatically through their individual phase-shift feeder ports."

Jason moved closer toward the display to see exactly what Orion was pointing at.

The AI continued on—talking about a wide array of missile systems, some of which were standard aim-and-fire dumb missiles; others had complex tracking algorithms, and some were packaged with nuclear and fusion warheads. It seemed to Jason they had a virtual cornucopia of missile and tracking capability that could be custom-configured on the fly. Only time would tell how The Lilly's diverse arsenal would impact their ability to come up against the Craing. The AI completed her presentation on the ship's various shielding technologies, also configurable on the fly. Jason was mentally and physically exhausted. It seemed the ship was nearly ready for what he had in mind. He thanked Orion for her time and headed back to the bridge.

Chapter 6

Jason arrived on the bridge at the same time as Lieutenant Perkins. He suspected it wasn't an accident, which was fine. Jason sat in the command chair for the first time. No one else was on the bridge.

"Any word from the admiral?" Jason queried.

"We try every hour on the hour according to a pre-arranged contingency such as this. But there's nothing: no signal, no FTL transmission indicators—" Perkins shook his head, looking sadder than Jason felt himself.

"You're close to my father," Jason remarked, not sure if it was a question or statement.

"He's an amazing man, Captain. He's been more than my captain over the years—more like a—" Perkins stopped.

"He's been like a father to you," Jason said, completing his sentence. "It's all right, Lieutenant, it seems I may have viewed my father poorly. I've always thought the worst of him, when in actuality, it seems he's sacrificed much more than I could imagine."

The lieutenant simply nodded his head and smiled. Jason needed to change the subject. He'd need Lieutenant Perkins' help, especially over the next twenty-four hours. "Do we have the capability to connect outside, via cellphone signal from The Lilly?"

"Sure, what did you have in mind?" Lieutenant Perkins asked, curiously.

"Lieutenant, the crewmembers on this vessel are unprepared for what is about to ensue."

"And what is that, sir? Our standing orders are to make haste to the Altar system. To be honest, we should have headed out several days ago."

"When we reunite with the admiral, back at the Altar system, my intent is to show up there holding a big stick. From now on, we're going to be the schoolyard bully. To do that, we're going to have to orchestrate differently from the admiral's way of doing things. Are you OK with that?"

Perkins seemed to mull this over a while before answering. "I'm with you, sir. Just tell me—tell all of us what you want us to do— we're all more than ready to get the hell back into the fight."

Jason smiled, and mentally ran through everything he'd thought about over the past few days. He pulled out his iPhone and scrolled through his many contacts. "There's close to one hundred men and women listed here. Many of them are single and have limited family ties. I'd like to recruit them into the Alliance. Starting with this one here, Billy Hernandez." Jason held up his cell phone to the lieutenant.

Perkins took the phone from Jason and looked through the contacts.

"Lilly, activate the forward section display. Transfer the contents of this device to the ship's database and post the first and last names so we can see them. Oh, and let's number them as well." The names appeared in three columns alphabetized and numbered. The lieutenant looked over to Jason. "So who stays and who goes?"

Jason reviewed the list of military personnel one by one, instructing AI to scratch anyone who was married, had children, or had other compelling reasons to stay on planet Earth. By the time he was finished, the names of sixty-three Navy SEALs remained. Jason nodded to Perkins and stood. "Lilly, please transfer this list to my ready room and prepare to initiate communications via their cell phone numbers."

When Jason arrived back at the captain's suite, Dira was in his ready room working at his desk, a virtual terminal hovering in the air.

"Good evening, Captain," she said, a bit startled by his presence.

"Evening, Dira. Mollie in bed?"

"Yeah, she fell asleep about an hour ago. She was pretty worn out."

"Well, I wanted to thank you for all the time you're spending with her. I know it's not in your job description to play babysitter to the captain's kid."

"No, it's my pleasure. There's nothing going on in Medical right now, and Mollie's just plain fun to be around. I feel like a kid again."

Looking at Dira sitting there, he wondered about her and her own life. What had she'd given up to be here on The Lilly? He'd have to make more of a point to talk to her. She was interesting, and those eyelashes were a bit captivating.

"I have a few more things to tie up before I turn in myself," Jason said. "Oh, and I've called for a 0600 staff meeting."

"Yes, sir. I'm assuming it will be held here in your ready room?" Dira asked, getting up and heading for the door.

"Yes, right here—and thank you again, Dira. Perhaps after the meeting we can bring in Mollie and discuss this whole Zoo situation."

"That would be fine, Captain." Dira left and Jason immediately took her seat at the desk. "Lilly, initiate a phone call to Billy Hernandez."

* * *

Jason was the last to arrive in his ready room. By the time he'd gotten Mollie up and they'd shared a quick breakfast together, he was already running late. The small conference room was filled, leaving only one opening at the head of the table. Jason took his seat and looked around the room. Ricket sat directly to his right and Lieutenant Perkins to his left. Others in the room included Chief Horris, representing Engineering, Dira for Medical, Orion for Gunnery, Jack from the Zoo, and McBride for Helm and Navigation.

"Thank you all for attending," Jason said, making eye contact with each of them around the table. "Unless notified to the contrary, this meeting will take place every morning. Today, I'd like to start off with something positive." Jason stood up and looked down at Lieutenant Perkins. "Please stand up, Lieutenant." Perkins, confused, stood up and nervously pushed his hair away from his forehead. "Lieutenant Perkins, as Captain of the United Planetary Alliance vessel The Lilly, I hereby congratulate you on your promotion to the rank of Lieutenant Commander and, subsequently, XO of this vessel." Jason smiled and held out his hand. Stunned, Perkins shook the captain's hand and acknowledged the applause from his friends and fellow officers. "Until we can get you a brand new set, please accept my own, previously worn, lieutenant commander clusters." Jason handed them to his new XO. Perkins looked down at the clusters in his hand. "XO, I'll be asking a lot of you over the next few weeks. Hope you're up for it."

"I'm up for it, Captain, and thank you for your trust in me."

Taking their seats, Jason moved on to the next order of business. "Now, I'd like each of you to report on the status of your individual departments. It is my intention to depart within six hours. Everyone in this room was contacted by the XO yesterday. Subsequently, I know all of you were up late last night writing your departmental reports. This morning you'll be speaking about your department's Strengths, Weaknesses, Opportunities and Threats. Over time you'll become more accustomed to writing comprehensive reports of this type and how to get the most out of the information they provide. With limited staffing on The Lilly, we'll each be doing more than one job—including me. These reports are the first step toward us becoming better prepared, which will lead to more effective organization and strategic decision-making skills. Understood?"

Jason could see from the frowning looks on his staff's faces that they were less than thrilled. Well, they'd just have to get used to it. If the crew were to be successful in battle, then their current lack of discipline, non-existent cross-departmental communications, and overall laziness would have to be eliminated. Jason tapped twice and then once more on the tabletop, which brought up a virtual tablet—the others around the table followed suit. "Okay, looks like I have everyone's SWOT report except for yours, Jack."

Jack, the Zoo caretaker, was wearing the same stained overalls. He looked as unkempt as he had yesterday and was also the only one who'd not brought up a virtual tablet.

"Sir, my computer skills are not—" Embarrassed, Jack looked down, almost childlike. "I can audio-interface just fine and the droids, well, they can communicate like everyone else. But writing reports and such, I'm not very good in that regard." The others in the room kept their eyes on their tablets.

"Jack, we each have a unique skill-set here. No one in this room, or anywhere else on this ship, can effectively do the things you do. We'll work out the report writing aspects; perhaps Ricket can come up with an alternative approach." Ricket looked up towards Jack and nodded.

"What I would ask of you, as well as the rest of the officers in this room, is to ensure you are presentable and wearing a proper uniform denoting your rank or position on this ship. Again, I want to be airborne later this afternoon, so let's move on with our reports. Only the highlights. I'll read the details later."

One by one the officers discussed their department issues using the SWOT analysis format. At the end of the meeting, Jason asked Jack, Dira, and Ricket to stay behind. For the last ten minutes of the meeting, Jason had seen Mollie walk by the doorway several times—her not so subtle way of reminding him to not forget about their Zoo meeting.

"Mollie, why don't you come in here and sit down?" The rambunctious eight-year-old rushed in and sat between Dira and Jack. Jason winked at her and couldn't help but smile at her enthusiasm. "Mollie, I know you are excited about the Zoo and working with Jack, but I first need to have a better understanding of what the area is all about and the various safety aspects." Jason looked over at Ricket.

"The Zoo operates independently of the

AI," said Ricket, looking over to Jack for confirmation. "In fact, we now believe it was designed to be shared between multiple vessels."

Jason shook his head and frowned. "What does that mean, shared?"

"Perhaps a whole fleet of Lilly-type ships would be able to access the Zoo the same as we do," said Ricket. "And activation of the Zoo chamber has only come online within the last year. Yet animal care still took place while the ship lay dormant, prior to being discovered by Gus and the admiral fifteen years ago."

"Also," said Jack, "The Lilly has DeckPort-type access to each of the natural habitats, but it is only the animals we ourselves have contributed to the Zoo that we are responsible for, and for their continued upkeep."

Jason's brow furrowed. "Wait, so who's taking care of the other animals if it's not us? What other ships are currently sharing the Zoo? And more important, is that a potential security issue? What's keeping crewmembers from other vessels from infiltrating the ship, via the Zoo?"

"All good questions," Ricket replied. "Those issues, and others, were my initial concern as well. As we have long surmised, the indigenous inhabitants of this ship, and possibly others like them, have long ceased to exist. There are no other active vessel port systems, like our own to the Zoo here on The Lilly, accessing the natural habitats."

"So who's been taking care of all these

animals?" Jason asked, still confused.

"Their natural habitats are in a reality physically located on another planet or planets, probably a world with similar environmental characteristics to those of Earth. But animal care here is completely automated. Whatever is needed in the way of food stores, or anything else for that matter, is handled similarly to how we've discovered weapon armaments are handled here on the ship—utilizing that JIT-type process used in conjunction with the manufacturing phase synthesizer."

"Bottom line, no one can access The Lilly via the natural habitats—you're absolutely sure about that?" Jason asked, emphatically, looking first at Ricket and then at Jack.

"The security protocols for accessing the ship are independently controlled. It would be impossible to bypass the encrypted access codes. Codes that I've personally configured."
Jason looked over to Mollie and Dira. Both had been following along with interest. "What is it you'd be doing, Mollie? How would you be helping Jack?"

"Some animals are all alone in their havitats." Mollie said, with a quick glance over to Jack for approval.

"Habitats," he said, then nodded for her to continue.

"Yeah, habitats, and some of these lonely animals need human contact. Some of these animals hate the droids and do bad things to them." Mollie looked again to Dira and Jack, making sure she had said everything correctly. Dira had covered her mouth, doing a poor job of holding back a giggle. Jack was shaking his head.

"There are only a few of these special cases—most have mates or other same-species cohabitants in their environments. But animals, such as Raja, pine for physical contact. Others, some that are too dangerous to come into actual contact with humans, enjoy having a living being visibly close by—even if standing outside of their habitat."

Mollie nodded her head at Jack's explanation.

Dira chimed in. "Mollie's already made several new friends. Of course Raja, but also the Drapple, and the saber-toothed tiger, and even the cute little brine hog."

"I love the brine hog, Dad! But he looks so sad. I think it's because he's missing an ear."

Jason nodded, and thought for a moment. "What's a Drapple?" he asked everyone, having trouble keeping a straight face.

Dira answered first. "That's that big worm thing you saw jump out of the aquatic habitat."

"Oh yeah, I think it smiled at me," Jason said, quietly considering everything he'd heard. "Okay, here are my conditions for Mollie working with Jack in the Zoo. They are non-negotiable."

"What is non-netopial?" Mollie asked, confused.

"Non-negotiable. And that means you have

to agree to my terms," replied Jason. "First, I want a printed list made of the various animals presently in the Zoo—including their quantities. On that list I want to know which ones are dangerous, poisonous, or anything else that could be harmful to humans. Second, while inside the Zoo area, Mollie needs to be supervised…"

"Well, I'll always be around," Jack interrupted.

"No, someone other than you, Jack. No offense, but if you're working or preoccupied with your duties, then Mollie's not being watched."

"If I'm not needed in Medical, I may be able to watch her. Just maybe," Dira said, smiling over at Mollie.

"Yes!" Mollie said, with two little fists raised in the air in triumph.

"I'm not through yet," Jason said, admonishing her with another wink. "Third, I will be informed when Mollie is entering and leaving the Zoo." Jason looked over to Dira and she nodded back, silently acknowledging she would ensure all his conditions would be met. Jason sat there and considered it all. The pregnant pause lingered longer than Mollie could stand.

"Oh, come on, Dad! Are you going to just sit there like that all day? I've got work to do," Mollie questioned, exasperated.

"Okay, get out of here. And don't forget my conditions."

* * *

It was mere minutes before the scheduled time to embark. Jason wondered if he had been avoiding this moment. Perhaps he should have done what his father requested and gotten the ship quickly airborne and heading toward the Altar system. But doing so, he knew, would have been a recipe for failure. He'd just have to deal with the admiral and any admonishments, if and when they met. If what the admiral described in his latest text was true, the dire situation with the Craing, then the last few days they'd spent preparing could go a long way towards making a real difference. Over the last few hours the crew had really come together and acted with more professionalism then he had witnessed in the past.

The Lilly was all buttoned up, with the ramp secured and all external connections terminated. Several small maintenance drones would remain behind to watch over the underground aquifer base. Jason looked around the now-bustling bridge. Perkins was seated next to him; McBride was at the helm at the most forward console. Ricket was one level up, seated at the console directly in front of Jason. Both Chief and Gunny were manning stations at the side consoles.

"Lilly, I'd like to address the ship."

"Ship-wide channel is now open."

"Attention. This is the captain.

Momentarily, we will be disembarking from our underground base. You have all worked hard over the last few days to prepare the ship as well as yourselves for what lies ahead. Understand— shortly we will be tested in battle. The Lilly will be tested in battle. There's a Craing cruiser in Earth's upper orbit. We'll intersect with that ship later today. But first we have a quick stop to make. Secure your areas and prepare for immediate departure. Captain out."

"Helm, initiate 100 percent phase-shift configuration and plot an outpoint directly topside."

"Phase-shift initiated and plot outpoint locked." McBride looked back over his shoulder towards the captain. Jason took one more look around and nodded to the young pilot. "OK. Let's go."

McBride smiled and turned back forward. He tapped a combination onto the pressure sensitive keys at his virtual console. The ship shifted. "We're stationary 200 feet above ground, sir," McBride reported. Ricket had explained the phase-shift process in more detail that morning: it required tremendous amounts of power—too much for it to be used during FTL or even standard sub-light travel. But for small leaps through virtually any material, solid or otherwise—up to several miles—it worked like a charm.

The command center's 360-degree display indicated that the ship was hovering directly over the scrapyard. In the distance, Jason could see his small ranch-style home, which still seemed to be intact. His eyes were drawn to the smoldering, burnt-out remains of Nan's minivan.

"Status?"

"No contacts, sir. Skies are clear," Orion reported from the comms station.

"Take us into sub-orbit and then back down to the provided coordinates."

The ship moved away from the scrapyard and quickly gained altitude. The ground disappeared in a blur replaced by the approaching darker blue stratosphere. The Lilly leveled off and soon began to descend back towards Earth.

"We'll be in range in thirty seconds, sir."

"Multiple contact. Twelve F-18 Fighters have been deployed," Orion said, surprisingly calm-voiced.

"Location?" Jason prompted.

"They're already wheels up—and pretty much right where we're heading: Air Station Meridian, East Central Mississippi."

"Ricket, can they lock missiles?" Jason barked—louder than he'd intended and nervous that he'd already made a crucial error.

"No, we are jamming their radar, infrared, and any of their other signaling capabilities," Ricket replied, "but they can fire their on-board projectile weapons. Seems right now they are just taking pictures."

"Gunny, can our comms talk to them?" Jason asked, with the hint of a smile.

"No problem, Captain. Channel's open."

Several of the F-18 fighters were clearly visible on the display. On the closest, its external missiles could be seen, including 2000-pound JDAM warheads, Sidewinders, and AMRAAMs. Jason knew from experience the pilots would be following predetermined courses of action. After what had happened in San Bernardino, these boys would be more than a little nervous.

"Attention, deployed F-18 Fighter squadron and centralized command unit of Air Station Meridian: Greetings. We're a non-hostile, repeat, non-hostile craft dropping by to take advantage of some of your famous southern hospitality. We'll be gone before you know it."

"Lots of chatter out there, sir—they're being ordered to engage," Orion said, looking over to Jason.

"We're in position, sir," said McBride, "based on the GPS coordinates provided." They were now stationary, hovering fifty feet above the eastern-most airbase runway.

"Lilly, initiate a phone call to Billy Hernandez."

"Dialing now, sir," Lilly's somewhat unfriendly voice responded, followed by the sound of a ringing phone line. Jason looked to his right and saw Perkins, as well as several others on the bridge, holding back chuckles.

"Speak to me," the deep voice answered.

"We're here, Billy."

"Hey, Lieutenant Commander—Welcome!

Yeah, come on in, we're ready as we'll ever be."

Jason commanded McBride to initiate the phase-shift process. Within the blink of an eye The Lilly shifted again. The wrap-around virtual display instantly changed from a bright sunlit afternoon to a dark interior location—bands of light filtered through small gaps around a large double door at the front of the hangar.

"How long before we're detected in here, Ricket?" Jason asked, still somewhat amazed they had accomplished their plan so well.

"All signatures are dampened. The only way we'll be discovered is if we are visually identified."

"Excellent. XO, you have the con. Lilly, lower the aft gangway." Jason got up and headed off the bridge. "And Gunny, you're with me."

Chapter 7

"Um—Sir, you need to be wearing a sidearm," Orion said as they made their way down the corridor toward the closest DeckPort.

"We're still on home soil, Gunny. I don't see—"

"Sir, with all due respect, we don't know who or what will be waiting for us. Let me do my job—let's get you outfitted with a weapon. A quick stop at the gunnery?"

Jason held his hands up in resignation, "Lead the way."

* * *

Checking through his newer memories, those that were post HyperLearning, Jason found knowledge on the operation of the particular hand-held pulse weapon at his side. Now, walking side-by-side along the corridor with Gunny—six foot three at least, and over two hundred pounds of muscle—Jason sensed the raw physical prowess of the woman. Jason, a ten-year Navy SEAL veteran, along with his team members—some of them waiting in the hangar below—were battle-hardened, trained warriors. But he had a feeling Orion could hold her own. Once at the lower level airlock hatch, Orion entered the appropriate code and the large hatch began to swing open.

"So external access hatches like this one need to be opened manually?" Jason asked.

"That's right, sir. Our NanoCom devices only work on opening internal bulkhead hatchways and doors. Not really sure why; a good question for Ricket."

Once the hatch had swung itself free, Jason moved to walk down the extended gangway, but Orion put her arm out, blocking his way.

"Sorry, sir, but protocol has your security detail, namely me, clearing first." Orion drew her sidearm and slowly continued down the gangway. Jason followed behind, knowing she was right. The massive navy hangar had been emptied of other crafts, but The Lilly merely a few feet of fore and aft room to spare. Jason's eyes still hadn't adjusted to the near total darkness; crisscrossed stripes of bright yellow sunlight beams made it difficult to see. Dust particles and smoke hung silently in the air. Jason recognized the pungent smell of Billy's Gurkha-brand cigar.

"How you doing, Billy?" Jason shouted out in a raised voice that echoed around the hangar for several seconds. Orion, now by Jason's side, slowly turned 360 degrees, weapon outstretched.

"So is this my new replacement?" a deep Latino voice answered back. Then the bright red embers of his cigar illuminated Billy's smile, ten yards away. Someone flipped a breaker and bright overhead lights filled the room. Billy stood relaxed; forty more SEALs stood equally relaxed behind him.

"You can put your weapon away, Gunny;. we're among friends," Jason said before taking several long strides to embrace his friend. At close to six five, Billy Hernandez towered over Jason. The room was eerily quiet and Jason turned to see what was up. The SEALs were looking at The Lilly, all dumbfounded. Orion, too, had turned around to see what had caught their attention.

Jason stepped over closer to the ship and turned to face the group. "I'd like to introduce you all to The Lilly."

"Forget the ship, who's the girl?" Billy blurted out, eyeing Orion's curvaceous backside. The other men laughed briefly, but most kept their eyes on the ship. Orion glanced up at Billy and scowled, then looked over at Jason and scowled at him as well.

Jason continued: "Those of you I spoke with on the phone yesterday already know about our mission. Others of you have been told secondhand. The simple fact that so many of you made it here on such short notice from all over the country speaks volumes."

"You had us at Hello," another SEAL barked from the back of the group—followed by a new chorus of chuckles.

Quickly attempting to get through his comments, Jason continued on. "This ship— well, she just might be Earth's answer to the massacre that took place in San Bernardino several days ago. I'm sorry, but we only have a few minutes before we need to lift off. Believe me when I tell you, Earth is in more danger than any of you realize." This announcement sobered the group; the men knew about extreme danger—better than most.

"I don't know when we'll be back. And if that's an issue, this is probably not the right cruise ship for you. Those who are coming onboard, check-in here with Gunnery Officer Orion; she'll log you in and get you situated."

Jason was surprised to see that most of his former shipmates, even those who'd participated in the foray against the Somali pirates' raiding of the Christina, were all present. After several big bear hugs and extended pats on the back, each of the men joined the line and eventually disappeared up the gangway.

Bringing up the rear, and with the airlock secured, Jason used his NanoCom to order McBride to go ahead and shift out of the hangar to a predetermined, hopefully deserted, location several miles away.

The forty-one new crewmembers were led directly to the Mess Hall on Deck 2 at the forward section of the ship. Orion had assembled a team of five Lilly crewmembers, including Dira, and even Mollie, to help with ship orientation and living quarter assignments. Jason wasn't quite ready for these SEALs to have full access to the ship. Several things needed to happen first, including a rotation of HyperLearning sessions for everyone in Medical. By the time Jason walked onto the bridge, The Lilly was situated in the middle of the Chihuahuan desert—140,000 square miles of absolute nothingness. Perkins stood at the forward section of the display, looking out at the vast sandy plains.

The AI announced, "Captain on Deck," along with the boson's whistle. The XO turned to the captain.

"Our new guests getting acclimated?" Perkins asked.

"Yeah, I'd forgotten what a rowdy group they can be. I've asked Ricket to reconfigure the five MediPods. We'll start rotating the men into Medical within the next hour—then they can spend tomorrow in their bunks recovering." Both men smiled, knowing first hand how uncomfortable they would be over the next twenty-four hours.

"What can you tell me about that Craing cruiser up in orbit? Jason asked, changing the subject.

Perkins leaned over a nearby console and tapped a series of keys. The forward section of the display changed to a rotating model of a Craing cruiser. "It's the largest of their cruisers, actually considered a battle cruiser—nearly twice the size of The Lilly. Craing weaponry is far more advanced than anything the Alliance has been able to produce so far—that's why they keep getting their asses kicked."

"How will The Lilly stack up?" Jason asked

"That's anyone's guess—but I'm starting to think she'll hold up just fine."

"Size of its crew?"

"Between two and three hundred. They typically have a complement of fifty or so fighters. Captain, even their light cruiser is a formidable opponent. We would typically want to have five or six Alliance cruisers with us before going up against one of them."

Jason pointed to the Craing vessel. "Can I get a view of the inside of that ship?"

Perkins made a few more keystrokes and they both looked at the display. "This is a best-guess scenario based on our most recent active scans. The Craing ship has relatively few compartments, and significantly more open space than Alliance ships. The Craing put little effort into creature comforts. Other than their Overlords, crew personnel are packed together like sardines. That leaves them more room for cargo, and oftentimes the cargo is slaves," Perkins said, tight-lipped. Jason looked at the display, trying to come to a decision. But his thoughts were interrupted by the sound of an incoming hail. McBride, who was now sitting at the comms-console, turned to the captain.

"We've got a priority one hail coming in from the admiral, sir," the ensign said, excitedly.

"Go ahead and put it on screen, Ensign."

If possible, the admiral looked even more tired, more defeated, than he had previously. Jason took in the scene; a makeshift bandage had been wrapped around his father's forehead. His uniform, torn and open at the collar,

115

exposed another gash on his neck. In the background, a haze, probably smoke, added a foreboding look to the already deteriorating scene.

"It's good to see you're still alive, sir," Jason said.

"For now, anyway. As bad as this must appear to you, we've actually had a bit of good luck. Where exactly are you?"

Jason sat back and hesitated before answering. Damn, this was the one area he wanted to avoid getting into just yet. "Earth was attacked, as you predicted it would be—apparently they tracked The Lilly to her general location. Several of our fighter squadrons were quickly destroyed, and hundreds of locals were herded onto several Craing cruisers. Unfortunately, Nan was among those taken."

Jason's father took in a slow deep breath. "She'll be held, probably for several weeks, maybe months, interrogated, and with luck sent to a work camp. I'm sorry Jason—this must be very difficult for you. What about Mollie—they don't have her, do they?"

"No, she's here on The Lilly. She's handling it as well as can be expected. And she's pretty much taken over the ship."

The admiral smiled, and then became serious. "Are you on your way to the Altar system now?"

"No, sir. We have left the underground base but—" Jason paused, seeing Perkins subtly shaking his head, "—we made a quick detour.

Currently we're in Texas."

"Texas, what the hell are you doing in Texas? I explicitly—"

Jason interrupted the admiral just as his voice had begun to rise. "Here's the situation, sir. First, I've picked up my SEAL team: 41 battle-tested hard-asses ready to fight for the Alliance. Second, Ricket discovered an on-board manufacturing device that will allow us to make all of the ship's weapons operational. And third, we're going to make a visit to a Craing light cruiser sitting in Earth's high orbit. We're going to board her, and I'm going to find out where they've taken Nan. After that, well, I haven't quite figured that part out yet."

Jason stopped talking and watched for his father's reaction. Angry at first, red faced, his nostrils flaring—but then something in his face changed. Perhaps it was a sudden realization. Or was it resignation? The admiral nodded several times before speaking: "That's exactly the type of bullshit I hoped you'd bring to the party, son." Smiling now, the admiral continued with, "I'm not going to second-guess your command decisions, Jason. You tend to land on your feet and you take ballsy risks, something I think I stopped doing a long time ago. If we have any chance of surviving this war, it will be because the right people took bold moves."

"Thank you, sir. And what was the bit of good news you mentioned?" Jason asked.

"An old adversary has joined the fight. Still not close to what is needed to go up against the

Craing, but a neutral planetary system just got in the game. We've been downloading this intel and other information across the data link. Let's talk in a few days. I still need you here at the Altar system, Jason. Don't get yourself killed."

"Aye, sir." Jason looked over to Perkins and gestured to cut the transmission.

Chapter 8

Jason wanted to check on the new crewmembers. He'd heard that Mollie was helping out and he wanted to see what she was up to. Over the last few days, he'd become more familiar with the DeckPorts. Before, he would pass by them in the corridors without knowing what they were. Not all of them looked the same, especially if they remained idle too long. Then they would turn solid and look more like a regular hatchway. But DeckPorts had a colored frame around their perimeter—color-coded, though Jason hadn't completely figured out that part yet. Jason exited the starboard forward Level Two DeckPort and for the first time he felt somewhat at home. He heard familiar noises: talking, arguing, laughing, and even singing. He realized he'd never been to this part of the ship.

The mess hall was one of the larger areas of the ship, spanning the width of The Lilly. What hit Jason first as he entered the hall was the aroma. It was wonderful—was that pot roast? Most of the crew had already filled their trays and were finishing up. Jason crossed over to the cafeteria-style counter and examined the wide selection. Behind the counter was a familiar-looking crewmember.

"Plimpton, isn't it?" Jason asked. He remembered passing the chubby-faced Seaman

Apprentice on his first day aboard. "What do we have here?"

"Big spread tonight, sir, with all the fixins: Pot roast, mashed potatoes and gravy, French green beans, hot biscuits, and peach cobbler for dessert." Plimpton took the captain's plate. "Load it up, sir?"

"Oh yes, thank you. So who cooks all this? We have a chef onboard?"

"You're looking at him, sir, although here on The Lilly there hasn't been the opportunity to do much cooking, what with our easy access to food replicators and such."

"Well, I think that's certainly about to change," Jason said, turning away with his tray of food and surveying the mess. He spotted Dira seated next to Mollie several tables over. Mollie seemed to be the center of attention and must have said something funny, because the five SEALs seated at the table were chortling. Jason recognized one of the guys, Lieutenant Morgan—something or other. He'd leaned over and whispered something in Dira's ear. She smiled, turned, and whispered something back into his. Did she linger there a while? Never really liked that guy much, Jason thought to himself.

"Got room for one more?" Jason asked loudly above the hall's noisy chatter.

"Dad! Sit next to me," Mollie screamed. Her enthusiastic smile beamed up at him. Jason caught Dira's eye and she smiled. An uncomfortable quiet came over the table while

Jason buttered his biscuit and dug into his food.

"Quite a ship you have here, Lieutenant," Morgan said, breaking the silence. "Something right out of Star Wars, or is that Star Trek?"

"My dad's captain now, not lieutenant commander, see his collar?" Mollie interrupted, never to let the obvious go unnoticed. Jason knew that Morgan was perfectly aware of his new rank. Smiling, Jason nodded his head and took another heaping bite of pot roast. This is just what we do, Jason thought to himself. It wouldn't be the navy without a little shit-slinging. He knew shit-slinging could go both ways, so he'd bide his time.

Dira collected her tray and got to her feet. "Well, I need to get back to Medical and relieve Ricket. We've started the HyperLearning process and all five of the MediPods are in use—including the one with your friend Billy," Dira said, smiling at Jason and then at the others around the table. "…and Mollie, I'll see you tomorrow." The men all watched as she walked away, including Jason. Interesting how her spacer's jumpsuit seemed to fit her perfectly, in all the right places. Dira took a quick glance back over her shoulder and smirked when she saw the multiple eyes checking out her backside. Out of his peripheral vision, Jason saw Mollie scowling at him, so he put his full attention back on his supper. Several more crewmen joined their table and then several more after that. Eventually, everyone in the mess hall turned around in their seats and had, in a sense, joined the captain's table.

A seaman from across the room yelled over to Jason, "Hey Captain, what ever happened to that animal Billy snuck onboard the Tripoli. What was that damn thing, a baboon?" The room erupted in laughter.

"It was a lemur, Wilkins. And if you also remember, Billy spent a night in the brig for that stunt. I think everyone on the Tripoli was bitten at least once. Had to be the meanest damn animal in the South Pacific," Jason shouted back. Mollie smiled, enjoying being part of the good ol' boys' camaraderie.

Another sailor called out, "Hey, Captain, are we gonna offer up some bad-ass to those aliens up there? Maybe a little payback for what they'd done to our boys in California?"

The room went quiet; all heads turned towards Jason. He didn't answer right away and when he did, he put his hands over his daughter's ears. "Yeah, we're going to fuck them up—we're going to fuck them up in a bad way." The mess hall erupted in a hail of hoots and hollers. They were a team again, and for the first time Jason felt good he was their captain.

* * *

Jason woke in the middle of the night to the sound of Mollie crying. Recently, she asked if she could leave her light on, something to do with nightmares. He got out of bed and made his way to her room and crouched down next to her bed.

"Hey there, sweetie, what's going on?"

"I miss Mommy. I miss her so much. Why can't we just go get her?" Mollie asked, her eyes red and full of tears.

"Soon. I promise, we're going to do our very, very, very, very, very best to get her back with us," he replied, giving her a reassuring smile.

"Don't try to make me laugh, Dad. This is serious."

"I know it is, kiddo. I don't like to see you hurting like this. Hey, want me to hang out here for a while? Maybe until you go back to sleep?" Mollie nodded and let her eyes close. Jason gave her a hug and a kiss and scooted up on the bed next to her. He leaned back against the bulkhead and took a deep breath.

"Dad? Can I call her? Like on her phone?"

"No, I don't think so, sweetie."

Before Jason drifted off to sleep, he wondered if he would be able to keep his promise to get Nan back. Was she still alive? He'd done a good job not letting his mind go there—until this moment.

* * *

One more person had been asked to join the 0600 staff meeting, and in spite of looking less than 100%, Billy Hernandez was hanging in there. His attention was on Ricket, obviously not sure what to make of the small mechanical man. Ricket was in the middle of an explanation.

"…even if Nan had her cell phone on her person, obviously there are no cell tower services thousands of light years out in space. With that said, the Craing ship itself would have the capability to forward those signals—just as The Lilly can do. But this is all academic— unless we have supervisor-level access to an internal Craing network," Ricket explained, seeming intrigued by the prospect.

"Well, it was just a thought—Mollie gave me the idea last night and I wanted to throw it out there—even if it is a bit far-fetched. Let's move on. Billy, I know you're not feeling all that great, but with your help, I'd like to work out a tactical strategy to board and take over the Craing ship. Think your guys will be up for that?"

"Yeah, we'll be up for that, Captain. I'll get some training maneuvers scheduled for tonight." Billy smiled with his typical machismo-flair and a quick wink across to Orion.

Orion scowled at the militarily-lax gesture. "If we have some time, I'd like to test the rail guns today and some of the other weaponry that's recently come online. I have ordnances available that I'm clueless about. There's a solid rocky ridge a quarter mile long and eight hundred feet high several miles to the east. I want to put some holes in it," Orion said, matter-of-factly, looking at Jason. It took a moment before the others around the table turned to look at Gunny; no one really sure if she was serious. Jason knew—she was.

"Scan for life signs. Make sure you don't take out a weekend camper or a Boy Scout troop. But sure, have at it."

* * *

On the bridge, Jason, Orion and Ricket prepared for weaponry and JIT ordinances tests.

"We'll be testing multiple criteria today, including accuracy, reload rates, any overheating issues, explosive yields for various ordnances, and more. Of course, here at sea-level atmosphere, results may be significantly altered from the vacuum conditions of space. The AI knows to compensate for all measurement calculation variances."

"Any significant difference between The Lilly's rail guns and, say, those typically used on Alliance ships, or on Craing vessels?" Jason asked his gunnery sergeant.

Orion nodded, as if expecting the question. "The velocity of the projectile is dependent on two things: the length of the rails, and the power of the current being applied to the rails. The Alliance ships, and even the Craing for the most part, use longer rails. Not so with The Lilly; the rails are ridiculously stubby. I'm curious how enough velocity can be generated for the guns to be effective. I guess we'll find out," Orion said with a shrug. Ricket had been walking back and forth to several different consoles. Every so often the bill of his baseball cap would rise up— pointing toward Orion or Jason—as he listened to what had caught his interest.

"We are ready," Ricket announced, pulling himself up onto a nearby chair and entering something at the virtual terminal. The forward display changed orientation and increased the zoom level. The distant ridge-line now completely filled the display.

"Lilly, what's the composition of the ridge being targeted?" Jason asked.

"Commonly known as granite. It consists of coarse grains of quartz of 10-50%, potassium feldspar, and sodium feldspar. These minerals make up more than 80% of the targeted rock ridge-line. Other common minerals present include muscovite and biotite," the AI replied in a flat tone.

"So, I'm correct when I say the target area is solid?" Jason reaffirmed.

"Yes, that is correct, sir."

"And the thickness across the ridge?"

"Between five hundred and thirty, and six hundred and twenty-three feet at its widest," the AI replied.

"That's a mother big piece of rock," Jason said under his breath. "I'm ready when you are, Gunny."

"First, we'll be testing the forward rail gun system utilizing a solid non-explosive ordnance with a fifteen-second burst. What is important to remember, Captain, is that we have no on-board stores for these ordnances. This is as much a test of the phase synthesizer's JIT manufacturing capability as it is of the guns themselves." Orion was at the weapons console and entered several commands. Small tracking cross hairs locked onto a specific rock outcropping on the display. Jason felt a slight vibration as the forward rail gun deployed on the lower hull of the ship.

"Charging rail guns," Orion said, then looked over to the captain.

"Fire at will, Gunny."

The gun fired in rapid succession—for fifteen seconds a blur of dark streaks shot off in the direction of the targeted rock area. When the dust settled, the face of the rock outcropping was gone, leaving a perfectly symmetrical opening several feet in diameter.

"Lilly, how deep was that penetration into the rock face?" Jason asked, leaning forward in his seat.

"One hundred sixteen feet with no discernible deviation, Captain," the AI responded.

"And now, Captain, the same test with both forward and rear rail gun systems deployed," the Gunny said, excitement creeping into her voice. Both guns fired in rapid succession—for fifteen seconds there was a blur of dark streaks in the directed targeted rock area. There was considerably less dust, and the face of the rock outcropping was virtually unchanged.

"Lilly, how deep was that second penetration into the rock face?" Jason questioned, his brow furrowed.

"Three hundred-eight feet with no discernible deviation, Captain," the AI responded.

Jason looked over to Orion. "How would these results compare to those of comparable Alliance weapons?"

Orion was shaking her head. "I've never seen anything like this, Captain. For such a short burst to inflict that much damage—it's impressive to say the least. Lilly, using the current ordinances, how long can the rail gun systems sustain continual firing?"

"Rail gun systems will overheat with prolonged firing lasting in excess of thirty minutes before requiring a four minute cool-down period."

"That's also impressive, Captain," Orion said. "A factor or two, or even three times better than anything we currently have in the Alliance arsenal. I'd like to try a few of the more exotic ordnances now. They're listed on the selection menu, but I'm not real sure what they are. Do you have any idea, Ricket?"

Ricket shook his head. "Minimal descriptions are available—I might be able to access more over time."

Orion selected a different set of ordnances from the display menu. "Let's try these," she said, looking over at Jason for approval. "These are called PQR ordnances, and I'll bring the burst duration down to five seconds to be safe." Jason sat back in his chair and waited for the next test to begin.

Both guns fired in rapid succession—almost immediately the ground started to shake. The five-second burst of bright white streaks shot off in the direction of the ridge. A large plume of dust filled the air and obscured the ridge-line from view.

"What the hell was that?" Jason asked, excitedly. As the dust started to settle, it became evident that a section hundreds of feet across had been completely and totally obliterated—leaving two separate ridge-lines where there previously was one.

Ricket nodded his head in appreciation. "I believe that PQR ordnances have anti-matter characteristics."

"Sorry, Captain, I had no idea of the potential damage... we should probably hold off on any more testing until we're in open space." Orion looked down at her console, embarrassed.

"There's so much we don't know about this ship," Jason said. "But I agree with your assessment." He was hailed via his NanoCom. "Go for Captain, what can I do for you, Billy?" Jason asked aloud, holding two fingers to his ear. He had discovered that was the common crew practice when communicating.

"If you're done blowing up mountains, we'd like to commence training maneuvers. We'll be staging men and equipment external to the ship. From there conducting four-team raids into various access points."

"Has everyone completed their HyperLearning?" Jason asked him.

"Yes, but with the exception of the new weapons and the ship's advanced technologies this won't be all that different from other raids we've conducted. We'll need to ensure we have the element of surprise and the sooner we get started with these maneuvers, the better."

"Understood. You better get cracking then, Lieutenant. Give me a progress report in four hours."

"Aye, Captain. Billy out."

"Contacts approaching from the east and south, sir," Orion announced. "Looks like a squadron of F-18s—Yeah, they are the same ones from Air Station Meridian. Orders, sir?"

The display, still depicting the decimated ridge-line to the East, showed six of the jet fighters approaching at high velocity. "Try to contact…"

Orion interrupted Jason mid-sentence— "Captain, we have incoming. Multiple missiles."

"Can you destroy them?"

"No time—we only have seconds and the ship's still configured for test mode."

"Ricket, what will those missiles do to The Lilly?" Jason asked, desperation in his voice.

"There will be no damage to the ship itself," Ricket replied, evenly.

That was good news, but something else nagged at the back of Jason's mind. "Shit, Billy's maneuvers!" Jason blurted. Using his NanoCom, he hailed his friend.

"Go for Billy. What's up, Captain?" Billy queried, but abruptly cut the connection.

"Lilly, get me a high-up visible of the ship and surrounding perimeter," Jason commanded. The display changed to an elevated view showing The Lilly and two of Billy's four-man SEAL teams running flat out. Still at fifty yards—they were scrambling to get back to the ship. The display flashed white and The Lilly shook. The sound of muffled explosions at the outer hull reverberated as additional incoming missiles found their target. Everything went quiet. Incapacitated by shock and then disbelief, the bridge crew momentarily froze. "XO, get a team to attend the wounded. Orion, connect me to that squadron leader before they commence another run—hurry!"

"Channel is open, Captain, but they're not talking to us," Orion said. "But they will hear you."

"This is Captain Jason Reynolds of The Lilly, the United Planetary Alliance vessel you have just fired upon. This is a non-hostile vessel with U.S. military personnel aboard; I repeat, this vessel has U.S. military personnel aboard." Jason listened for some kind of acknowledgment.

"This is Admiral Malinda Cramer, commanding officer at Air Station Meridian. You will comply with the following directives. First, you will prepare to be boarded and allow full access by U.S. military personnel. Second, you will relinquish all weapons and..." Jason cut off the admiral.

"Ma'am, I apologize, but that's simply not

going to happen. And I feel once you understand the situation, you'll support our continued actions."

"Captain Reynolds, was it? When a foreign vessel enters United States air space without prior clearance and then proceeds to fire a nuclear weapon—let me be perfectly clear, nothing short of a declaration of war will be levied on the responsible nation. The seriousness of this is monumental."

"Admiral, are you aware of the alien vessel in high orbit around the planet?"

"Of course," she replied, her irritation mounting.

"Our single most important initiative right now is to either capture that vessel or destroy it. This vessel, the one you sent three AIM-7 Sparrow missiles at, was unaffected, although the eight U.S. SEAL team members conducting training maneuvers on the ground were most likely killed. If you think we can't destroy anything the U.S. military, or any other military force could throw at us, I suggest you take another look at that solid granite ridge-line." There was a pause and Jason could here papers shuffling—undoubtedly, the admiral had been handed a dossier by her support staff, bringing her up to speed on who she was talking to.

"You're a Navy SEAL, Lieutenant Commander. You're the late Admiral Perry Reynolds's son—am I correct?" the admiral queried Jason. "I knew of your father. A fine officer."

"Yes, ma'am. I was previously a SEAL commander on the U.S. Tripoli; presently Captain on this vessel. And yes, I am Admiral Perry Reynolds's son, guilty as charged. Although he's still very much alive." Jason said, knowing how far-fetched that must sound.

"Captain, Admiral Reynolds has been reported missing, most likely dead, for over fifteen years. Are you telling me this information is incorrect?"

"Yes, I discovered this fact myself just a few short days ago—this was his ship. Admiral Reynolds has been fighting an interstellar war with an alien race called the Craing. And yes, I do know how absolutely ridiculous that sounds. The ship in high orbit around Earth is a Craing light cruiser. Their intentions are to infiltrate Earth."

"And the reason your father didn't work through normal government or military channels?" the admiral asked Jason, disbelief in her voice.

"You're asking the same questions I had, ma'am. It's important that you understand the Craing have been preparing this invasion for many years. They are patient and this isn't their first infiltration. From what my father has indicated, human-like Craing beings have infiltrated the highest levels of our government and military. There was no one in authority here he could trust. But right now, I need to attend to my fallen crewmembers. And by the way, I see one jet fighter, in fact, military vehicles of any kind approaching—it will be destroyed and any resulting deaths will be on your head." Jason needed to get off the bridge. "Please contact your superiors and we can resume this conversation, let's say two hours from now." Jason got up and headed for the exit. "You have the con, XO," he declared over his shoulder.

Medical was a flurry of commotion. Four of the MediPods were already filled with injured SEAL team members, and Dira was helping to situate another man into the remaining capsule. Fresh blood covered the bottom half of her grey jumpsuit. She looked up when Jason arrived. "What the hell happened out there?" Dira asked him, her tone accusing. "I need Ricket; where's that damn robot?" Just then Ricket darted into Medical.

Beginning with the first MediPod, he checked on each of the displays, made adjustments where needed, moving on then to the next pod, and then the next. Jason looked through the small observation window on each of the MediPods, then rushed into an adjacent semi-circular room configured with twenty or so hospital-type beds, each bed perpendicular to the curved bulkhead. Here lay three more men with varying degrees of injury. Billy Hernandez occupied the centermost bed.

"Captain, over here." Billy beckoned Jason with a wave. His sleeve had been cut away and a bandage encircled the top portion of his arm.

"How's your team? What's the extent of your injuries, Billy?" Jason inquired, evident concern in his voice.

"Twenty-five were in the mess hall feeding their faces. Sixteen of us of were on maneuvers. Of those, half were on the far side of the ship— just inside the fighter bay. Then all hell rained down on us. I'm fine, but Lieutenant Morgan here has, um—"

"Cavitation wounds," Dira interjected, entering the room. She quickly moved to the side of Morgan and checked his vitals. "He should be OK, once we get him into an available MediPod. Unfortunately, some of the men there won't require any further medical attention."

"How many injured—what's the count on fatalities?" Jason asked, aware that Dira still hadn't looked at him.

"From what I understand, all the men who were outside the ship were vaporized. I'm sorry." Dira said sympathetically to Billy.

"Those were eight of the finest men—" the words caught in his throat. Overwhelmed by emotion, Billy blinked his eyes in rapid succession.

Dira continued on for Billy: "The eight men outside the ship were killed, two more standing in the open fighter bay are also dead. It looks like the remaining six will recover."

Jason nodded and took another look around the room.

"Where's Mollie right now?" Jason queried.

"She's fine. I asked Seaman Plimpton not to let her out of his sight and to take her down to the Zoo."

The captain's brow furrowed. "The cook?"

"Yes, the cook. He's also super responsible and someone I trust." Dira moved on to attend to an unconscious patient with several burns on his upper torso and face. "I was going to let you know as soon as things settled down here."

"Thank you. Is there anything else I can do to help? You need other support staff?"

Dira nodded. "Billy mentioned several of his boys below were also EMTs. They're already on their way up."

Jason looked at Billy. "I need to return to the bridge."

Billy pulled an IV tube from his arm, swung his feet off the bed and stood. "And I've also got work to do," Billy said.

Jason looked over to Dira, who gave a resigned shrug. "Just try to take it easy, Billy. You've been through a lot."

He nodded and headed out of Medical.

Jason found Ricket still helping with the MediPod casualties in the next room. The two EMTs had arrived and were busy helping out: one was using a vacuum device to remove blood off the floor, while the other was positioning a dead SEAL into a body bag.

"Captain, we have company," Perkins transmitted into his NanoCom.

"On my way." Jason was already running for the bridge. Ricket looked up and followed close on his heels.

Chapter 9

"Well, Admiral Cramer obviously didn't take your threats to heart, Captain," his XO said, watching the scene unfold on the display console.

Jason shook his head. "Those approaching transport helicopters are U.S. Army-led. They're following their own command structure."

"Captain, we've got troop movement and a convoy of tanks rolling across the desert in our direction," Orion reported from her console.

"How far out, Gunny?"

"They're twenty minutes from our position. We're being hailed by the admiral—it's been two hours."

Jason said, "Admiral, this is Captain Reynolds."

"Captain, by now you have undoubtedly noticed the activity off to your north."

"Army deployment. We talked about this, Admiral," Jason bristled.

"Let's just say the army was not receptive to the navy negotiating on their behalf. Leaving that subject for the time being, I've been on the horn non-stop for the last hour to the Pentagon, Joint Chiefs of Staff, as well as to the president. To be honest, there's very little consensus between them all."

Jason continued to watch as several Apache-attack helicopters landed, joining the distant formation. The last thing he wanted to do was fight against the same people he was trying to protect. "From the looks of things, our military forces have decided to go on the offensive. Let me ask you this. What will it take to change their attack plans from being adversarial, to working together with us in fighting a mutual threat?"

"They simply don't trust you, Jason. As far as they're concerned, you're still a Lieutenant Commander in the U.S. Navy, up on charges for second-degree murder, as well as being AWOL."

"There's more than a few of us who are AWOL on this ship. Let me ask you personally, Admiral. Do you believe me?"

There was a longer pause than Jason hoped for, but the answer eventually came. "Yes, as I said before, I knew your father—know your father. I've looked through your records and you are a fine officer, although monumentally impetuous. I'll back you, Jason. I'm just not sure how far that will go."

"Thank you, Admiral, that means a lot to me. But the simple fact of the matter is we, and that means us here on this ship, as well as everyone else on this planet, don't have much time. A Craing fleet is en route; unfortunately, you'll have to take my word for it."

"I do, others won't," the admiral said with regret.

Jason had the beginnings of an idea, "I take it this conversation is being monitored, even by the Joint Chiefs of Staff—yes?"

"That's probably a good assumption."

"Okay, I have an idea. Probably relates to that impetuousness you just referred to. Admiral, I'll get back to you within a half hour, if that's acceptable. Oh, and please convey my apologies to Army higher command for the trouble they've gone to out here, but we're leaving Texas."

Jason gestured for Orion to cut the connection. "XO, let's get the ship prepped for another flight. McBride, set a new course, this time for Washington D.C. I'd like to be off the ground in ten minutes. Orion, have Billy meet me in the mess hall with the remainder of his team. XO, you have the bridge."

Billy had assembled his team as instructed. Jason entered the mess hall and, as usual, Ricket was not far behind. Using his virtual tablet, Jason enlarged the display to several feet out in diameter, and proceeded to outline his plan. Billy had put on a new jumpsuit and seemed no worse for wear. He and his men paid close attention to what would be expected from them.

There were more than a few open-mouthed blank stares. Billy smirked, "So you're really not shitting us—we're doing this?"

* * *

Back in the command chair, Jason checked his tablet one more time. Ricket had configured it to access the Internet. Even with the incalculable processing capabilities of the AI, Jason still felt more comfortable Googling certain things.

"We're ready to lift off, Captain," the XO said. Jason looked up at the display, curious how this new view was even possible—maybe from a piggybacked signal from an orbiting satellite? The Lilly truly was something to behold, the sweeping curve of her matte-black hull, and the overall simplicity of her lines—set against the stark contrast of the surrounding desert landscape. At a parameter of several miles up, he saw four military fortifications had been erected. Each one appeared like a small anthill with a flurry of activity—little black ants moving this way and that.

"When you're ready, McBride, take us up to low orbit and then back down to the specified coordinates"

The ensign acknowledged the command, although he looked even more nervous than usual. The ship lifted off and hovered for several moments before it made a gentle sweep upwards toward the stratosphere. Jason looked toward the rear of the screen's 360-degree display, which showed the ascending view from the ship's stern. He wondered if the hundreds, if not thousands, of military personnel were looking up at her swift ascent, and were disappointed there wouldn't be a fight today.

"Again, everyone, this only works if we have the element of surprise. Billy, you in position?"

"Aye, sir. Teams are in position—one forward and one aft," Billy replied.

"Sir, we're starting to make our descent," McBride relayed from his seat at the helm. The display changed from the dark nothingness of the upper stratosphere to the rapidly approaching North American eastern seaboard and the bright blue Atlantic to the east. "We're at 1,000 miles, Captain," said McBride. "Shields and signal dampeners are up."

Perkins, seated next to Jason, leaned in close, careful not to be overheard by the rest of the crew. "Sir, are you really sure there'll be enough room? The Lilly's got quite a substantial backside, if you hadn't noticed," Perkins whispered, and then sat back in his chair.

"I think we'll be fine, XO," Jason said, with as much confidence as he could muster.

"600 miles and closing, sir," came from the helm. "400 miles—200—100—25…" Washington, D.C. sprawled before them, the recognizable shapes of the Capitol building, the long quad that stretched between the Washington and Lincoln monuments, and then the winding blue of the Potomac River. And there, on the far side, was their destination.

"Go ahead and phase-shift now, Ensign," the captain ordered, his eyes locked on the display. The view instantly changed from a picture postcard view of Washington, D.C. to a series of drab, seven-story concrete buildings that encircled the ship.

"Shift successful, Captain. We are on the

ground in the center courtyard of the Pentagon building."

"Thank you, Helm. Extend our shields ten yards around the ship. Open aft and forward gangways," Jason ordered. "Billy, make a perimeter around the outside of the ship and stay within the shields. Orion, connect me with the admiral again, please," Jason said, with the hint of a smile.

Admiral Cramer's loud and angry voice filled the bridge. "What the hell have you done, Reynolds? Do you have any idea of the repercussions a stunt like this... hold on, I've got the Secretary of Defense on the other line." The bridge went quiet; all eyes were on the captain. "Okay, I'm putting the defense secretary through," she said, sounding thoroughly disgusted.

"Captain, this is Benjamin Walker, Secretary of Defense. Seems you've paid us a little visit at the DOD. Would you like to explain?" he asked, as calmly as if he was talking about the nice spring weather.

"I apologize for the dramatics, Mr. Secretary, but half measures were never going to work. I think we all know that."

"But landing in the Pentagon center courtyard, Captain? We were already sitting at DEFCON 2. This has brought us to DEFCON 1. Each branch of the military's been deployed."

Jason was prepared for that response. "There's a clock ticking, and far too much is at stake—the fate of our country—the world.

We're simply not going to play any more games. You have a unique, one time only opportunity to be an active participant in how things will transpire. This ship, like it or not, is humanity's only ace in the hole. I suggest you, and whichever chiefs are present, come aboard for a more in-depth discussion."

"I beg your pardon, Captain?" the Secretary of Defense said, incredulously.

"Come on over, it's perfectly safe—bring your own security detail. But before you decide, remember, I could have just as easily put this ship down on the South Lawn of the White House. If you're not inclined, or you're too busy, perhaps the president will be more accommodating." The reply took several long moments.

"There's a lot that has to be undone here. To be honest, I'm not even sure it can be. Give me ten minutes, Captain—I can't believe I'm agreeing to this."

Jason smiled at the bridge crew and turned to his XO. "Find Plimpton and let him know we're having guests for dinner."

All six of the sixteen Chiefs of Staff, the Secretary of Defense, as well as a security detail, emerged from The Pentagon building onto the inner courtyard. It was early evening and The Lilly's running lights were on, giving the ship an impressive first impression. Standing at attention and saluting, Billy and his team lined up in two rows. Jason, standing at the rear gangway, also saluted as the contingent of officials approached.

As the impressive group approached with star-studded shoulders, oversized stripes, and chests ablaze with ribbons, Jason was momentarily intimidated. He recognized Benjamin Walker. His broad shoulders, large square head, topped off with a mane of thick black hair, contributed to his air of strength and authority. The group came to a stop and reluctantly returned the captain's salute. Walker's face fell when he noticed several large trees had been toppled and now jutted out sideways from beneath The Lilly's wide keel.

"Thank you for the nice reception, Captain," the Secretary of Defense said cordially. "Just so you know, at this moment there are more than a few crosshairs trained on both you and your crew, as well as this vessel."

Jason had noticed multiple sniper rifle barrels protruding from upper floor windows. In the air space above the Pentagon, helicopters circled relentlessly.

"With that said," the secretary continued, "I'd like to make some quick introductions." The Secretary of Defense and several appointed chiefs huddled forward into a semicircle around Jason at the base of the gangway. "Captain Jason Reynolds, this is Chairman of the Joint Chiefs of Staff, General Brian Carter, United States Marine Corps; Chief of Staff of the Navy, Vice-Admiral Harold Brightman; Chief of Staff of the Army, General Eric Slayton; and Chief of Staff of the Air Force, General Peter

Bickerdike."

"Welcome, gentlemen. Please follow me."

Chapter 10

The military chiefs and a select few of their security detail were led directly to The Lilly's lower level mess hall. It was clear the Joint Chiefs would need to stay in constant contact with their aides and other subordinates outside the ship. Jason had worked out a system with Billy and the other SEALs. Each would be assigned to a chief, which would ensure that no one was left unescorted. There was reluctance from the Joint Chiefs' security detail concerning the use of the DeckPorts, but eventually Defense Secretary Walker barreled his way in front and murmured something about them needing to grow a pair. The others then followed suit, giddy as children on their first Disneyland ride.

Jason was surprised to see the mess hall had been transformed into a formal meeting room. Tablecloths had been spread over pushed-together smaller tables and the cafeteria counter was hidden behind a temporary bulkhead. A ten-foot virtual display hovered in the air at the far end of the hall. Jason had to smile when he recognized the suspended image of The Lilly— one that had been taken by an F-18 fighter earlier, at Air Station Meridian.

"Please be seated, gentlemen," Jason said, taking his own seat at the head of the table. He watched as the three security men took up positions against the bulkhead walls while the group of older men, mostly in their fifties and sixties, took their own seats around the table.

Watching them, he couldn't help but think about his father's warning concerning Craing human-like beings who had infiltrated into the highest levels of the government and military. Who here was, in reality, a Craing? Jason held two fingers up to his ear and turned slightly away from the group of men before him and quietly said, "Captain to Ricket."

"Go for Ricket," the mechanical voice came back.

"Ricket, I'd like to ask you a quick question," he said, turning away. "Would it be possible for you to detect if any of the men currently onboard are actually Craing beings?"

"Only with direct sensor contact, sir."

"In that case, please come on down to the mess hall. Captain out."

"I'd like to bring you all up to speed on the course of events that have brought us here. Much has happened in just a few short days," Jason said, addressing the group.

The Chairman of the Joint Chiefs of Staff, General Brian Carter, shook his head, an exasperated expression on his face.

"General Carter, you look distressed. Please feel free to speak your mind," the captain said with patient forbearance.

"This little meeting is totally inappropriate—sitting here with some kind of self-appointed emissary from who or what— who knows? The audacity to think you can

147

barge your way into the Pentagon and have us sit here like little school children; frankly, it's insulting." The Chairman of the Joint Chiefs swiveled his bald head around, back and forth several times, looking for support from the others.

Secretary of Defense Walker raised a conciliatory hand towards his fellow staff member. "Brian, why don't we just hear Captain Reynolds out? For God's sake, we're already here." This brought several smiles from the others and temporarily mollified the general enough from making any more comments.

"Thank you, Secretary Walker. I guess I'll start at the beginning—" Jason described what had transpired over the preceding few days, including the discovery of the mechanical man, Ricket; the subsequent shooting of his daughter; the mad dash to The Lilly; and the multiple conversations with his father, Admiral Perry Reynolds. Certain technical and tactical information regarding the capabilities of the ship was of course withheld from the visitors. Jason went on to describe the Craing light cruiser and the events that led to the abduction of his ex-wife. Questions arose from the defense secretary and the six joint chiefs. They understood that Jason was an unwilling participant over the course of events. With the exception of General Carter, they seemed more conciliatory toward his predicament and subsequent landing at the Pentagon.

Secretary Walker raised his hand again for

everyone to be quiet. "What is clear is the United States needs this technology. What's required, Captain, is to bring you under the umbrella of the United States government and its military apparatus."

Jason smiled and slowly shook his head. "Sorry, Secretary Walker, but that would be the worst thing we could do. Lilly, please bring up an overhead view of our current location." Jason turned and saw the display change to a high-up nighttime perspective showing The Lilly sitting in the Pentagon's courtyard. "Right now, the Chinese Ministry of State Security in Beijing, the Russian Federal Security Service in Moscow, the Inter-Services Intelligence agency in Pakistan, and a score of other international security agencies around the globe are all studying this same satellite image. Instability, even with our allies, is inevitable and has already begun. You'll be in-fighting amongst yourselves as much as with the Craing." Just then Ricket, still wearing his LA Dodgers baseball cap, entered the mess hall and stood to Jason's left.

"The sharing of technology will be the single most influential factor for the survival of Earth's societies. To stay free from the Craing, or even other interstellar adversarial influences, Earth's technology needs to advance rapidly." Jason paused for a moment to look around the room before he continued on. "This planet needs to embrace space travel with the implementation of faster than light, or FTL, technology. This will open up new opportunities for commerce with other worlds. Unfortunately, warfare is as much a reality in space as it is here on Earth."

Ricket pointed toward the display while it simultaneously changed to a view of open space: an inky black background with twenty bright objects, within a diamond-shaped formation.

"What are we looking at here, Ricket?" Jason asked, perplexed.

"This view is of the Craing fleet en route to Earth," Ricket replied succinctly. "Each of those four objects is a cluster of five hundred Craing vessels—a total of two thousand ships. Each five hundred-ship cluster contains what is called a Battle Dreadnaught. It's five miles long and five miles wide." Ricket used a laser-type pointer. "If you'll notice, this cluster of five hundred ships here, with its own Battle Dreadnaught, has broken off and is headed straight for the Sol system—us."

The officials began to talk amongst themselves. Eventually, Secretary Walker looked up. "What is the time frame?" he inquired, heavy concern on his face. Ricket looked up to the captain, then back to Walker.

"They are no more than five days from Earth," Ricket replied. The group of men looked back at Ricket with stunned expressions.

"Excuse me, I'd like to introduce you to Ricket, our Science Officer, whom I mentioned earlier." Ricket then proceeded over to the table and, one by one, introduced himself and shook the hands of each of the Joint Chiefs, and the Secretary of Defense. When he had completed shaking each of their hands, Ricket turned to Jason and pointed to General Peter Bickerdike of the Air Force, and nodded. Using his NanoCom, Jason hailed Billy.

"Go for Billy," the deep voice replied.

With his comms, Jason said, "I need an armed detail on standby—but take no action just yet."

"Got it, we'll hold for your go."

Jason took a breath and looked directly at the highest commanding officer in the room, the Chairman of the Joint Chiefs, General Carter. "Sir, I have the unpleasant duty to inform you that one of the men in this room is Craing. We need to know how you would like to proceed?"

"What do you mean by that? One of us— the Joint Chiefs? That's not possible. Each one of us has been vetted—top-level security backgrounds—it's simply not possible." Worried, each of the men looked at one another. All except General Bickerdike, who never took his eyes off Ricket. The security detail standing closest to the door reached for the gun at his hip. At this movement, the other two drew their weapons and stepped up to the table in-between the Joint Chiefs. Jason pressed back into his chair. He'd rarely been on the receiving end of this kind of situation and his hands twitched toward the gun at his waist. He did not drop the gaze of the man who had his gun pointed at his head.

"At ease, men," Carter commanded. "Let's just settle down and take a breath. Captain, can you provide unequivocal proof of this infiltration?" Carter asked.

Jason looked to Ricket, who in turn nodded his head and turned toward the large display screen. The conference room, now from Ricket's distinct perspective, was displayed. Jason noticed that each person was partially transparent, as if viewed through x-ray vision. Everyone's internal organs, blood vessels, muscular and skeletal systems—all were clearly depicted. Ricket zoomed in to the form of General Bickerdike, and then zoomed in again to focus on a close-up of his torso area. General Bickerdike, as clear as day, had two hearts—one directly above the other.

"In addition to the obvious physical abnormality, chromosomal and other markers are significantly different than those of human species—but nearly identical to those of the Craing," Ricket said.

Secretary Walker and the others turned their attention to Bickerdike, who merely sat back in his chair with a resigned expression on his face. The chiefs started to squirm and shift in their seats. Heads nervously turned this way and that. General Carter caught the eye of his lead security officer and gestured for him to take the general into custody. Bickerdike stood without ceremony and was quickly escorted from the mess hall. Jason's father had warned him of the possibility of an infiltration, and why he had avoided involving the government and military all those years. But something didn't add up—one more thing he'd have to discuss with the admiral. With a Craing fleet mere days from Earth, there could be no avoiding the sobering realization that life on planet Earth was about to dramatically change.

General Eric Slayton, the Army Chief of Staff, asked, "Ricket, can you provide some kind of test, something our own personnel could administer here on Earth?" Ricket looked to Jason, who responded back with a nod.

"Yes, with slight modifications to your standard DNA tests, the hidden chromosome markers can be flagged," Ricket replied in his usual, even-toned voice. Again, Jason thought this was strange. Why the hell hadn't his father offered the government this same option?

"On a more positive note," Jason interrupted, "I'd like to continue our discussions. There is technology here beyond your imagination—if you're interested to learn? We can start with a quick meal and a more in-depth look at the capabilities of the ship."

The visitors conferred amongst themselves for a moment and then enthusiastically nodded their heads in unison. Those in attendance were about to receive a strategic and military advantage. The opportunity to see The Lilly's capabilities first hand was, as Jason knew it would be, impossible to resist.

Plimpton, with the assistance of two seaman apprentices, had been waiting in the wings to start the dinner service. Callurian wine was poured, followed by leafy green and blue salads, with an assortment of dressings from distant planetary systems. The main course was similar to prime rib, but made from the tender meats of a Bamba steer from the Saram system. Dessert was simple American apple pie, a la mode, with coffee. For the most part, Jason only picked at his meal. Conversation was better than expected. Most likely, reality had set in—their need to make this relationship work was clearly at the forefront of their minds. They knew that Jason and The Lilly could have just as easily dropped in for dinner in Moscow or Beijing.

It had been a long day and Jason missed Mollie. Using his NanoCom, Jason contacted Dira, something he hadn't done before and felt strange doing.

"Go ahead, Captain, what can I do for you?" Dira said, nervously.

"I'm looking for Mollie, is she with you?"

"Yes, we are playing a game—of course."

"Would you and Mollie care to help me give a tour of the ship to our guests?"

"We'd love to. Are you still in the mess hall?" she asked.

"Yeah. How about I meet you in Engineering—oh, and let Chief Horris know we're on our way."

"Sure, see you soon. Bye bye," Dira replied—not using the standard military comms jargon, which Jason, for some reason, found endearing.

Having consumed six bottles of Callurian wine, The Lilly's guests were a tad unsteady on their feet, awestruck and loud. Ushering them out of the mess hall and into the corridor was a feat in itself. After several days on the ship, the technology was commonplace to Jason. For the visitors, it was mesmerizing. By the time they converged at the DeckPort, their facial expressions revealed child-like incredulity at what they were witnessing. Ricket, who stayed at Jason's side, periodically looked up at him with a confused expression. It had crossed Jason's mind more than once during their tour that it would be tough to recognize these seven men now as being among the top leaders of the free world.

Horris greeted the distinguished visitors as they entered Engineering. From behind the group, Jason gestured with his open hand that he wanted to be out of there in five minutes. The Engineering chief nodded, and proceeded to explain the intricacies of the exotic Antimatter Drive to the best of his ability. As they stood in the middle of the main engineering room, with its open space above to multiple decks, the tour group spun and gaped at the sheer size of the propulsion systems and the advanced technological capabilities of the vessel.

Dira and Mollie arrived within several minutes. Mollie gave her dad a hug and looked around at the group of middle-aged men. "Who are they? What's with the costumes?" she asked, looking up at her father, slightly confused.

"Well, they are in uniform, Mollie—just like we wear uniforms. Theirs are very dressy-type uniforms, bedecked with many medals," Jason replied.

Dira had moved over to the Joint Chiefs of Army and Navy and introduced herself. "Hello, my name is Dira," she said, in what sounded like a British or Australian, accent—similar, but definitely different. "You won't be able to pronounce my last name since I am not from your planet, as you may have noticed from my different physical appearance," she said, smiling and pointing to her light violet skin and extended eye lashes.

"Where you from, sweetheart?" General Carter asked her, obviously enamored with the exotic-looking crewmember. Dira's eyes glanced over to Jason in response to the politically-improper sweetheart term. "I'm from a planet in the Altar system called Jhardon," she replied, smiling. To the whole group, she said, "Now, if you will all follow me, I'd like to show you our medical facilities."

Mollie rushed forward to the head of the procession and took over the job of tour guide. "My name is Mollie Reynolds and I'm Captain Reynolds' daughter and I work in the Zoo," she said, very official-sounding for a little girl.

This generated more questions.

"How old are you, Mollie?"

"What is the Zoo?"

Jason hung back with Secretary Walker as the tour progressed out of Engineering into the corridor. "There's a few things I'll need your help with for everything to work out, sir," Jason said.

"I'm not sure what I can do, but I will certainly try," the square-faced man said, and looked as though he meant it. "But you know how government red tape is."

"We'll need to bypass the red tape; in fact, we'll need to expedite things."

"Well, stop beating around the bush, Captain. What is it you're looking for?"

Dira had taken over the tour again when they reached Medical. The group moved inside and stood before the five MediPod units—two were still in use by injured SEAL warriors. "These medical capsules, we call them MediPods, provide full-body diagnostic screening, as well as administer a comprehensive range of medical treatments."

Mollie stepped forward and put her hand on the MediPod closest to the door. "This is the MediPod capsule they put me in when Ricket shot me in the heart," she said.

Navy Chief of Staff said, "Well, it looks like you've recovered well, young lady. Was the process painful?"

Mollie shrugged and said, "I don't know… not really—I was dead."

The men began another barrage of questions targeted to her. "What do you mean, dead? Like dead dead?" Secretary Walker asked, looking first to Dira and then to Jason for confirmation. "What is she talking about, how is that possible?"

Jason stepped forward with his hands up. "I know you have lots of questions, but there's still much we don't understand, gentlemen. We've figured out how to operate many things, such as the MediPods and the ship's drive systems, but we are still working on fully deciphering the ship's technology."

The Navy's Chief of Staff said, "But the implications. The impact these capsules could have on everyday life—they could revolutionize the medical industry here on Earth."

Next stop was the bridge, where the invited guests were introduced to the rest of the officers and crew. They also had the opportunity to speak with the AI. Jason noticed the group was getting a bit overwhelmed, asking fewer questions. Before ushering them off the ship, Jason had one more stop to make. He looked around for Ricket and saw his baseball-capped head at the back of the group. "Ricket, can you take us to the flight bay? I'm not entirely sure how to get there," Jason queried.

"We can DeckPort directly to the bay—just have everyone make a closed fist as they enter the port, like this:" Ricket held up a small fist and walked into a nearby DeckPort. Dira got everyone's attention and instructed the men to do as Ricket had done.

The flight bay was quiet, totally deserted and sat in near-darkness. Ricket triggered the overhead lights and the large hangar-like room came to life. The bay took up three partial decks and spanned the width of the ship. Six dark red, single-man fighter crafts lined the aft bulkhead and two shuttle crafts sat side-by-side at the forward bulkhead. Both sides of the ship could be opened to outer space via large sliding bay doors. Standing in front of the assembled Joint Chiefs of Staff and appointed Secretary of Defense, Jason knew everything came down to this: their audacious landing here at the Pentagon, the wine and dining, the tour—all of it. For Jason and his crew to have any success fighting the Craing, getting the support of these men was imperative.

"Earlier today, we lost ten SEAL heroes at the hands of the United States government. Men who had dedicated their lives to protecting this very nation were struck down without provocation or reason." Jason's statement sobered the visitors as they uncomfortably squirmed and looked down at their feet. "Hopefully, you now realize our intentions are sound. So I'm asking you to step up and do the right thing." Jason finished and looked back at each of the men.

"What do you want us to do, Captain?" General Walker asked.

"The Lilly currently has a complement of sixty-two crewmembers, although 200 would be optimum. We're dangerously understaffed to conduct the type of campaign necessary to go up against the approaching Craing fleet. First of all, we have no pilots for these six fighters, or for the two shuttles. We have barely enough bridge crewmembers for a single shift, let alone a second or third. We are undermanned in virtually every department. So we need your help—and we need it tonight." The silence in the room was deafening. The older men's faces were impossible to read.

Admiral Brightman cleared his throat and looked up. "By this time tomorrow, you'll have ten Navy Top-Gun pilots at your disposal. The families of the deceased Navy SEALs will be informed of their terrible loss, and the posthumous awarding of the Navy Medal of Honor will soon be issued. Your current complement of Navy SEALs will have any AWOL charges against them dismissed, and each will continue to receive full pay and benefits in accordance to their rank while on loan to The Lilly. I'll also ensure charges are dropped for you as well, including those having to do with the Somalian pirate incident. You'll also be officially promoted to the rank of Navy Captain. Will that suffice for a start, Captain? Personally, I can't think of anything that is more important than this endeavor." Admiral Brightman stood tall and at attention.

"Yes, sir, and thank you."

Not to be outdone, General Carter spoke up: "Captain, I'm sure each of our military departments would be honored to have representation onboard: Navy, Army, Marines, and Air Force. We'll get started on that immediately."

"Thank you, sir. Lieutenant Perkins has the

roster of open crew positions. Also, please inform our sister allied nations that they too will have crew representation on The Lilly—that is, as time permits us to do so in the future." Jason's reply reminded his visitors that he still had every intention of keeping the mission on a multi-allied level. They nodded, although with far less enthusiasm in that regard. Jason informed them they would be lifting off within the hour and returning to Texas and the wide-open spaces of the Chihuahuan desert.

Chapter 11

Jason left word with his XO to move the 0600 meeting to 0900 that morning. After a quick breakfast, Jason and Mollie left the ship, ready for some fresh air and exercise. The Lilly had been set down between two granite ridges, three miles east of their previous position in the Chihuahuan desert. He'd scrounged up his old backpack and they were exploring nearby cliffs when two large Sikorsky UH-60 Black Hawk helicopters approached from the east and set down behind the ridge.

"Looks like we have company. What do you say we head back?" Jason asked Mollie, already heading down the rocky landscape.

Mollie shielded her eyes from the bright morning sun and looked down at the helicopters. She scowled and said, "We sure get a lot a of visitors lately, Dad."

"Well, The Lilly is going to be pretty popular for a while," Jason told her, not liking the looks of things below; armed soldiers, piling out the rear of both crafts, were in assault formations. The Army helicopters had tried to come in fast and quiet. Out of habit, Jason held two fingers to his ear and accessed his NanoCom. "Captain to XO."

"Go for XO, Captain."

"Secure the ship and put up the shields. We've got assault teams approaching from behind the ridge," Jason commanded.

"Already done, sir. We've also got multiple missile locks on us coming from land and air-based vehicles. Orders, Captain?" the XO asked. Jason had a hard time connecting the actions unfolding before him with the sincerity he'd felt from General Carter and Vice-Admiral Brightman.

Jason and Mollie quickly crouched down on a rocky ledge: a perfect perch to view the action below. "Who's on comms this morning? I need to talk to Secretary Walker."

"I can patch you—give me a quick second, Captain," the XO replied. Jason watched as four ten-man Army assault teams converged, breaking into two larger teams. They were still several hundred meters away, but he judged by their crouched, weapons held high, forward movement, that they would reach the ship in just a few moments.

"This is Walker," the deep voice of the Secretary of Defense boomed in Jason's ear.

"Secretary Walker, this is Captain Reynolds, and I'm currently watching as an Army assault team converges on The Lilly, not to mention there are missile locks detected from multiple sources. I thought we had an agreement, sir."

"We did, Captain. What you are seeing is the U.S. military at odds with itself. Not quite a coup, but close."

"How is that even possible? It's not like we're a third-world nation."

"You're preaching to the choir. For now, you're on your own. Army Chief of Staff General Slayton apparently had divergent views last night. As of right now, the U.S. Army has every intention of taking that ship of yours. As far as they're concerned, it's just too valuable of a resource to be left in your hands. The good news is your requested Navy pilots, as well as a Company of Navy SEALs, are cooling their heels at Air Station Meridian out of Mississippi. I need to go—the president is on the line. I'll get back to you." The Secretary of Defense hung up.

"Captain to XO," Jason said, watching as the army assault crew approached his ship.

"Go for XO, Captain"

"Perkins, initiate a shift to several hundred miles from here. You can come back and get us later."

"No can do, sir. Ricket is working on it, but the phase-shift option and several other systems, including shields, are offline."

"Offline? How the hell did they go offline? The ship's just sitting there," Jason asked, getting nervous about the assault teams approach. Not so much for The Lilly and her crew, but for the approaching Army personnel who had no idea what they'd be up against.

"Ricket thinks it could be sabotage," Perkins replied.

"Hold on, XO. Captain to Billy."

"Go for Billy, sir. We're locked and loaded just waiting for your orders."

"Energy weapons only, on stun. Is that clear?"

"Understood. Definitely looking forward to putting the spank on the U.S. Army," Billy said, not even trying to hide his excitement.

"They are sixty meters out, approaching west and east of the ship. Deploy now, and be careful. Captain out."

Jason and Mollie watched from their above perch as the scene unfolded below on the desert floor. Both gangways deployed simultaneously. Two SEAL teams rapidly moved down the ramps with weapons held high. Each SEAL was equipped with new, full-body hardened combat gear. Their helmet heads-up display (HUD) provided a full virtual representation of their surroundings, including the position of the approaching two Army assault teams. Jason felt a fleeting pang of jealousy. Not only would he miss out on the action, but the use of the new assault gear. Billy, in the lead, looked up at Jason's hidden position and gave a quick salute.

"Showoff," Jason said. Obviously, Billy's HUD had detected his and Mollie's life forms along with all the others. Jason was tied into the SEAL team's comms. But this was Billy's operation. He was totally in his element.

"Captain to XO," Jason said into his NanoCom.

"Go for XO."

"Can you scan for the Army comms signal and patch me in?"

"Yes, and I have already been monitoring.

You're now patched in."

Both sides were surprisingly quiet—the result of redundant training; soldiers at this level didn't need micro-managing. The invading troops moved quickly and Jason had the uneasy feeling he'd greatly underestimated the capabilities of the U.S. Army.

"Ricket to Captain"

"Go, Ricket."

"General Peter Bickerdike of the U.S. Air Force was not the only Craing to come aboard last night. Escorts, aides, and their assistants were constantly moving in and out of the ship. That's when we believe numerous Craing devices were planted. We've found two. There are still several more disrupting the AI."

"Hold on. Let me get this straight. With the advanced level of technology on this ship, saboteurs couldn't be detected?" Jason barked back.

"We believe we've rectified the problem," Ricket replied.

"XO to Captain," Perkins broke in, excitedly, "We have a new contact, sir." Jason realized right then that the Army assault team was a diversion. Probably keeping from sight something much larger. "It's the Craing ship, sir—she's left high orbit and is on a direct course for The Lilly." Jason's mind reeled. The implications were staggering. Had the U.S. Army been infiltrated and aligned with the Craing? Jason's ears rang with his father's reluctance to work through government and military channels.

"Ricket, do we have weapons capability?"

"No, sir"

"What do we have?" Jason barked back.

"Only those systems not controlled directly by the AI—I'm surprised comms are even working."

"So no shields, no weapons, no ability to phase-shift away?" Distant gunshots echoed off the rocky ridge.

"Not right now," Ricket replied evenly.

"Billy for Captain."

"Go, Billy."

"We're taking fire, sir," Billy said, out of breath.

"You're going to have to handle them— we've got bigger problems."

"We've already rounded one of their teams up and incapacitated them. But you've got a four-man team moving around the east ridge, coming directly at you. They must have stayed behind on one of the Black Hawks. Jason, they know your position; you have mere minutes."

Jason grabbed Mollie's arm and pulled her to her feet. "We've got to scramble, kiddo," he said, trying not to frighten her more than necessary. Jason looked up towards the top of the ridge-line, which looked to be several hundred feet above them. "Come on, let's keep moving," as he picked up the pace. More gunshots rang out below on the desert floor.

"I'm scared, Dad," Mollie said, looking up with tears in her eyes.

"I know, little one, me too, but I have an idea. Just keep moving up toward the top of the ridge, OK?"

"Captain to XO," Jason said.

"Go, Cap."

"Can you connect me to Admiral Malinda Cramer, commanding officer at Air Station Meridian?"

"I'm on it," Perkins replied.

"Billy, what's the status of that Army four-man team?"

"They've split up, looks like they're trying to flank you on two sides. I'm on my way but still a half-mile out. One other thing, they're not coming up as human on my HUD—think they're those hybrid Craing-human things."

Jason's NanoCom beeped. "Captain Reynolds, this is Admiral Cramer."

"Admiral, are you aware of our situation here?" Jason asked her as he helped Mollie climb over a large rock formation and climbed up next to her.

"Yes, and it's a cluster-fuck, Captain. No one's real sure how to respond to the Army's actions. We're a bit stymied."

"I need air support and quickly. I'm being chased up a damn ridge-line by an Army assault team. We'll be the two individuals wearing shorts and running for their lives."

"Seriously? Can't your fancy spacecraft help you, for God's sake?"

"Not right now. Seems it's broken."

"Let me see what I can do," she said, and

168

disconnected.

Jason and Mollie made slow progress up the ridge. They heard the sound of automatic weapons below and then the thump thump thump as bullets pummeled the ground nearby. Several ricochets pinged-off rocks just inches from Mollie's head. "Why are they shooting at us?" Mollie screamed.

"Keep your head down!" Jason barked, looking over his shoulder and mentally vowing to put a bullet in whoever would shoot at a child.

"Billy to Cap."

"Go," Jason ordered as he tried to shield Mollie from another barrage of bullets.

"Looks like one of the teams has held up down below, while the other one is closing in. I'm still a third of a mile out," Billy said, sounding frustrated.

Jason looked up. They were more than seventy-five feet from the top of the ridge, but then what? What would they do? The good news was this last section of the ridge had larger rocks to shield them from gunfire.

"Mollie, I want you to do something for me," he whispered, knowing that sound easily bounced off the rocky walls. "I want you to continue up the ridge and—"

"No way! You're not leaving me up there alone," she spat back, fear in her eyes.

"It's only for a few minutes. I need to check on something. I'll be right behind you—just get started, OK?" Jason told her, trying hard to look confident and that everything would be okay.

"You know, I really hate you sometimes," she said, scowling down at him as she reluctantly kept climbing.

Jason quickly moved back down the ridge to his previous location where there'd been rock protection. He could hear the soldiers moving down below.

"XO to Cap," Jason heard in his comms.

"Go," he whispered back.

"Craing ship is approaching. They have weapons lock."

"Get everyone inside; batten down the hatches." At that moment The Lilly came under fire. Bright bursts of blue light thundered from the Craing ship that now hovered no more than a mile to the west. A cockroach—lifelike and menacing, slow and deliberate—it approached. The Lilly shook while the bombardment continued. The incredible heat turned the sandy desert landscape to molten glass. Several more rounds were fired close by and pinged up towards the top of the ridge, where Mollie would most likely be by now. Jason knew he'd have only one chance. The two soldiers were less than ten feet from his hidden position. But the rock he hid behind would not shield him once they came around the next bend.

The noise from below was near deafening as The Lilly continued to take relentless fire. Jason took a deep breath and readied himself. In one continuous motion, he pulled himself over the rock and leapt. He caught them by surprise, as both had turned to watch the ship being pummeled. They were Army Rangers in full assault gear. The Ranger on his right took the full brunt force of Jason's body, as he was knocked forward and his face careened into solid granite. The Ranger's M4 rifle continued its fall down the mountainside, end-over-end and out of reach. Using the unconscious Ranger's body and his protective vest as a shield, Jason reached for and unholstered the soldier's side arm. Startled, the other Ranger was already wildly shooting, never pausing to consider the life of his fellow Ranger. The rounds kept firing into Jason's human shield, until the Ranger's clip emptied. Jason pushed off the dead soldier and brought up the 9mm Beretta and, without hesitation, put a bullet between the Ranger's eyes.

"Ricket to Cap."

"Go."

"We now have minimal shift capability," Ricket said steadily.

Jason watched as the Craing ship landed, continuing its onslaught of plasma pulse fire. "Phase-shift to the top of this ridge. Make sure you're back far enough, out of direct line of fire. Also, make sure you don't put her down on Mollie's head. She's up there somewhere." Jason turned to see waves of heat rising from the ship's still fiery hot hull. Then, in the next instant, The Lilly was gone. Relieved, Jason turned to make his way back up to the top of the ridge-line. The first bullet hit Jason in the back of his shoulder; the second tore through flesh and bone at the side of his head.

Chapter 12

Jason was on the ground looking up. He felt wetness on his back—the bullet had gone all the way through. He could feel the tingling of nanites already at work repairing the damage. The two Army Rangers were advancing up the hill faster than he'd expected and were now just several feet from him, rifles poised to take a shot.

One of the Rangers spoke into his comm unit. "We've got him. He's alive, but he looks to be in critical condition with a round to the head. Confirmed. We'll transport now," the Ranger said, and moved to lift Jason. The Ranger's face exploded into a bloody mess. He'd taken a round to the back of his head fired from an M4 rifle Billy had found, several yards down the mountain. Almost immediately, the second Ranger's face disappeared—an almost identical headshot.

Crew from The Lilly arrived from the top of the ridge just moments later. Strong hands lifted Jason onto a stretcher and then headed back up the hillside. Billy was one of those who carried him.

"You look like crap, man," he said with a grin.

"How's Mollie—on board?" Jason asked, worried.

"Yep, except for some scratches to her

knees, and worrying about you, she's fine." Billy leaned over closer to Jason. "Nanites already doing their thing. Weird as hell; a minute ago I could see your skull—wound is pretty much closed now. That's some weird shit, man."

* * *

Dira and Mollie were waiting at the top of the gangway for the men to bring Jason aboard. Both looked relieved to see that not only was he alive, but barking orders to be put down. Mollie rushed over and hugged her father, then preceded to yell down at him, "Don't you ever leave me alone like that again! I was scared to death!"

"You got it, I promise," he said. Dira was attending to his injuries. When he looked up, their eyes locked. He saw worry in her eyes, and then embarrassment. She frowned. Once finished with a temporary field dressing, she turned on her heels and stormed off.

Jason got to his feet. He was sore, but he'd live.

"Captain to Ricket."

"Go for Ricket," the mechanical man replied.

Jason, now halfway to the bridge, queried on the ship's status. "How we doing on internal systems, Ricket? Weapons online yet?"

"Not yet, Gunny's working on that. Maybe five minutes."

"What's the condition of the hull?"

"Critical. Definitely cannot take another barrage like that last one, at least not without shields."

"You're not giving me much to work with here, Ricket. What's the farthest we can phase-shift away in her current condition?" Jason asked, hating the sound of desperation creeping into his voice.

"Up to three miles; unfortunately, that keeps us within easy range of the Craing guns."

"Keep working on it. I think I have an idea. Captain out."

Jason rushed onto the bridge to surprised faces.

"Captain, the Craing vessel has powered up its thrusters. She's been scanning us and knows we're sitting here on top of this plateau, defenseless. She's getting ready to come finish us off." Jason stood motionless for several moments in thought, then looked over at Perkins.

"XO, how many Craing are onboard that ship. Have we scanned her?"

"Yes, about one hundred seventy-five."

"Bring up that diagram again, the internal ship configuration."

"Okay, but there's no way to board her without getting our systems online," the XO replied, incredulously.

Jason studied the display and activated his NanoCom. "Captain to Billy."

"Go for Billy. What's up, Captain?"

"I hope you and your men are still suited

up. Prepare to board and take that ship." Jason said, wondering if he was about to condemn The Lilly and her crew to a terrible fate. "And scrounge me up one of your new full-body combat suits." Jason looked over to his XO: "Prepare to phase-shift in exactly two minutes."

"To where?" the XO said, bewildered.

Jason hurried over, close to the forward display, and pointed: "To right here—we'll only get one chance at this so don't screw it up." Jason turned to leave the bridge, "And the bridge is yours. I'll stay on comms."

"Yes, sir," Perkins replied, at first a bit confused. Then he nodded his head in appreciation. Jason left the bridge and headed for the nearest DeckPort.

* * *

Billy, holding his own helmet under his arm and dressed in a dark red hardened combat suit, was waiting for Jason in front of the aft airlock. The embers of his cigar flared and a cloud of white smoke filled the air. Jason shook his head, but now was not the time to lecture his friend about smoking onboard.

"These suits are a little tricky getting into the first time," Billy said, standing next to a second open combat suit. "You have to step into them feet first, one at a time—doing things in the right order." Billy proceeded to show Jason exactly how to fit himself into the suit and latch each section shut as he went. Over his NanoCom, he heard the XO's nervous voice,

"Thirty seconds to phase-shift." A nearby SEAL handed Billy a helmet.

"This will adjust to your own physiology. You'll discover that you pretty much know how to operate everything already. Your previous HyperLearning tests took care of that. Well, mostly." Billy placed the helmet over Jason's head and secured the airtight latch mechanism.

"Your helmet's heads-up display is configured to work with your nano-devices as well as react to eye movement," Billy said. "All very intuitive, it just takes some getting used to."

Another SEAL handed Jason a high-powered pulse assault weapon.

"That's set to burn through flesh and blood but not the hull," Billy said with his typical smile. Jason just nodded. The countdown in his head was at three, two, one...

"Phase-shift completed," came the voice of the XO in Jason's ear. Jason was extremely relieved the comms still worked, now that The Lilly was sitting in the belly of the Craing vessel, three miles from their previous location. The forward and aft gangways were being deployed and SEALs were scurrying out with weapons held high.

Billy's voice came over Jason's comms, "Kinda brings new meaning to the old saying if you can't beat em, join em, don't it?"

"Let's keep the chatter down, boys," Jason said as he took in his new surroundings. The Craing vessel's enormous cargo hold had fortunately been almost empty, although several large crates in one corner had been obliterated by The Lilly's shift. So large was the hold, two of The Lillys could fit together, side by side. Dark and lurid colors were muted to dreary shades of grey. Jason and his team of SEALs moved forward, taking short, tentative, steps as they investigated the hold. His visibility was limited. The air was thick and moist and caused condensation to form on his visor. He wiped at the front of his helmet. It was as if a stagnant, putrid cloud hung suspended throughout the ship.

"Nice, cheery place you brought us to, Cap," Billy's voice stated over his NanoCom.

They broke into five teams: Lion, Bear, Zebra, Tiger and Cougar. The latter stayed put to watch the perimeter of The Lilly. Lion and Bear teams headed forward, while Tiger and Zebra headed aft. Jason and his Lion team headed off down the port corridor of the ship. Billy and team Bear moved forward on the starboard side corridor. Jason quickly realized he needed to change his HUD settings to display life signs. Immediately, over one hundred orange symbols came into view laid on top of a virtual representation of the Craing ship.

Apparently, The Lilly and the SEAL teams were still undetected. Jason and his four team members were a formidable sight in their oversized protective combat suits, streamlined helmets, amber-colored backlit visors, and large plasma pulse rifles. They moved forward and took up the full width of the corridor. Jason and his Lion team passed multiple small, about five-foot high, closed hatchway doors along the corridor. Two life signs approached from a perpendicular corridor ahead. Jason signaled his team to hold back and they watched as two Craing crew members emerged in front of them, at the point where the corridors intersected. These three- to four-foot high beings looked remarkably similar to Ricket, with their greyish skin, thick and creased, hide-like, short stubby arms and legs, and the same triangular-shaped heads and large eyes.

Two Craing were stunned and left lying on the floor, even before they had a chance to react. The majority of the Craing crew seemed to be concentrated in one section of the ship, about sixty meters from Jason's current corridor position. More signs of life began to show up in this section of the ship along with noises, like soft murmuring sounds, emanating from down the corridor. Off to the right was a wide entranceway. According to Jason's HUD, it led to another chamber. Actually, to the largest area of the ship, even larger than the hold where The Lilly was parked. The chamber, taking up much of the deck they were on, was opened to ten decks above. Flashing over the entrance was a series of symbols. Although Jason had no idea what they meant, the HUD had figured it out and displayed the translated text: Meal-Time.

"Billy to Captain."

"Go for Captain—you seeing what I'm

seeing, Billy?"

"Yeah, we're just outside the other entrance. I'm seeing close to a hundred life signs here and another hundred humans up above."

"Another hundred humans?" Annoyed with himself, Jason realized he had his HUD set to ignore other human life signs.

"Crap, you're right." Once changed, the HUD filled with close to one hundred bright blue symbols.

"Ricket to Captain," came the mechanical voice in Jason's ear.

"Can't talk right now, Ricket. I'll get back to you." Jason disconnected while he edged closer to the entrance and peered inside.

Scattered about the room were ten stone-like tables, each big enough to sit fifteen to twenty Craing comfortably. Ornate woodcarvings, some as large as automobiles, encircled the room. Hanging down from the walls were long, intricately painted banners. Scenes of early Craing warriors holding spears and riding elaborate carts, perhaps chariots, into battle—much like the early Egyptians—although much of the effect was lost due to their short stature. A golden statue of a large lizard-like creature dominated the center of the room. Here, the smoky haze filling the air was the worst Jason had experienced yet—dark and foreboding, where the only light came from flames flickering upward from ten round caldrons. Each table was open in the middle where a Craing, Benihana-style chef stood serving his guests. Back and forth, he'd turn to the caldron and then back to those around the table, serving each in turn.

Jason now realized that these cauldrons were actually more like giant cooking grills. He scanned the room. Obviously, these meal times were part of some kind of religious ceremony. A repeating mantra had begun and droned in the background. Each of the Craing stopped and lowered his head, as if in reverence or submission. Jason watched and wondered if they were praying to the lizard statue in the center of the room.

"Captain, you seeing this shit?" Billy hissed over his comms.

"Yeah, I'm seeing it," Jason replied, still mesmerized by the scene.

"So these are the aliens that are terrorizing the universe? I just don't get it, Cap."

A loud cracking noise, what sounded like snapping twigs or small bones being broken, echoed around the large chamber. The Craing suddenly turned and faced the forward bulkhead in unison, and bowed several times in rapid succession. When the sound came again, in unison they all turned forty-five degrees to face another bulkhead and bowed again. They did this a total of four times—north, south, east, and west—giving homage to whatever or whomever. Eventually, the strange sounds stopped and the Craing returned to their meals.

The caldrons around the chamber hissed

and splattered as pieces of meat were thrown onto the grills. One of these flashes illuminated the open areas above. Looking up, Jason saw what looked like little fenced-in alcoves. Jason looked down at the eating area and then back up at the surrounding four vertical walls, filled with alcoves and long encircling catwalks. Somewhere at the back of his mind, he'd already put the pieces together. That the alcoves above were actually cages and that the pieces of meat on the cauldron grills were human arms, legs, and even a side of human ribs. Moans and screams had been filtering down from above all along. But that was nothing compared to his most recent realization. Somewhere, way off in the distance, high up above, he could hear the familiar Boom Boom Pow ringtone. Nan's cell phone.

Ricket must have configured the Craing AI to forward cell calls. Jason took a slow deep breath. It was all he could do to keep himself from shooting every one of these barbaric Craing right here and now. Jason looked back to his team; four dimly lit faces stared back, with gaping jaws and wide eyes. They had each set their HUD displays to piggyback onto Jason's. They'd seen exactly what he had seen.

Jason hailed Billy. "Let's get these… whatever the hell they are, rounded up and secured. They don't seem to be armed. Have Cougar team prepare a mock brig back in the hold area."

"You got it, Cap," Billy replied.

Both Lion and Bear teams rushed in simultaneously, with weapons aimed at the Craings' heads. The unarmed, near naked Craing turned this way and that. Astonished to see their vessel infiltrated, without warning, the small aliens scurried around frantically. Jason thought it strange—the act of raising one's hands must be the universal sign of submission. Each of the startled Craing crew was ushered out into both side corridors. An alarm klaxon sounded. That same dreadful sound Jason had heard near the scrapyard.

"Captain to Ricket," Jason said.

"Go for Ricket," the mechanical man came back. "Captain! I've made cell phone connection to…"

Jason cut him off, "Yes, I know what you've done. I heard the phone ringing. Is she all right, is she hurt?"

"I do not know. She did not answer. But the phone is located on deck nine right above your current location," Ricket said.

"I'm investigating. What's going on with The Lilly?" Jason asked, finding it nearly impossible to concentrate.

"Shields are now operational. Orion says the weapons are still down, but she's making good headway."

Jason ran for the nearest of the four lifts, surprised by the archaic slide-up metal gate and exposed cables and its old-fashioned pulley system above. After several tries he figured out the control lever and the lift slowly began to rise. The lift itself was coated with a splattering of a sticky-syrupy mixture of congealed blood and God knew what else. The second deck came into view through the metal mesh gate. The cages here were empty; only an occasional piece of torn off flesh, an odd finger, or an errant tuft of hair remained, stuck fast in the rough metal flooring.

Decks three through seven were a repeat of the same: empty cages and just as disgusting. Jason tried to keep his mind from venturing too far toward hopelessness and the growing possibility that Nan had recently been dismembered, carved up, and grilled on an open flame below. His stomach turned, and he fought the urge to retch. The lift was coming up to floor eight and immediately things looked different. Complete bodies, stationary, some sprawled out on cage floors, obviously dead. Others stripped down and partially dismembered. In a cage off to the right, Jason saw a familiar shape. An aluminum walker. Two florescent-green tennis balls still secured to its front legs. Jason's mind flashed back to Nan helping an elderly man across the desert as they were ushered into the alien ship. This ship. Rolling carts, similar to hotel maid's carts, were positioned down the catwalk in front of several of the cages.

The closest had an assortment of tools and cutlery—a strange type of saw lay atop a bloody cutting board with congealed blood and tissue, still wet. The carnage was horrific. Jason wanted to pull his eyes away but couldn't. The lift was coming up on the ninth floor. Again, more bodies. Movement now. At least some of the people on this floor were still alive. All hog-tied, with their hands and feet secured tightly behind their backs. Faces looked out from behind the bars of cages with fearful eyes. Louder now, it repeated, Boom Boom Pow. Jason turned his head from side to side to get a better fix on its location. The lift came to a stop and he rammed the lift gate open. He turned left and ran down the catwalk, listening for the phone. Surprised faces watched him run past.

"Hang on. You're safe now. I'll be back." Jason repeated these heartening words over and over again as he ran down the catwalk, making sure he made eye contact and looked as reassuring as possible. The cell phone ringing got quieter. Jason backtracked, slowing to a walk. He looked in each of the cages, one-by-one, where terrified eyes stared back at him.

He found Nan's cage. Back in the corner was a woman, not moving. Her hair covered her face. Jason pulled on the cage door. It was locked. He stepped back to assess the lock. Like the lift, it was a simple, old-fashioned mechanism. Positioned on the catwalk, out of arm's reach, was a release lever. He pulled it and the door released with a loud clang. Jason flung the door open and rushed to the woman's side. She stirred. Carefully, Jason moved the hair from her face and with both hands cradled Nan's scratched and bruised face. Her eyes opened halfway and then went wide. Realizing he still had his helmet on, he used one hand to disengage its front latch and pulled the helmet over and off his head. Then, carefully, he pulled the gag away from her mouth. He kissed her forehead.

"You're safe now, you're OK," Jason said to reassure her.

Staring back at him in disbelief, Nan tried to talk, but started coughing instead. She swallowed, tried again, "Get me the fuck out of here, Jason!" she screamed. Jason almost smiled.

"OK, OK… let me free your hands and feet." Looking behind her, he realized he'd need a key for the metal shackles. "I have to leave you just a quick—"

"Don't you dare leave me here, for God's sakes, Jason, please don't leave me here!"

"I'm just getting a key. I'll be right back." Jason kissed the back of her head, ran from the cage and headed off down the catwalk to one of the carts parked at the far end of the floor. He saw more terrified expressions and heard muffled cries for help. This cart was relatively clean. The Craing's tools-of-the-trade were still lined up on its metal cutting board. Jason, near frantic now, looked for the keys. He pulled open its cabinet-like doors and rifled through more cutting implements, letting them fall to the deck plates with a clang. Frustrated, he moved back up to the top shelf, where those items ended up on the floor as well. Finally, he found them hanging from the push-handle, swinging from a thin chain. He yanked it free and ran back toward Nan's cage.

As if she'd been holding her breath, Nan exhaled and relaxed, somewhat, when Jason was back at her side. As he worked the lock, Nan looked back over her shoulder. "How's Mollie? Oh God, Jason, tell me she's all right."

"She's perfectly fine. You'll see her soon."

Jason got the lock open. He gently opened the shackles on her wrists and ankles and threw them on the cage floor. Slowly, Nan straightened her legs and pulled her arms back around. Relief spread across her face. "Thank you, Jason, I didn't think I'd ever—" Nan pulled him into her arms and buried her face in his shoulder. Her tears turned to sobs, her body shook uncontrollably. Eventually, she looked up and kissed Jason on the mouth. Slowly, she pulled away and tried to stand. Off balance at first, she managed to stand upright. "Oh my God, turn around," she said.

"What do you mean, turn around?" Jason replied, not understanding.

"Just turn around. I've got to pee, Oh, my god, I've got to pee!"

Jason turned around and heard the sound of urine hitting the side of a metal bucket. He checked in with The Lilly.

"Go for XO."

"What's the status on the rest of the Craing ship—they obviously know we're here?"

"Captain, they've cordoned off this deck

from the rest of the ship. Our sensors indicate there are still another hundred Craing onboard that we'll need to contend with. Also, Admiral Crawford came through with additional troops, but the Craing are shooting at anything that moves out there. So we're on our own till we take out their weapons." Just then Orion hailed Jason.

"Go ahead, Gunny."

"Weapons are back up, Cap."

"Excellent! XO tells me that Admiral Cramer delivered on her promise and is standing by with a company of SEALs. So we need to do something about the Craing's onboard weapons. Is there any way The Lilly can target them from inside the hold?"

"From inside this ship? Are you serious?"

"Of course I'm serious. Yes or no?" Jason barked.

"I guess... yes, that shouldn't be a problem. Give me a few minutes to figure it out, though."

When Jason turned around, Nan was buttoning her pants. "You OK to walk?" he asked, putting an arm around Nan's waist and carefully helping her take a few steps.

"I think I can walk, I'm alright."

In front of her cage on the catwalk was a procession of other released prisoners. Jason's team was already ushering them to the lifts. Five at a time were being moved below to the bottom deck. In the distance, Jason heard weapons begin firing, then a hail from Gunny.

"What do you have, Gunny?" Jason asked

her, into his NanoCom.

"I'm working with Ricket on the best way to target the Craing weapons. I'll need a few more minutes on that."

"Good work, Gunny."

Jason and Nan reached the lift and shuffled on with three other women captives. As the lift made its way downward, they looked up at him, each with tears in their eyes. An elderly woman mouthed the words "thank you," reached up and gently touched Jason's face. When the lift came to a stop, Jason pulled open the lift gate and helped everyone out, moving them past the Craing meal hall, and into the far corridor. Jason watched as Nan's eyes locked onto the fiery caldron grills and then looked up, into his eyes. She knew exactly what they were, what they were used for. Jason's team had assembled their Craing prisoners outside the large chamber, but everyone was moving into the corridor. Too high off the ground to escape, they sat along bulkheads in groups and were provided water.

"I want to get you onto The Lilly, so you can see Mollie and get cleaned up. How's that sound?" Jason asked, as the two of them continued down the corridor.

"That's fine. I don't know what The Lilly is, but just get me out of here."

Chapter 13

When Nan entered the captain's suite, Mollie screamed and ran into her mother's open arms, almost bowling her over.

"Mom, I missed you so much."

"I missed you too, sweetie," Nan said, stroking Mollie's hair.

"I wanted to be a big girl, for Dad and everyone, but it was really hard."

"I'm so proud of you, Mollie. You are a big girl."

As they hugged in the captain's ready room, Jason rushed back to his bedroom to collect some of his things. He'd put Nan there so she could be closer to Mollie, and he'd bunk in one of the officer's open quarters. Long term, he wasn't sure if Nan would want to stay onboard or not, but for the time being, this was the safest place for both her and Mollie. Jason arrived back in the ready room with arms loaded up with his officer's jumpsuits, his old backpack, and assorted odds and ends.

"Jason, I'm not kicking you out of your room…" Nan said, with a furrowed brow.

"I'll be right next door. This way you're with Mollie. Hey, I'm in and out—crazy hours."

Earlier, on their way into the ship, Jason had given Nan an overview of The Lilly, and what had transpired over the past few days. When he mentioned the part about landing the ship in the Pentagon courtyard, Nan stopped him with, "You did what? You landed this spaceship at the Pentagon? Who'd do that sort of thing?" she spat. After some explaining, she almost understood his reasoning, but not completely; especially the fact that Mollie had been onboard during the whole escapade. Jason told her his father was still alive and leading the United Planetary Alliance, and about the impending attack by the quickly-approaching Craing fleet.

Mollie was still talking a mile a minute, and Nan looked exhausted.

"Mollie, let's give your mother some time to get cleaned up and rest," Jason said, pulling his ex-wife to her feet and leading her to the back bedroom. "Washroom's in there. The bed's surprisingly comfortable. I'd like to have you checked out in Medical when you're up to it as well. If you need to talk—you know… about your whole ordeal—"

"Thank you, Jason." She pulled Jason closer, so Mollie couldn't hear. "I was unconscious during some of it. When I woke, it was so awful. I heard their screams. Jason, they cut these people up—alive. I knew I'd be next. I kept waiting for that cart to pull up in front of my cage." Nan headed for the washroom, turned and looked back at him before closing the door.

Jason turned and headed for the door. "Can you watch over her, kiddo?" Jason asked, looking over at Mollie.

"I'll take good care of her, Dad."

* * *

Jason made it back to the bridge just as Orion and Ricket had begun targeting the Craing weaponry systems. An elaborate virtual representation of the Craing ship, with targeting vectors crisscrossing in multiple directions, was displayed with bright yellow lines.

"What's the status on taking out their weapons, Gunny?"

"Just making sure we don't kill ourselves in the process—or take out crucial Craing systems. We're going under the assumption you'll still want this ship to be operational once we've taken her."

Ricket looked up from the console and said, "The biggest problem is keeping the Craing bridge intact, as well as these two primary drive systems, here and here," he said, pointing up to their locations on the wrap-around display. Jason had a hard time concentrating on what the mechanical man was saying, having just encountered the Craing—of which Ricket was clearly the same species.

"But we think we have it. Short micro-bursts using our four plasma cannons, which will give us a wider selection of shooting angles," Ricket said, already back at work at his console.

"How about the Craing crewmembers being held in our makeshift brig, and the released captives still out in the corridor?" Jason asked, concerned.

"As of right now, the targeting vectors don't put anyone in a direct line of fire," Orion said, "that is, unless someone moves."

"Go ahead, Gunny, fire when ready," Jason commanded, taking a seat in the command chair. Displayed in red, the four plasma cannons snapped into position on The Lilly's outer hull. The gimbal-mounted cannons immediately started to rotate, track and then lock onto their pre-programmed targets. The cannons started to fire in unison; bright red vectors overlapped the yellow ones indicating the new shooting solutions. Within thirty seconds the firing stopped.

"Weapons destroyed, Captain," Orion said, a confident smile on her face.

"Nice work, Gunny, you've redeemed yourself from blowing up that mountain yesterday." This brought chuckles from the other crewmembers. Jason looked up at the virtual display, still hovering above their heads. "Gunny, other than the ones we've taken prisoner—can you display the positions of the Craing—those on other decks?" Jason asked, the seed of an idea forming.

"Here you go. Craing are represented by the orange symbols now displayed throughout the ship on decks two through ten."

"Is there a way to target them without blasting through the outer hull?" Jason asked, looking from Orion, then to Ricket, and then over to his XO. Both Perkins and Orion shrugged, not sure. But Ricket's expression seemed to convey there was a possibility.

"Not everyone on those decks could safely be targeted. Not without destroying engineering and bridge sub-systems. But certainly here, here and here would be no problem." Jason looked on as Ricket drew virtual circles around various areas on the ship diagram. "That's approximately ninety-three percent of the Craing crew."

As tempting as it would be to assassinate all the Craing crewmembers in one fell swoop, Jason didn't feel comfortable in doing so. At least not without giving them the option to surrender first. "Ricket, can I address the Craing crewmembers throughout the ship?"

"Yes, it would need to be translated to Terplin, their native language—but Lilly will do that for you." Jason watched Ricket closely, wondering how much the possible killing of hundreds of his own kind was affecting him.

"Lilly, please translate the following and have it broadcast ship wide."

"Yes, sir, whenever you are ready," she said, in her usual no-nonsense voice.

"Crewmembers of the Craing Vessel. This is Captain Jason Reynolds of the United Planetary Alliance vessel, The Lilly. You must immediately lay down your weapons and surrender. We have freed your captives, taken over one hundred Craing crewmembers into custody, and have destroyed your vessel's main weaponry. Every one of you is currently being tracked and will be killed unless you relinquish any weapons you have and surrender. You have one minute to comply." Jason nodded for Orion to cut the connection. All eyes were on the display. There was no movement at first, but then, slowly—the orange dots started to move.

"Captain, we have Craing crewmembers, from multiple decks, heading down to Deck 1," Perkins announced.

"Armed?"

"No, sir. Looks like they're surrendering."

This all seems too easy, but a hail from Billy interrupted his thoughts. "Go ahead, Billy."

"What are we supposed to do with all these guys? Looks like hundreds of them—they have their hands up—docile as little lambs."

"Round them up, Billy, secure their hands. Find out who their captain is and who their other officers are. Ask Lilly to help translate for you. The rest of them I want confined somewhere outside of the vessel. Let them stand in the sun for a while."

"Ricket, Orion, you're with me. XO, you have the bridge and once we're off The Lilly, shift her out of here. Just in case they've booby-trapped this bucket, I want her to be at a safe distance."

* * *

On the way off the ship, Jason needed to find a new helmet. He'd left his in Nan's cage, and there was no way he was going back up there. Orion, and even Ricket, had quickly dressed in hardened combat suits and carried pulse rifles. On the other side of the hold, Billy and his Bear team were waiting, their guns pointed at six Craing crewmembers. Several moments after Jason, Orion and Ricket joined Billy, The Lilly disappeared. Startled, the six Craing officers jumped and looked nervously between one another. Seeing Ricket, they became noticeably more uncomfortable. Jason hadn't quite figured out the various Craing expressions, but he was pretty sure what he was seeing was hatred.

"Who do we have here, Billy?" Jason asked, eying the six Craing.

"Their equivalency to captain, XO, pilot, chief of engineering, and two others. I'm not sure what the hell they do."

Jason nodded and quietly watched the Craing for several more moments before speaking again. "Will they understand what I'm saying?"

Billy nodded. "They seem to understand everything we're saying just fine. I think they've been interacting with humans for quite some time. This one here, the one with the gold medallion, is their captain." Jason had been studying the various medallions around each of the Craing's necks: one bronze, one copper, another silver or platinum, and the captain's gold one. Jason walked over to the Craing captain.

He stared at him for several more seconds until he started to fidget and looked away nervously. Jason reached down and pulled the golden chain from around the Craing captain's head. Jason held the chain and looked at the medallion for several moments before placing the chain around his own head and positioning the medallion in the middle of his chest.

"Make no mistake, Craing. This vessel has one captain and one captain only—and that's me." Jason looked over to Orion and Ricket and nodded. Unceremoniously, the medallions from the other officers were removed and placed around Orion's and Ricket's necks. "Ricket, these Craing crewmembers are going to take us on a little tour. By the time we're through, you're going to know everything you need to know in order to fly this vessel into orbit and beyond."

"Yes, sir. Although I probably do not need the tour to be able to do that," Ricket said, now returning a blank stare back at the Craing crewmembers.

"Humor me. Let's start with the bridge," Jason replied, as they headed off toward the forward section of the Craing vessel. Jason was hailed by Lieutenant Commander Perkins. "Go for Captain."

"Captain, I have Admiral Crawford—hold."

"Captain Reynolds. This is Admiral Crawford. Is this a good time to get a status report?"

"Yes, in fact it is, Admiral. The Craing ship

is ours. The Craing crew has been taken into custody—unfortunately, we still need to figure out what to do with them. Right now, I'm aboard their ship and we'll be taking command of it shortly."

"What exactly are your intensions with that ship, Captain? Needless to say, we'd like to get our hands on her—their technology just may save this planet," she said, sounding somewhat desperate.

"Here's my problem, Admiral. And it's the same one my father faced. I have no idea who I can trust. It's evident the Craing have infiltrated into high levels of the government and military. The Army is compromised. Just this morning I took two bullets from a team of Army Rangers, both of whom were Craing-human hybrids. I've been thinking about this dilemma and I'm afraid if this is going to work, a new branch of service needs to be formed from scratch. It will be an outpost of the United Planetary Alliance. No one gets in without being fully vetted and tested. Anyone who joins up will be on extended loan from their corresponding service branch, but will not report to the U.S. military, our government, or any other chain of command." Jason knew what he was proposing was a lot to chew on; in fact, much of it had only gelled now that he was speaking with the admiral.

"Captain, that is simply preposterous! What makes you think—"

Jason cut her off. "And one more thing, Admiral. I trust you. And I'd like you to lead this outpost. Think about it and please talk to Secretary of Defense Walker. He's another one I trust. We're in serious need of military support—men, women, and logistical support. As of right now, we have two well-equipped interstellar vessels. There are three more in Earth's orbit that I'll need to bring under my control, if we are going to stand up to the approaching Craing fleet."

"I am, for no better word, speechless, Captain. I'll contact Secretary Walker and get back to you." Jason had thrown a lot on her plate and he only hoped he hadn't scared her off. One thing was for sure, he would need help from those who had already proven their honesty, grit, and courage.

The Craing bridge wasn't much different from the rest of the ship—dirty and a strange combination of highly-advanced technology and almost 19th century mechanical machinery. Ricket had taken the lead and was moving about the bridge, accessing their systems via touchscreen keyboards, not unlike what 21st century Earth used. As Jason stood back and watched Ricket do his magic, he watched the Craing officers and their resigned, almost calm demeanors. "You, the one who was captain of this ship. Why no resistance? Why have you made it so easy for us to take this vessel?"

The Craing officer looked up at Jason and didn't respond at first. Eventually, he straightened up and held Jason's stare. "In four hundred years no one has ever breeched and boarded a Craing vessel. It was immediately evident that your technology was far superior to ours. We have disgraced our heritage—we have allowed our Overlords, the eaters of the conquest, to be taken prisoner. Death will be our only reward now. All we ask is that you make it swift and as painless as possible."

"That might not be possible. You see, one of those prisoners you had locked up in those cages, way up there on the ninth deck, well, she's very special to me. And the thought that you would have carved her up to be eaten by your—what did you call them? Your Overlords? Well, I think I need to ensure you'll stay alive for a very long time."

"It is a great honor to be presented to the eaters of the conquest. I do not understand your anger."

Jason hadn't intended to shoot the little captain. But he really had no choice. Like the pirates on the Christina, sometimes the universe is just better off without the riffraff. Jason raised his pulse rifle, squeezed the trigger, and watched the Craing's body catapult across the bridge. Fortunately, for the Craing officer, the rifle was set to stun.

"Orion, have these other Craing clean-up this mess. Ricket, continue with the ship-wide tour and ensure that we can get her into orbit as soon as possible. Be prepared to teach the rest of us how to fly this thing."

Ricket looked over at the unconscious Craing captain and then back to Jason. "What about damage to this vessel? We can't very well go into orbit like this." Ricket then went back to what he was doing. Jason looked over at the Craing crewmembers and raised his eyebrows. They returned the gesture and nodded their heads in unison.

"We'll fix, we have many parts and can patch the hull. We fix everything," the Craing officer said. Jason thought he might be the same Craing who'd worn the silver medallion.

"Good. Let's get to it then. And we'll need to have the weapons systems repaired as well." Jason looked over at Orion and said, "Have Billy send-up several SEALs to watch over them. No Craing goes unescorted. But with their help maybe we can get this tin can up and running faster than if we're left to do it ourselves." Jason left the bridge without saying another word.

Chapter 14

Jason had Ricket deploy the vessel's gangway. He returned to the lower deck of the Craing ship and stood there, looking out at the rustic Chihuahuan. The Craing Overloads were now assembled by the right front landing strut. The other Craing crewmembers were held farther back where there was some semblance of shade. SEAL sentries kept weapons pointed in their direction. Jason heard them before he saw them. The thump thump thump of four large Chinook helicopters. There was an incoming hail from his XO.

"Go for Captain."

"We have our Top Gun pilots arriving now, as well as another one hundred fresh SEALs. Looks like Admiral Crawford really came through for us. And it could be in just the nick of time. Those three Craing Cruisers that left have now reentered Earth's orbit—I imagine they're wondering what happened to their other ship."

"Keep your eye on those ships and let me know if there are any developments. Where'd you set down?" Jason asked, looking off toward the horizon.

"Don't worry, it's safe to phase-shift back now." Within several moments, The Lilly appeared twenty meters off the bow of the Craing ship. Startled, Jason thought to himself that Perkins was having way too much fun phase-shifting all over the place.

As Jason descended the Craing ship's ramp, The Lilly's forward and aft gangways descended. He saw his officers, including Lieutenant Perkins, Chief Engineer Horris, and Dira. Ricket and Orion were still on the Craing ship—they had a lot of clean-up work to do. Jason met up with his crew and they all turned to watch men and equipment pouring out of the Chinooks. Billy and his teams acted as the welcoming committee and it became obvious that many had served together previously. He never tired of watching the open jaws and double takes of career-hardened military men when they first set eyes on The Lilly, not to mention the larger Craing ship. Dira eyed Jason and smiled. "I checked on your wife—she's doing fine."

"She's my ex-wife, but thank you just the same." Jason wondered why he felt the need to clarify his marital status to Dira, and realized this situation could get complicated. The ten Top Gun pilots were approaching. He'd thought SEALs had a certain over-confidence, but these Navy pilots brought a whole new meaning to the word swagger. Dressed in their standard drab green flight suits and carrying their helmets under their arms, the eight men and two women came to attention in front of Jason and his crew and saluted.

"Welcome. I'm Captain Reynolds," he said, returning their salutes. "Who's the leader of this group?" He closely watched their faces. They were all lieutenants, according to the rank on their flight suits. Without hesitation, the shortest of the men stepped forward and saluted again. A flicker of irritation was apparent on the other pilots' faces.

"That would be me, sir. Lieutenant Craig Wilson. Not only completed the U.S. Navy Strike Fighter Tactics Instructor program, but achieved Top Gun status, above and beyond the others in my group."

"So what makes you their leader, Lieutenant Wilson?" Jason asked, amused.

"Because I stepped up, sir. I always step up."

"How do you feel about flying in space in a craft we know very little about and without an instructor?" For the first time Jason noticed a hesitancy in the pilot's confidence. Jason smiled and addressed all the pilots. "We do have a certain amount of training, something called HyperLearning. You'll go to sleep in a coffin-like box and wake up knowing things you don't recall learning. Dira here is our Medical doctor and will help you get situated and start your HyperLearning sessions over the next few hours. Any questions? Good, dismissed."

Dira stepped forward and shook each of their hands, and they proceeded off as a group toward the ship. One by one, the Chinooks lifted off and headed toward the horizon. Chief Engineer Horris stood with his hands in his pockets, which only accentuated his bulging belly. "You like screwing with them," he said, more of a statement than a question.

Jason nodded and smiled, then pointed to the insect-like Craing vessel, like a wide green grasshopper ready to hop away. "What do you know about Craing propulsion drive systems?"

"They're very similar to most of the Alliance Drive systems. So I guess quite a bit. Why?" Chief Horris asked, looking at Jason with a slight scowl.

"Because that big green tin can over there has recently joined our fleet. Now you're engineering chief for her as well as The Lilly. Obviously you can't be in two places at once. You'll need someone you can count on to watch over the Craing ship's engineering. Let me know before we lift off who that will be."

Chief Horris frowned, nodded, and shuffled back toward The Lilly. Jason was about to return to the ship himself when another helicopter made an approach and landed, this time a smaller Apache. He knew who it was right away. Wearing navy blue and grey camos, Admiral Crawford headed straight for him. With short red hair and fair skin, he guessed she was approaching fifty, but she was an attractive woman in her own right.

"Captain Reynolds, I presume?" she asked, all business.

"Yes, Admiral," Jason said, saluting. "An unexpected visit. To what do I owe the pleasure?"

"Drop the dumb-ass act, Captain. You

know perfectly well why I'm here." He saw that the admiral had kept a smile on her face, which was a good sign. "I've come to see things for myself. With three more Craing vessels buzzing around in orbit, your ship, ships—are more than just strategic, they're essential."

"No offense, ma'am, but I'll need to confirm you're human before I can let you onboard either ship."

The admiral, somewhat nonplussed, pushed out her ample chest while looking down, and then back up again at Jason, with a slight smile on her face. "Son, you're not going to find anyone more human than me, but do what you have to do."

Jason hailed Ricket and waited for him to come back on NanoComs.

"Go for Ricket."

"I need your assistance outside the Craing vessel."

"I'm very busy, Captain. I'll be done here—"

Jason cut him off, frustrated. "Just get down here; you can return to what you're doing in a few minutes."

"Aye, sir," Ricket replied.

Jason proceeded to give the admiral an outside tour of both ships, similar to what McBride had done for him several days ago when he'd first been introduced to The Lilly and her crew. Admiral Crawford listened intently and asked intelligent questions. He knew, having been in her same position, that she must be feeling overwhelmed. Jason intentionally did not warn the admiral about Ricket—being something more than alien, but also machine. She showed no reaction whatsoever when Ricket approached. Although she did look over to Jason with a quick glance—letting him know she knew his game.

"Admiral Crawford, I'd like to introduce you to Ricket, our Science Officer."

"Good afternoon, Admiral Crawford, nice to meet you," Ricket said, shaking her outstretched hand. Ricket immediately looked up at Jason and nodded his head, seemingly bored with this same routine. "She's as human as you are, Captain. You do know there's now an automated way to do this—yes?"

"Thank you, but I'm fine doing things this way, at least for now, Ricket."

The small mechanical alien shrugged. "Yes, sir. If there's nothing else, I'd like to return to the Craing vessel to complete my tasks."

"Thank you, Ricket." Jason then turned back to the admiral. "Before you board, Admiral, I need to know if you're coming onboard as a U.S. Navy officer, or as a member of the United Planetary Alliance? As I mentioned, we need to create an outpost here on Earth, one that is separate from the influences of government and military persuasions."

"And these two ships will come under my authority in that position?"

"No. The Craing ship will, and perhaps others shortly. But The Lilly is, and will remain, an independent asset."

The admiral nodded, her expression indicating she wasn't completely satisfied by Jason's answer. "That little greet and meet with Ricket—he vetted me, didn't he?"

Jason nodded. "Yes, as he did the Joint Chiefs of Staff, which is why General Peter Bickerdike of the U.S. Air Force is now held in a brig somewhere in Washington."

"Who would I report to? You?" she asked with a sardonic smile.

"Yes, ma'am. Although we're still figuring some things out, and that may change once Admiral Reynolds has a chance to weigh in on it. We'll get in contact with him shortly, I hope." The last thing in the world Jason wanted to do was to take on added responsibility. Commanding a single spaceship was one thing, but a fleet of alien vessels? Not to mention an outpost. He would gladly hand over the task to Admiral Crawford, but he didn't trust her yet, or where her true loyalties lay.

"We'll need a base for this outpost, one outside the reach of all political, as well as geographical, influences."

Jason was encouraged by her train of thought. "I agree; any thoughts on the matter? Any suggestions?"

The admiral smiled and slowly looked around, taking in the vast desert landscape.

"What do you think of right here, on the Texas-Mexico border? Two hundred square miles of desolate, undisturbed Chihuahuan desert. A province unto itself. Not American, not Mexican." It was clear by Admiral Crawford's expression, she'd not only given the prospect consideration, she'd already made it happen.

"What will we name this province?" Jason asked, fairly certain she had an answer for that as well.

"Earth Outpost for the United Planetary Alliance—the EOUPA. Isn't that what you wanted?" she asked, exasperated. When Jason and the Admiral turned and headed toward The Lilly, he noticed all the Craing prisoners were gone.

Chapter 15

After reading his father's accounts of the Alliance's devastating defeat by the Craing, Jason almost felt guilty he'd captured one of their vessels so easily. Admiral Crawford, sitting next to him in his ready room, was still reading the same report. If the FDL incoming communications indicators were correct, both admirals would be talking to each other within the next few minutes. Jason realized the irony of it all; the one thing his father had kept secret and out of the war with the Craing, was the one thing that could have defeated them: The Lilly. You won't destroy Craing ships by blasting away at their shields. You phase-shift right into the belly of their holds and infiltrate from inside. Ridiculously simple—profoundly effective.

Lieutenant Commander Perkins entered the room, followed by Ricket, Billy, Lieutenant Craig Wilson, the new Top Gun hot-shot, and Orion. Each had previously met Admiral Crawford and they now formed into a group to strategize about the three Craing vessels orbiting above Earth.

A question had been tumbling around in Jason's head for the last few hours. "Ricket, my first question is about the phase-shift technology on The Lilly. Can it be duplicated? Do we understand it enough to transfer that technology to something else, say a fighter? When that Craing fleet arrives with their 500 ships, some of them won't have anywhere near the needed inner space for us to phase-shift into their hulls. But fighters…"

Ricket thought for a moment before answering. "Yes, and you've already seen three examples of that technology." He pulled off his baseball cap and scratched the top of his head. The rest of the crew were long used to his strange looks, but the admiral was more than a little fascinated by his near-transparent skin, and the continual mechanical goings on all over his head.

Jason let that sit for a while and smiled. "The shed. Those metallic-glowing-cylindrical things in old Gus' tool shed. What the hell were you doing with them?"

Orion spoke up first, giving the mechanical man a sideways glance. "He was keeping them a secret, Captain. Ricket's always keeping something a secret," she scoffed, with more than a little accusation behind her words.

Before Jason could chime in, he noticed Billy had a strange look on his face, like a painted-on smile. Then he noticed some movement under the table. Billy and Orion were playing footsies, kicking at each other like damn children.

"It's because there's still a mole onboard, right?" Perkins asked, beating Jason to the punch. Ricket nodded, but said nothing.

"That's one more thing that needs to be

dealt with," Jason said, glancing over to the admiral before continuing. "So, did you use that phase synthesizer on sub-Deck 4B to create the new phase-shift devices? What would it take to make enough for each of the fighters and for the two shuttles to be outfitted?" Jason asked, and then scowled at Billy to knock it off.

"Anything the phase synthesizer constructs or duplicates happens instantaneously. The truth is, items are made even before we request them," Ricket replied in a matter-of-fact tone. His statement pulled Admiral Crawford away from reading the report.

"What the hell are you talking about?" she questioned, her brow furrowed toward Ricket.

For some reason, Jason found her annoyance funny and had to hold back a chuckle.

"Many aspects of the ship deal with piggybacking onto the multiverse. And no, none of us fully understand these principles, but the original designers of The Lilly certainly did. We're making incremental progress, at least in regards to utilizing those capabilities." Ricket paused, collected his thoughts, and then continued. "To answer your question, I should be able to make as many as needed. But that's not the problem. The problem lies with integrating the units into current systems and providing them with enough power. Even with that said, these fighters will temporarily be without thruster and weapons prior to making a phase-shift, and they'll need to get in close, within a mile of the Craing ships."

"It's not like the Craing are going to let our fighters just mosey up and then wait while our new gizmo takes effect. And, by the way, does anyone know where all our Craing prisoners are?"

Billy sat up and nodded his head. "Yes, sir. Temporarily, we've put them into their own cages on the Craing ship. It seemed appropriate."

"I like it," Jason said, smiling. Just then he, and it looked like everyone else at the table, was being hailed.

"Go for Captain."

"Contacts. The three Craing cruisers have entered Earth orbit. They've locked onto both The Lilly and their own ship," said McBride

Jason looked over to Ricket and Orion.

"Can we get the Craing vessel's shields up?"

Ricket brought up a virtual console. "Yes, they're up now. We'll need to stop working on any hull patches as long as the shields are active."

When Jason looked over to the admiral, she shrugged and said, "Oh no, I'm not staying behind. You couldn't pry me off this ship with a crow bar."

* * *

The Lilly lifted off within three minutes. Jason had a basic plan of how he would engage the Craing vessels, but he'd still have to play some of it by ear. Billy was ready with three separate 30-man SEAL teams, allocated to Bear, Lion, and Zebra, each wearing hardened combat suits and carrying plasma pulse rifles.

Ricket was busy with a new project. One Jason wished he'd thought of before they'd blasted the hell out of the other Craing ship's weapon systems.

"How we doing with that, Ricket?" Jason asked the mechanical man, now hunched over and working at his Science Officer's station.

"I have two possibilities: if one doesn't work, the other one might."

Jason let out a long breath. Both the admiral and his XO sat next to Jason, who was seated in the command chair. They continued to stare at Ricket.

McBride at the helm said, "We're in orbit, sir. Three contacts—it's the Craing vessels and they are moving to intersect."

"We're in weapon's range, Captain," Orion said.

"In range for phase-shift in three minutes, based on our current trajectory and speed," came from the helmsman.

"How much time will we need between jumps, Ricket?" Jason asked.

"Depends on how close we can get to their ships. The closer the better. If it's within one-mile, regeneration time is less than eight minutes."

"Lilly, segment the wrap-around display for

each of the external quadrant views as well as helmet cams for Bear, Lion and Zebra team leaders," Jason ordered.

The display changed. On the forward segment, a Craing ship was quickly moving into view. On other display segments, jerky helmet cams showed SEAL teams waiting at the forward and rear air locks.

"They're powering weapons, Captain. Firing their plasma cannons. Our shields are holding," Orion reported. The admiral was on her feet, pacing. Jason felt her eyes on the back of his neck. He knew she was getting impatient. She wanted him to fire back.

"Captain, are you going to just watch them? Are we mere spectators here, or will you get your ass in the game?" Quiet came over the bridge, and all heads turned to see Jason's response.

"Two things, Admiral," Jason said, not taking his eyes off the display. "One, I don't report to you. Please remember you're here as a guest. Two, The Lilly's guns are for the most part untested. They could irreparably damage that Craing vessel. So let me ask you—do you want an operational vessel to add to your fleet or one that is shot to hell and useless?" Jason knew this confrontation was coming. Better to get it over with now rather than later.

The admiral was flustered and obviously not used to being confronted this way. "Well, do something!" she shot back, sitting down in a huff.

The Lilly had not slowed and continued to barrel down on the Craing cruiser. "They must think we're crazy," McBride said. "Ramming speed…" he added, in an exaggerated deep voice.

"Prepare to phase-shift to the vessel's hold. Same as before, Ensign."

"We're at one mile, Captain," McBride reported.

Jason looked around the bridge, then gave the command. "Go ahead and shift."

* * *

Bear Team, led by Billy, made its way down both gangways. Looking up at the segmented display, the Craing ship's hold looked nearly identical to the captured vessel. Dark and lurid. The bridge watched through multiple helmet cam videos. It was apparent that this hold was not empty; in fact, it was nearly full.

"Go for Captain. What have you got, Billy?" Jason asked in response to the hail.

"They look like tubes or some kind of pods. Yeah, they look like pods," Billy responded.

"Pods with Craings inside?" Jason asked, fairly sure he already knew the answer. Billy positioned his helmet directly over one of the pods. An elderly man's face, apparently unconscious, was visible through a rectangular window. A row of small interior lights partially illuminated his sallow skin and exaggerated the dark creases on his face.

Jason watched the display change as Billy stepped back and provided a wider view of the hold. Easily, several hundred pods had been destroyed. Lives ended. Perhaps human prisoners awaiting a fate worse than death. It was apparent to everyone on the bridge that the Craing had anticipated their move. Perhaps they had been in contact with the first vessel and stacked the pods here as some kind of deterrent to a phase-shift.

"Hold your position, Billy. I'm joining team Bear," Jason said, rushing toward the bridge exit and saying over his shoulder, "XO, you have the con. And Ricket, your priority is back on the miniature phase-shift devices."

* * *

Jason quickly suited in a combat suit. Equipped with a pulse rifle, he hurried down the gangway and met Billy and the rest of team Bear. Like last time, they broke into five squads, with one staying behind to guard The Lilly's perimeter.

"Looks like we have Craing combatants both forward and aft headed our way. Wait—not Craing. I don't know what the hell they are," Billy said, while he stopped to evaluate his own HUD readings.

Ricket broke into their comms. "I've never seen these readings; they're not human-Craing hybrids, nothing like those who are on earth,

Captain."

Jason's thoughts flashed back to Air Force General Bickerdike and his bizarre two beating hearts. Jason hailed Perkins.

"Go for XO, Cap," Perkins responded over their comms.

"Get The Lilly off this tin can. Shift away now!" Jason commanded, fearing a trap. Within moments, The Lilly shifted away without a sound.

The alien beings pouring into the hold were unlike anything Jason had expected to see. Not short and grey like the Craing, and not humanlike as General Bickerdike. These hybrids were easily seven feet tall, one thousand pounds of muscle—somewhat humanoid, but with a head not dissimilar to that of a rhinoceros, with protruding center horns and all. They wore thick leather-like battle gear. Pulse weapons were strapped to one wrist, and they carried some kind of battle hammer in the other. These hammers easily weighed hundreds of pounds.

As three rhino-warriors, one-by-one, charged into the hold, Jason and Billy simultaneously dropped to one knee and fired their phased plasma rifles. Jason went for a headshot on the left rhino-warrior, while Billy went for a center mass chest shot on the other.

They kept coming: one with a bloody socket where his eye had been, and the other with a two-inch blast hole in the middle of his chest. These beasts lived for battle. The short four-foot high Craing were fine conducting wars from the protection of their warships, but they weren't soldiers. This kind of in-your-face confrontation required seasoned, skilled fighters—warriors. Jason realized now why the three Craing ships had left orbit. They needed to bring in reinforcements.

Billy adjusted his aim and continued to shoot. Several of the rhino-warriors went down with a floor jarring crash. The Craing had set up this surprising ambush; a trap had been laid. More and more rhino-warriors were charging into the hold from four separate corridors. According to his HUD, there were as many as seventy-five of these beasts aboard, compared to Jason's task force of less than thirty men. Most of them, fortunately, were taking cover behind stacks of the remaining pods and crates. The beasts attacked with wild abandon—almost frenzied, but without the U.S. military's tactical precision that trained soldiers would exhibit in battle. These guys were all about brute force and brawn.

Up ahead, a rhino-beast had made it through the line and was charging one of the SEALs. He too dropped to one knee and fired repeatedly. The beast kept coming. The SEAL took the brunt of the rhino-beast's onslaught in his mid-section. His heavy battle armor was unable to keep the razor-sharp horn from penetrating through the front, and then out the back of his combat suit. The beast, using his hammer to dislodge the now dead SEAL from his horn, looked around, and charged directly toward Jason.

He brought up his weapon, positioned his laser sights right above the creature's horn, and fired. A burst of blue plasma shot into the beast's forehead. The rhino-warrior went down like a sack of potatoes.

Nearby, Jason saw Billy had lost his weapon and was dodging a rhino's horn. Like a matador, he danced this way and that, barely avoiding being skewered. He then took a glancing blow to the shoulder. Fortunately, it didn't penetrate his battle armor. Quickly, Jason aimed and fired at the beast from across the hold. Three bursts went into the back of his head. The rhino-warrior stopped and stood motionless, almost defying gravity, before there was the inevitable crash to the floor. Billy turned to see who'd saved his life. Seeing it was Jason, he casually saluted his friend, retrieved his weapon, and went right back into the fight. More rhino-warriors were moving into the hold—they were so large, so wide, they needed to enter one at a time. Ten SEALs now lay dead on the hold's floor.

A hammer struck another SEAL, removing the top portion of his head. Blood and tissue sprayed in every direction. They were taking too many casualties. Then, without warning, something smashed down on the top of his own head—something from behind. He went sprawling to the floor. Jason's visor had cracked, obscuring his view. His head felt like someone had dropped a dump truck on it. Then he saw the hammer that was again on its way back down. He had just enough time to roll to his left. The hammer struck an inch from his helmet. The sound of the metal weapon hitting the hold's metal sub-flooring rang out like a gong. The rhino-warrior brought his weapon up for a final blow. Jason kicked out, planting the hardened toe of his boot right where he imagined the beast's family jewels would be. Obviously in excruciating pain, according to the look on his face, the rhino-beast took it like a man and held steadfast. Then two blasts from a nearby SEAL made the creature's head explode, covering Jason in blood, bone, and grey flesh. Jason wiped the mess off his damaged visor.

Something was nagging at him in the back of his mind, something he remembered learning in grade school about rhinos in Africa... Then he had it.

Jason set his comms for the general band. "Be ready to go to night vision, we're going dark in here. Shoot the lights, all of them!" Jason commanded. In between taking shots at the beasts, the SEALs pointed their weapons up towards the overhead lights. One by one, they exploded and the hold went totally black. Their night vision optics switched on automatically. The rhinos were blind as bats and stumbling around. Several had fallen and were crawling around on all fours. Watching them, it was almost pathetic. Jason felt uncomfortable killing them this easily. Being taken as prisoners would not be an option for these huge warrior-beasts;

they'd rather fight to the death.

"Do it quickly. Shooting them right above the horn does the trick," Jason said, without any malice in his voice. Within minutes the hold was clear. According to his HUD, all other alien life forms on the vessel were Craing. Jason hailed The Lilly and had her phase-shift back to the hold.

Jason, along with the rest of Bear team, headed directly toward the Craing bridge. He commanded another SEAL team to clear the rest of the vessel, round up any remaining Craing, and lock them up in their own cages. As evident from comms reports, the Craing on this ship were somewhat prepared to fight back, yet no match for the battle-hardened SEAL teams. Where the rhino-beasts were true warriors and fought with honor, even passion, the Craing were fearful and cowardly. Any concern that the Craing would self-destruct their own vessels to keep them out of enemy hands was dismissed. It wasn't uncommon for the Craing, especially the Overlords and officers, to whimper and grovel when apprehended.

Once Jason entered the Craing bridge, he contacted Ricket.

"Go for Ricket," he replied.

"Remotely, can we navigate this vessel from The Lilly?"

"What did you have in mind, Captain?"

"I want to capture this ship, along with the other two, take them out of orbit and park them back in the Chihuahuan desert. Can you do that remotely?"

Ricket was quiet for a moment, then spoke up. "I'd need to set up three virtual helm stations, right here on The Lilly's bridge. To configure that, I'll have to access their bridge as well as their AI. I'll be right over."

As Jason and his team waited, he looked around the Craing bridge. Again, it was dirty and a strange mix of new and old technology. Billy had assembled the Craing bridge officers into a group and sat them down on the floor. They wore the same gold, silver, copper and bronze medallions. Jason took the gold medallion from the Craing leader and placed it around his own neck.

"What can you tell me about the approaching fleet?" Jason asked.

The group of Craing officers looked nervously from one to the other. Finally, the captain spoke. "Please do not harm us. This is a great honor for your people. Understand, the Craing cannot be defeated. Our numbers are too great. We are bringing order all across the universe. Your world will be added to the Craing Empire, subject to serve the emperor's regime. This planet has been seeded for many years now. It is all but done; the only thing left for your people is obedience."

Jason watched as the alien spoke. He didn't shoot the captain, although the thought crossed his mind. What he needed was information. Truth was, Jason didn't think it would take much effort to convince any of them to spill what they knew. It seemed the Craing hierarchy was about fear and subjugation, certainly not about empowering their lower-level leaders. But that would be for Admiral Crawford and her people to determine.

Ricket entered the bridge, a satchel hung from around his shoulder. He went directly to the helm console and started unpacking a myriad of things, including fiber link-type cables, two small cell phone-size devices, and a larger box that everything connected to, including the helm of the Craing ship. Ricket held two fingers up to his tiny ear and connected to the AI. "Lilly, we're ready for navigation and systems tests," Ricket said.

Although Jason couldn't hear what the AI said back to Ricket, from his expression, it obviously irritated him. An uncommon emotional response from Ricket. He really didn't like the Lilly AI—that was apparent. After a few inputs and settings changes, Ricket turned to Jason. "This vessel is now under the helm control of The Lilly. Not only its navigation, but all systems ship wide."

Billy's team added the Craing bridge crew to the other captured prisoners. A small contingent of Allied crewmembers would be left onboard, primarily as a security detail.

* * *

Within ten minutes of being back onboard, they had shifted back into Earth's orbit to hunt down the other two Craing vessels.

The XO said, "Contacts—the two Craing ships. They're together."

"Distance?"

"Five hundred miles out, sir. We've been scanned and they're approaching fast."

"Make the announcement for General Quarters, XO," Jason said, now seeing the two Craing vessels come into view on the display.

"We're taking fire, Captain. Sustained plasma blasts to our aft. Not sure how long shields will last with so much hitting us all at once."

"Well, it's about time this ship was put to the test."

Two Craing warships attacked in earnest, and came at them from two opposing flanks, throwing everything they had at The Lilly.

"Captain, we have plasma fire coming from both battle cruisers. Every gun is firing. Shields are holding at 98 percent," Orion reported.

"Stay on course, Helm; bring us right up close and personal," Jason commanded.

"Yes, sir," McBride acknowledged.

"Multiple new contacts, sir. Craing Drone Fighters."

The wrap-around display came alive with additional activity. Fifty insect-like fighters emerged from both Craing vessels and quickly moved to engage The Lilly from multiple angles.

"Captain, the fighters are firing plasma as well as small rail-gun ordnances. Shields are holding at 96 percent."

"Captain, the AI is requesting automatic tracking and firing dispersal to engage the fighters," the XO inquired.

Jason watched the display as over one hundred ships fired continuously at their hull.

"Gunny, how far out are we from intersecting with either of these warships?"

"Still five miles out, sir."

"XO, let's see what the AI does with those fighters. But watch that we don't engage the battle cruisers. We need them intact."

Jason felt the bridge subtly vibrate beneath his feet as the big plasma cannons, two forward and two aft, snapped into position. Tracking, the gimbal-mounted cannons spun until they acquired proper firing solutions. Almost simultaneously all cannons fired. The display erupted in a blaze of plasma fire. Within ten seconds the screen was still.

Orion, speechless for several moments, shook her head and then spoke. "All fighters destroyed, Captain."

"We're now within two miles of both cruisers," McBride reported.

* * *

Jason ordered The Lilly to shift into the first Craing vessel's hold and dropped off two SEAL teams. They waited several minutes and then shifted directly into the other nearby Craing vessel and dropped off two more teams.

Then they shifted back out to open space. From The Lilly's bridge, they watched the action unfold from multiple helmet cams on the segmented display. As Jason watched the battles play out, he couldn't help but admire the rhino-warrior's unwavering courage under fire, and their passion. First on one ship and then on the other, the lights went out. The other alteration Jason had made to his battle plan was to issue secondary weapons: thick, massive projectile handguns that fired multiple narcotic-laced projectiles. This time, he didn't want to kill the rhino-warriors.

By the end of the day, all three Craing vessels had been captured, without any additional losses on the side of the Alliance. It took a little trial and error navigating the three Craing ships out of Earth's orbit simultaneously, but once Ricket, McBride and Perkins spent enough time at their makeshift remote control stations, they ultimately were successful and able to shift the ships to the desert outpost.

Chapter 16

The Four Craing vessels were situated in a large circular configuration on the Chihuahuan desert floor. Right in the middle was The Lilly. The Army had been infiltrated far more than the other military branches. Through a blitz of disinformation, they were quickly separating themselves. Admiral Crawford hadn't wasted any time procuring her own military assets from the Navy, Air Force, and Marines, but not from the Army. In a matter of hours, a city of tents and portable administrative structures had popped up all around the periphery of the small fleet of alien ships. Still a mere drop in the bucket compared, in magnitude, to the approaching Craing armada.

Ricket had come up with dozens of hand-held vetting devices: simply point and click, and you'd know if you were in front of a Craing-Human hybrid. With close to six hundred new personnel to the land base, thirty-seven of the military had been hybrids and taken into custody. But tonight was about celebrating their recent victories in Earth's orbit.

Jason hadn't seen Mollie and Nan since the previous day and he was excited to reunite with them. In the midst of Jason fighting the Craing, Nan had opted to move herself and Mollie to another two-bedroom suite along the officer's corridor. As Jason stood under a hot shower, he let his mind wonder to Nan. How was she dealing in the aftermath of such a traumatic course of events? Where do they go from here? What about Dira? An interesting woman. Was she a woman? Certainly beautiful in her own regard. She had been working non-stop moving people into the HyperLearning modules. Even Admiral Crawford had opted to get the procedure over with sooner rather than later. Wearing a towel around his waist, Jason opened his closet where, to his surprise, was a new, all white dress uniform hanging in front of his standard captain's jumpsuits. In Mollie's handwriting was a note, Wear this one tonight, Dad!

Halfway down the gangway, Jason stopped and took in the scene. They'd gone all out. Strings of colored lights had been strung high up in-between The Lilly and each of the Craing ships. A band was playing center stage; various crew members from Navy, Marines and Air Force units had joined together. They missed a few cords here and there, but for the most part Jason was impressed.

Across the impromptu courtyard, Nan and Mollie were setting out large vats of food on long tables. Both had dressed up for the occasion—Mollie in a floral party dress and Nan wearing a cream-colored blouse and a form-fitting black skirt. The courtyard was bustling with crew and base personnel. The band erupted with their own rendition of Sweet Home Alabama, prompting hoots and cheers from the growing crowd. Mollie was up on one of the tables dancing, then singing into a large wooden spoon. Jason laughed out loud and shook his head. Shy she isn't, he thought. Then, to his surprise, Nan joined her up on the table, laughing and singing into another spoon, as if they'd rehearsed this bit for hours. A growing crowd of onlookers formed to watch the performance. Nan didn't notice Jason had joined the group—then their eyes met and held. She continued singing, but now her singing was directed in only one direction, towards Jason.

The song ended to enthusiastic applause. Mollie and Nan continued to ham it up, taking bows and curtsies, and then both jumped down off the table. Mollie caught sight of her father and waved. Nan moved in close, wrapped her arms around his neck, and held him tightly, more intimately than he'd ever remembered her doing, even before they were married. Finally, when they separated, Jason's expression must have said it all. Why? She reached up and took his face in her hands, much like he'd done to her in that Craing cage.

"While lying there on that slimy disgusting floor, hearing the desperate pleas of the others and their horrific screams as they were slowly killed, I was resigned to my fate. Knowing that my time too was coming, I handed my life over to whomever, God maybe… Jason, when I saw you there, crouched before me in that cage, that you'd kept the promise you yelled to me while I was being taken onto that ship… Oh my God,

Jason, you came for me. As impossible and inconceivable as that could possibly be, you came for me." Tears streamed down her cheeks. "Thank you."

"You're welcome, Nan." He replied, wiping his own eyes.

Billy and Orion had joined the group, towering over everyone. By the goo-goo eyes they had for each other, they'd definitely progressed past the playing footsie under the table stage.

The music stopped and a hush came over the crowd. A detail of ten marines entered the courtyard surrounding three people: Admiral Crawford, Secretary of State Walker, and the President of the United States, Howard Ross. The president was a stout man in his mid-fifties and wore glasses. He had a brusqueness about his manner. He'd been compared to Teddy Roosevelt, and now Jason could see why. Like the parting of the Red Sea, the crowd, which had opened wide to the dignitaries, now came together to encircle them. The desert had returned to quiet stillness.

"Thank you for letting me be a part of your celebration, Captain. I will not be here long, but I felt it important to personally extend my gratitude to you and your team," the president said, shaking Jason's hand. He slowly turned to look at the crowd, then back at Jason. "In a matter of days, you've accomplished a staggering amount of success. My advisors had briefed me on the approaching Craing fleet. It was a foregone conclusion that an invasion was imminent. A dire situation for the country and the world. What their occupation would mean, I wasn't really certain. Perhaps slavery, mass-genocide…? But now we have hope, Captain, and sometimes that's all that's needed. A little hope." The president turned and looked at the small fleet of alien ships encircling the camp, smiled, and shook his head.

"Thank you, Mr. President. No victory would have been possible without the crew of The Lilly and perhaps, most importantly, that of my father, Admiral Perry Reynolds, who's been fighting the Craing in other star systems, light years from ours, for over fifteen years."

Jason knew what the next question would be, and he was about to signal Ricket on his NanoCom when he spotted a Dodgers baseball cap already moving in his direction.

"Mr. President, I'd like to introduce you to several people. This is my daughter, Mollie, and my former wife, Nan. And this is Ricket, our Science Officer aboard The Lilly."

Smiling, President Ross shook Mollie's and Nan's hands. "I am very pleased to meet you both. I heard we nearly lost you. I'm looking forward to hearing the details of your adventures."

Mollie stepped up closer to the president and gestured for him to bend down. "I was shot in the heart and actually died, Mr. President."

"Well, you're a remarkable young lady, Mollie, and that goes for your mother too," the president said with an appreciative smile. The president's eyebrows rose when he noticed someone shorter than Mollie looking up at him, someone not quite human.

"Mr. President," Jason said, "this is Ricket, our Science Officer aboard The Lilly."

The president took the mechanical being's hand while the crew held their breath, knowing their introduction was not merely a formality but an indicator of how far, possibly, the Craing had infiltrated into the highest levels of government. Jason watched the president's smiling face. It became obvious to Jason that he knew he was being tested; the admiral and Secretary of Defense Walker must have briefed him that his would be a necessary next step.

"Nice to meet you, Mr. President," Ricket said, and as quickly as he'd arrived, he scurried back off into the crowd. All heads turned to Jason, alarm on their faces. Jason put two fingers to his ear and spoke quietly for a moment, then turned back to the group. Knowing there may never be another opportunity to screw with the President of the United States, Jason hesitated, face stern.

The president stood there, brow furrowed in anticipation. "Well?" he asked.

"Oh, the handshake. Yes, yes—we're good, all good," Jason answered, maintaining the act.

President Ross looked relieved and turned to the Secretary of Defense as if to say, see, of course I'm human.

Jason was hailed. "Please excuse me for

233

one moment, sir." Jason turned and acknowledged the call.

"Captain, we have a problem on Craing ship 1. We're at the cages," Lieutenant Morgan told him.

"On my way," Jason replied.

"I need to attend to a small problem, but I'll catch back up with you shortly." Jason bent over and whispered something in Mollie's ear, then stood back up. "If possible, please stay a while longer, Mr. President. Mollie here is our most experienced tour guide. She'd love the honor of giving you an abbreviated tour of The Lilly, if that would be acceptable?" Jason asked. He noticed the president had already turned around and was looking at The Lilly with growing interest. President Ross looked over to one of his aides off to the side, who reluctantly nodded.

"Well, let's get this show on the road then," he said, excitedly. Jason shook the Commander-in-Chief's hand one more time and promised to reconnect shortly. He then ran off in the direction of the first Craing vessel. He wasn't exactly sure which ship was Craing vessel 1.

* * *

Jason arrived at the bottom deck courtyard area beneath the hundreds of metal Craing cages. From up above on the fifth deck he saw Morgan signaling down to get his attention. He took the lift and got off on the fifth deck, crossing over and joining Lieutenant Morgan.

To his surprise, Dira was there too. She averted her eyes when Jason got closer. She was wearing a long silk dress that left little to the imagination of what her slender body looked like beneath. She had applied her makeup in a way that must have been customary on her home planet of Jhardon. Her accentuated eyes and lips, her whole face, was nothing short of breathtaking. It took a conscious effort for Jason to break his stare and concentrate on the issue at hand.

The cage before them barely contained the seven-foot-tall rhino-beast. Blood dripped from around his large six-inch diameter horn. A bandage had been wrapped around his right thigh. Morgan had his weapon pointed at the rhino-beast. Jason noticed the gate at the front of the cage was distorted and bent out of shape, its broken latch mechanism lying on the deck floor.

"These cages won't hold them for long, Captain. There are a hundred and fifty of them, and this is the second breech in the last hour," Morgan said, eyeing the large beast.

"And they're hurting themselves in the process," Dira added, now looking at the captain. "I bandaged his leg earlier while he was unconscious. But he won't let me attend to his injuries around his horn."

The huge rhino creature stood before them, legs apart and hands on hips. His eyes were on Jason. "Can he understand me?" Jason asked.

"I understand you," the beast replied,

before the others could answer. The Lilly AI had been initiated earlier and was translating real-time.

"Why do you fight with the Craing?" Jason asked.

"To save our mates and offspring. Our planet has been conquered by the beings you call the Craing. Our male warriors must fight to ensure our species will endure."

"What is your name?"

"I am called Traveler. I do not have a mate or offspring, but I fight for those of my kind who do."

Jason looked up at the powerful warrior for a few moments before speaking again. "What if your world could be freed from the Craing. What if your warriors could regain their honor? What if we gave you back your weapons—your heavy hammers?"

The rhino-warrior stared back at Jason, blood still oozing from around his horn. "That is not a decision I can solely make for our warriors, our people. We loathe the Craing. Breaking the bonds of our captivity would mean everything. But the Craing are many in number. Thousands of planets have come under their tyranny. We fear for the lives of our kind. The risks of opposing the Craing are too great."

A booming voice came from an adjacent row of cages directly across the center open area.

"No! Traveler! It is time to regain our honor. It is time to bring freedom to our people," the other rhino-beast bellowed in a commanding voice. Like Traveler, he was standing at the front of his cage, with legs apart and hands on hips. Jason looked back to Traveler.

"The one who speaks is one of our leaders. He is called Three Horns. A great warrior and decision-maker."

Jason wasn't sure, but he thought Traveler was smiling—although his mouth was mostly hidden beneath several folds of grey skin. Jason turned to look across at Three Horns, and sure enough, he had two additional, albeit smaller, horns above his primary horn. He was nodding his large head and also appeared to be smiling.

"Can I trust you?" Jason asked, directing his question toward Three Horns.

"Can we trust you?" the beast replied back.

"Your warriors will fight with our warriors until we defeat the Craing, or die trying," Jason asked. "It may be a while before we can save your world."

"We will fight side by side with you, as brothers. But we will not be caged."

Jason took a step forward and swung open the gate to Traveler's cage and stepped aside. "You can release Three Horns, then follow us," Jason said to his crewmembers.

"Captain, I don't think that's such a good idea," Morgan said, blocking the rhino-warrior from leaving the cage.

"Stand aside, Lieutenant. These cages won't hold them long anyway, and we need to trust them. It's in our mutual best interest to work together." Jason gestured with a nod of his head for Morgan to step aside.

Because of their significant weight, the two rhino-warriors needed to be taken down the lift separately. Jason had an idea brewing— something that just might work.

Chapter 17

Jason had forgotten about the presidential tour in progress. He saw the small group had arrived at the Zoo and that Mollie stood in front of them, halfway down the corridor. She was talking and pointing up toward a rocky plateau fifty yards out. Two blue, eight-foot-tall carnivores were shredding a large side of beef.

"These guys in Hab 12 scare me. I think they're called Serapin-Terplins; we just call them Serapins and they're native to several planets. They look like raptors to me, but have fingers on their hands. Oh, and they have really pretty baby blue skin. Jack says we need to make sure they always have fresh meat in their habitat and lots of it." Mollie shrugged and was about to move on to the next habitat when Jason, Morgan, Dira and the two giant rhino-warriors entered the Zoo.

Earlier, the rhino-warriors had requested the return of their weapons; Jason agreed to their hammers but not to their energy weapons. Jason smiled and held his hands up letting everyone know that things were well under control. Just the same, the president's marine detail moved in front of the crowd with their weapons raised. Jason spotted Nan peering around one of the soldiers. Her expression was similar to that of the president's.

The rhino-warriors were fidgety, staring

first at the multiple rifle barrels trained on them and then at the two blue carnivores in the Zoo habitat.

"Please lower your weapons. I'd like to make some introductions," Jason said, as calmly as he could muster. Both Admiral Crawford and Defense Secretary Walker looked at the two rhino-warriors with concern and irritation showing on their faces.

"What the hell you doing, Reynolds? Do you realize how inappropriate this is—bringing two armed—uh—aliens near the proximity of the president?" Admiral Crawford fumed.

"I didn't bring them here to meet President Ross. No offense, sir, but we have other business to attend to. Just the same, please meet our new allies. Traveler and Three Horns are joining forces with us to defeat the Craing. We've learned that their world was conquered by the Craing, and their mates and offspring held captive while the male warriors have been forced to fight with the Craing or suffer the consequences. They have over one hundred and fifty warriors here and I need to find them accommodations."

Jack the Zoo's caretaker, standing quietly off to the side, had listened in, and Jason now had his full attention.

The president bullied his way through his armed detail and stood before the two rhino-warriors. "I'm Howard Ross and I'd like to personally thank you. On behalf of the country, welcome." The president held the stare of the two rhinos.

Traveler and Three Horns waited for the AI to complete the translation and then nodded. Three Horns looked over at Jason and did his version of a shrug. "Who is this small man who welcomes us to this strange place?" he inquired, sounding confused.

"Three Horns, he is our country's leader, our primary decision-maker."

Realization set in and the two warriors lowered their heads. "Forgive my rudeness, I meant no disrespect."

"Over the coming days I'd like to talk with you more, discuss our mutual goals and together plan how to defeat the Craing," said the president.

The two warriors did not answer; instead, they raised their hammers, knocking them together high over their heads. Instinctively, everyone covered their ears against the intense noise.

"I'm sure that's just a high-five gesture in their culture," Jason said to the group, not actually knowing any such thing. "Please, go on with your tour while I speak with Jack about the Zoo." Jason winked at Mollie and walked with his two new allies further down the corridor to where Jack was waiting for them.

"I have a strange request for you, Jack. Three Horns and his warriors do not do well in confined spaces. I'd like you to work with him. I'm assuming there are open, unused habitats available?" Jason asked, looking around at seemingly endless miles and miles of varying eco-habitat space. Jack did his customary scratching of his beard and appraised the two rhino-beasts.

"What are the living conditions on your planet?" Jack asked them.

Three Horns thought for a moment and then strode off toward the far end of the corridor. He stopped and stood gazing, hands on hips. Before him lay one of many ten-foot-wide openings into a massive habitat beyond. Three Horns pointed: "Much like this land. We stay here."

Jack shook his head, "No, no, that's already occupied." Jack and the rest of the group hurried down the corridor and stood next to the large beast.

"I'll find you a more suitable habitat, perhaps Hab 23. Let me check—"

"No, I have selected this one," Three Horns said, indignation in his voice.

Jack looked over to Jason for him to decide.

"See if you can make this work, Jack," he said, apologetically.

Jack accessed a small monitor mounted to an area of the bulkhead that divided the habitats from one another. "Well, this habitat contains the Furlongs. This actually might work. Just wait, one will show itself shortly." The two warriors soon became impatient and started to pace back and forth in front of the habitat. Finally, there was movement. A family of large bear-like animals had assembled in the distance, near the side of a stream.

"They look like regular bears," Jason said, somewhat disappointed.

"They are very similar to bears, mostly like the North American grizzly," Jack replied. Traveler stepped up closer to the habitat opening, where his horn penetrated the invisible field separating the habitat from the inside of the corridor. He was thrust backward and landed hard on his backside. Mollie's presidential tour group down the corridor turned around to see what the commotion was about. Traveler got back to his feet, no worse for wear.

"Can they share the habitat? It won't be forever," Jason asked, looking over to Jack.

Three Horns nodded his head affirmatively. "Yes, we hunt the Furlong bear—cook the meat on open fires." Jack looked over at Jason with an expression that said, see, this won't work.

"If you're going to stay here, temporarily, you cannot hunt the Furlong bear. It's an endangered species," Jason said, although he had no idea if that were true or not. "It's either here, with your food supplied by Jack, no hunting, or you and your warriors can stay back in the cages. It's up to you." Jason started to walk away, indicating it made no difference to him.

Three Horns, seemingly upset he'd said the wrong thing, replied: "Yes, we live alongside the Furlong bear. This will be our home while we join you and fight the Craing together."

Jason turned and nodded his head. Then he looked at Lieutenant Morgan. "I'm putting this project in your hands. Get the rest of the rhino-warriors situated. Work with Jack here and make sure we can retrieve them when needed."

"Yes, sir," Morgan replied.

* * *

Jason awoke as soon as he detected movement in his cabin. Out of the corner of his eye he spotted two amber spheres moving and hovering in the darkness. The lights came on when Jason sat up. Ricket stood at the foot of his bed.

"What the hell are you doing in here?" Jason asked, annoyed, and looked to see if anyone else had barged into his quarters in the middle of the night. "What time is it?"

"0400. Sorry to disturb your sleep, Captain. I have made some new discoveries, ones that may help us against the approaching fleet."

Jason rubbed the sleep from his eyes. "Wait for me in my ready room; I'll be right there."

Jason took a quick shower, got dressed, and was sipping coffee when he found Ricket waiting for him in the ready room. "Okay, what have you got for me, Ricket?"

"Best if I show you, sir," Ricket answered as he headed for the door.

* * *

The flight deck was in stark contrast to the last time Jason saw it. Where it had been quiet as a tomb before, it was a flurry of activity and sound now: the loud noise came from power tools and blasting rock-and-roll music. Jason smiled. He was starting to like these hotshots. Five of The Lilly's six sleek, dark red one-man fighters were at different stages of dismantlement around the flight deck. All of the newly-arrived Top Gun pilots were there. One was only partially visible up on a ladder, bent over a fighter's drive compartment, while another pilot, up in the fighter's cockpit, impatiently shouted down for a stabilization calibrator. How does he even know what that is? Jason wondered. Lieutenant Craig Wilson, the self-appointed leader of the team, was at the far side of the flight deck barking orders to three pilots sitting in their respective cockpits. When Wilson noticed the captain, he barked several more orders and walked confidently over to where Jason and Ricket were standing. He then came to attention and saluted.

"As you were, Lieutenant," Jason said, returning his salute. "I commend your diligence, everyone's, but what is it that required me to get out of my bunk at 0400?"

"Best if we show you, sir," Wilson replied with a smile. He turned on his heels and with a twirling index-finger gesture held high in the air, the three fighters on the far side of the flight deck simultaneously disappeared. Momentarily surprised at the disappearance of three of his fighters, Jason quickly realized what happened, and smiled.

Ricket moved to the main flight deck console along the bulkhead, entered something on the pad, and the twenty-foot-high flight deck doors began to slide open. Jason and the others congregated at the opened large bay doors. Dawn had given way to morning light; the sun was peaking above a distant ridge-line. Sitting fifty yards out in the desert were the three fighters. Jason nodded his head. "Good! So where are we now with the other three fighters?" he asked, turning toward Wilson and Ricket.

"Two more will be shift-ready within the hour. We still have one fighter that is totally inaccessible," Wilson responded.

"What do you mean by inaccessible?" Jason asked, looking over to one fighter still pushed back against the bulkhead.

Ricket took off his baseball cap and used it to gesture toward the lone fighter. "It's not a problem with the fighter, it's a system's issue; something with the AI not allowing access."

"Why would the AI not give you access?" Before Ricket could answer, Jason addressed The Lilly directly: "Lilly, are you monitoring this conversation?"

"Yes, Captain," The AI responded.

"What's going on with that last fighter? Why can't we access it like we did the others?"

"Original Caldurian configuration parameters do not provide adequate level clearance to access the Pacesetter fighter."

The fighter was not actually the same as the

others. It was slightly larger, more maroon than red, and it actually sat two pilots instead of one. Jason looked down to Ricket for his intake, but he was scratching his head again.

"Captain, this is new information for me. Like the AI itself, the ship's database and my own memory banks were wiped clean many years ago. Until now, I'd never heard any reference to the Caldurians, or anything about the original inhabitants of The Lilly," Ricket explained, his face showing a mixture of emotions, most of which Jason couldn't read.

Wilson interjected, "Sir, I'd like permission to start atmospheric, as well as outer orbit flight training maneuvers. HyperLearning can only go so far—we need time at the stick."

Jason nodded. "Permission granted; ensure you stay within the geographic confines of the outpost for atmospheric flights, coordinate all flights through the XO, and maintain constant comms contact." Jason brought his attention back to Ricket and the issue at hand.

"Lilly, why are you revealing this information now? What's changed?"

"Original Caldurian configuration parameters have been updated," the AI responded, her voice monotone, but borderline bitchy.

"By whom?" Jason asked, not liking the direction this was going.

"By the Caldurian."

Jason had to let that sink in for a moment. He could see why Ricket found the AI difficult to work with. Like pulling teeth, getting the full story was tedious.

Irritated, Jason continued, "Lilly, I require complete information. You seem fairly intelligent, work with me here. The old status quo, where you provided only minimum information, is not acceptable. "

"Yes, Captain, please migrate to AI standard operational mode," the voice replied flatly.

"What mode are we in now?" Jason asked, confused.

"What you would refer to as safe mode. As acting captain, only you have permission status to bring the Lilly AI fully online to operational mode."

Jason looked down to Ricket, "You didn't know any of this? Why wouldn't my father have done this years ago?"

"Your father found the Lilly AI most irritating. After a while he wouldn't even speak with it," Ricket replied, then shrugged his little shoulders as if his whole understanding of the world was flipped upside down.

"Well, you're the Science Officer, Ricket. Do I upgrade these parameters? Are there any dangers in doing so?" Jason asked, feeling he was in way over his head again. Ricket did not reply. He looked perplexed.

"Lilly, earlier you mentioned the parameters had been changed by the Caldurian. Are they still issuing you commands?"

"Yes, Captain."

Jason, now thoroughly irritated, wondered where the AI was physically located. He had visions of showing it his boot, or better yet, using it for target practice. The truth was, everything was at a crossroads. With hundreds of Craing ships on their way to Earth, their small efforts so far seemed too minor, too insubstantial, to fight off the imminent approach of the overwhelming Craing forces now only two days' travel away. Jason, his crew, and their distinguished guests had read his father's report. Two thousand United Planetary Alliance warships had been annihilated by a Craing armada. That same fleet was now approaching Earth. If something radical didn't change, and change soon, Earth's situation was hopeless. Jason didn't really see a choice in the matter.

"Lilly, who do you report to—me, or the Caldurians?"

"The Caldurians set the original parameters. I report to and follow your orders," the AI replied.

Jason looked one more time for some indication from Ricket. After a moment, Ricket nodded his head.

"Lilly, please go ahead and migrate to AI standard operational mode. Do it now."

"Would you like the cyborg you refer to as Ricket to also be migrated to operational mode?"

Jason saw both surprise and worry in Ricket's eyes. Obviously, he had never considered the fact that he was so closely tied to

The Lilly in this way. Jason was fairly sure Ricket was thinking along the same lines as himself. "How will it affect you? I mean—will you still be you?"

Ricket seemed to weigh the implications, "There is no way to determine this beforehand, Captain."

"Lilly, can that decision be made on its own at another time?" Jason asked.

"Yes, but it is not advisable."

"Do not update Ricket at this time, but continue with updating the AI to standard operational mode." Jason first saw relief wash over Ricket's face, but then he shook his head.

"No, Captain, please continue with my update as well. I would always wonder if I were operating at less than optimum. But thank you, sir," Ricket said with resigned expectation.

"Lilly, go ahead and update both."

"This process will take three minutes. All concurrent system processes will continue as normal and be unaffected, although verbal access will discontinue temporarily."

Almost immediately, Ricket became immobile, as if on pause. Wishing to give Ricket his privacy until the systems updated, Jason turned away. Still hearing the music in the background, he spent the time watching the fighters conduct their training exercises. They were flying in formation, skimming mere feet from the desert floor, only to swoop up at near-vertical angles toward the sky and disappear up into Earth's outer orbit.

Jason thought how wonderful it must be to fly like that. He envied these men and women for having that kind of freedom. Mostly out of curiosity, Jason accessed his own added HyperLearning constructs. Like flipping through virtual file folders at lightning speed, he found the stats under the ship's piloting section. He not only had the necessary learning to pilot the fighters, he alone had the learning and clearance for the Pacesetter fighter.

Precisely three minutes later, Ricket, whose eyes had been closed, were open and looking up at Jason. He took a long, deep breath and exhaled. Jason had never witnessed Ricket happy—until that moment. The smile was real, the gratitude was real and Ricket was still all there, and more.

"Good morning, Captain," Lilly said enthusiastically.

"Good morning, Lilly. First thing, please tell me what you know about the Caldurians and your current connection to them."

"Yes, Captain. I'd be happy to. The Caldurians are a race of humanoid descent. Their world is approximately three hundred light years from Earth. They pride themselves on being a peace-loving culture, one that thrives through its intellectual, artistic, and humanistic exchange with other world cultures. It was only through encounters with the Craing eight hundred years ago that the Caldurians were forced to integrate into their society both defensive and offensive weaponry domestically, as well as into their space-faring vessels. Attempts by the Craing to subjugate the Caldurian peoples failed. But approximately two hundred years ago, through the use of eight thousand nuclear-tipped missiles, the Caldurian world was destroyed."

A deep sadness filled Jason at the idea of an advanced society, one most Earthlings would certainly wish to aspire toward, destroyed.

"Lilly, you mentioned you are still taking commands from the Caldurians. If their world was destroyed, how is that possible?" Jason questioned.

"Not all Caldurians were killed. There were several off-world outposts, and they have survived. Their locations, as well as their numbers, are purposely kept secret."

"Thank you, Lilly," Jason said. His thoughts lingered on Calduria. A world destroyed so senselessly and, unfortunately, most probably the fate of his own world. One thing was perfectly clear: Jason needed to take the upcoming battle away from Earth, as his father had tried to do. His next thoughts turned to Nan and Mollie. Letting them remain on The Lilly while she flew into battle that could result in the death of everyone onboard seemed irresponsible. Yet, if they were defeated in space, would their fate be any worse than when the Craing ships came to subjugate Earth's populace? Jason realized that the decision rested with Nan, and he'd support her decision either way. Jason's thoughts were interrupted by

Ricket, who seemed to be contemplating something, nodding his head.

"Oh, now I understand," Ricket murmured to himself. He then continued aloud, "What I have discovered, to some degree, is that the original designers of this ship and its technology were intimately involved with navigating the multiverse, which of course are the infinite layers or membranes of separate universes that exist and coexist simultaneously. The concept of a multiverse has subsequently gone from speculation to one of science fact. What they accomplished that transcended all theory, at least that I am aware of, was locating a nearby multiverse membrane that operates in six dimensions versus our three dimensions. And it's that sixth dimension where everything exists in the realm of math... no physicality. That sixth dimension allows for mathematical conversations to take place and it is through these mathematical conversations, like your Google-search browser—but on a cosmic scale. Other membranes are not only located this way but easily accessed," Ricket said excitedly. Jason smiled and thought about what Ricket had discovered—now that he was operating at his full mental capacity. He also had become quite the little chatterbox.

Chapter 18

Jason spent the next day preparing The Lilly and the four Craing ships for departure. With a crew complement of 180, The Lilly was well staffed. The four Craing ships were subsequently assigned new crews from the outpost. Officers on those ships were quickly put through sessions of HyperLearning. In the end, though, Jason and his officers decided it was best to maintain control over the Craing ships remotely from The Lilly, at least until the 'green' officers got some experience under their belts.

On his way up from meeting Chief Horris in Engineering, Jason stopped off at Nan and Mollie's cabin. Early on, Jason had learned that if he simply stopped in front of a closed hatch, his presence would be alerted to those inside. When the door disappeared, Molly was standing there with a toothbrush in her mouth.

"Hi Dad, come in!" Molly said, and then quickly disappeared back into the suite. Jason noticed Nan had several spacer overalls over her arm. Although he knew it was her decision, he was disappointed that she was packing to leave.

"I didn't expect to see you again before lift off. Is that the right terminology, lift off?"

"That works," Jason said, looking around the cabin, which didn't appear too different from his own. Then he noticed Nan was actually hanging the overalls up in the closet. The relief on his face must have been obvious.

"Seriously, you thought we'd stay behind?" She shook her head in wonder. "It's not all that different from home, and, yes, someone has to do the laundry. The truth is, Jason, I'd rather be blown to smithereens up there in the stars with you than have those aliens get anywhere near Mollie and me back here on Earth."

"I'm glad, but I wanted it to be your decision," Jason said, noticing Nan had on her snug-fitting jeans again. She saw where his eyes lingered and smiled. "No time for that, Captain dirty mind, you need to keep your thoughts on saving the planet, remember?"

His face flushed. "All right, I'll check in on you two later." Then he remembered something else. "Mollie, did you come up with the four names I mentioned?" Jason asked out loud, not knowing where she'd run off to.

"I think so," she said, peeking her head around the corner. "Craing ship one is now called The Surprise, because we surprised the crap out of them; Craing ship 2 is now The Trickster, because they tried to pull a fast one over on us; the third Craing ship is now called Gordita, because Orion told me that it smelled like Taco Bell in there, and the fourth Craing ship is called The Last Chance because it was their last chance and they blew it. Do those kinda work, Dad?" Mollie asked tentatively.

Jason laughed out loud and nodded his head. "Oh, yeah, those work. I think I like

Gordita best, but they are all perfect."

* * *

Jason met with Admiral Crawford while standing outside near The Lilly's rear gangway.

"I'm sorry, Jason, but no one is oblivious to the bare facts of the situation. Even with a handful of fighters, c'mon, ten ships against hundreds? What are you thinking?" the admiral asked, shaking her head.

"Admiral, I learned a long time ago to play my cards close to my chest. On the surface, yes, the odds seem hopeless. Pathetic even. And I want it to continue seeming that way."

Frustrated, the admiral turned to leave and then turned back. "Well, then, you're doing an excellent job, Captain. Consensus has changed. We now feel it far more prudent to strategically place those vessels around the globe to protect key people. Use the shields and weapons on those ships here, where they can make the most difference."

Jason shook his head. "I'm sorry, Admiral, but I can't allow that. I've brought us this far, and I'm going to see it through."

As her gaze bore down on him, Jason took a long breath and looked around the makeshift courtyard. "As long as there's a mole onboard The Lilly, and hybrids coming out of the woodwork, I simply can't talk any more about my plans. As someone once told me during a dire situation There are many things you don't comprehend yet, but believe me when I tell you, not all hope is lost." As the admiral walked away, Jason only hoped it was true. Then he remembered one more thing and called after her, "Admiral!"

She turned back, her face red and angry. "What?"

"We've left you with a little gift," Jason said, gesturing to a large metal crate nearby. "Our phase synthesizer has been pumping out thousands of hybrid detectors. Get them in the hands of the people. While we're fighting the war in space, fight the war here on Earth."

The admiral turned her back on him and hurried off.

* * *

The captain's morning meeting in the ready room dragged on for hours. The overriding conflicting issue, one that kept raising its ugly head, was how to destroy the Craing fleet and still rescue potentially thousands of captives held in confinement cages aboard most of those same vessels. No matter how effective The Lilly could potentially be going up against the Craing fleet, a typical interstellar battle would not work. They needed to approach it from a different strategy.

Jason was the last one to funnel out of his ready room. He'd needed one last review with his officers. Everyone had their job to do; hopefully, they were all on the same page.

With only hours to spare before the Craing fleet reached the outskirts of the solar system, The Lilly and four Craing ships were as prepared as they were going to be. Jason ran through their latest strategy one more time in his head. Each of the former Craing ships, now Alliance vessels, had a skeleton crew of twenty, for a total of eighty. Of those crewmembers, the officers and key personnel had been brought over from the outpost and rotated through HyperLearning. Still green, but competent. Jason also totaled in the one hundred seasoned Navy SEALs provided by Admiral Crawford, plus the remaining fifty or so SEALs from Billy's outfit. Adding to that number were the ten new Top Gun hotshots. There were also one hundred and fifty rhino-warriors, and The Lilly's original crew of about thirty. He ran up the numbers in his head. A total combined crew of four hundred, or so, give or take.

Jason turned his attention to the bridge. Ricket had set up four remote consoles with virtual display configurations to mirror the captured Craing helm and sub-systems. Ensign McBride would pilot The Surprise, Gunny Orion, The Trickster, Lieutenant Commander Perkins, The Gordita, and Chief Horris, The Last Chance. Ricket would be at the console closest to Jason piloting The Lilly.

Jason gave the command and The Lilly and four Craing ships lifted off in unison. The bridge crew briefly looked at the wraparound display and watched as the outpost disappeared below them. He wondered if this might be the last time they'd ever see home. Jason noticed Billy standing near the back of the bridge, an unlit stogie hanging from the corner of his mouth. He, too, watched as Earth filled the display.

"Ricket, hold The Lilly's position here, outside of orbit. The rest of you go ahead and move your vessels to the assigned orbital coordinates."

The bridge crew had practiced this maneuver several times in simulations. Chief Horris, piloting The Gordita, was the weakest link—not a natural at helm control like the others. The display changed to a hovering 3D representation of Earth. Green icons representing The Surprise, The Trickster, The Last Chance, and The Gordita appeared on the display, and they each moved away from their current flight formation to positions that were equal distances from each other around the planet. Jason caught the helmsmen's eye. "Good job. Nice work all of you. Let's get back to your regular stations. Helm, take us to heading 2119." The Lilly moved away at just under sub-light speed. Earth became smaller and was soon swallowed up in the blackness of space.

"Just wanted to take in the view and let you know we're ready, whatever that means," Billy said.

"I know you are. And no matter what happens, thanks, Billy."

"Think everything of it," he replied,

flashing his big bravado grin. "Anyway, I've got work to do." Billy leaned in close: "Don't screw this up, boss. We're all counting on you." He gave Jason a slap on the back and left the bridge.

"Captain, we're picking up a hail. It appears to be from the approaching Craing fleet," Ensign McBride reported.

"Let's see what they want. Open a channel."

The view was somewhat familiar looking. It showed the inside of a gigantic Craing vessel, specifically the cages. But the proportions were different. The scale of what they were seeing was almost beyond comprehension. There were tens of thousands of metal cages, so many they disappeared into the far distance. Some prisoners appeared alien, some human. Mostly males, but there were females and children, too. Some were alive, some obviously dead, with portions of their body cut away exposing flesh, muscle, bone.

Several Craing workers were at their carts doing what they do; another was pushing his cart in front of the next cage. The bridge went quiet, everyone paralyzed by the visual carnage. Jason could feel his heart hammering in his chest, his pulse pounding in his ears. The Craing were using this video montage to make an impact. Then the view changed to a close-up of one cage.

It took a moment for recognition to set in. Jason's father was filthy, bloodied and showed signs of repeated beatings. In sharp contrast, the defiant look in his eyes showed anything but defeat. Angry, you bet, but Jason saw Admiral Perry Reynolds hadn't given up. The scene changed again. The smiling face of a Craing dignitary filled the screen. He wore a long green silk robe and some kind of headdress that towered several feet above his head.

"I am High Priest Overlord Lom for the Craing Empire. Here, the pathetic leader of the United Planetary Alliance awaits the honor of his fate, to be consumed by his conquerors. Understand, the Craing Empire can be benevolent. If you wish a quick and painless death for this human, as well as for our other captives, then return our vessels. Go back to your planet and await your fate."

Jason slowly stood and approached the forward display. He wanted these Craing bastards to see who they were talking to. But before Jason had a chance to speak, the Overlord's attention was pulled away. His eyes were locked on Ricket. With astonishment on his face, the priest made several attempts to speak, but nothing came out. Eventually he managed one word, "Emperor!"

Chapter 19

Ricket stared back at the forward display. Earlier he'd removed his baseball cap and it still sat atop his console. Eventually, he looked over to Jason and then back to the Craing priest.

"Is he looking at me?" Ricket asked quietly, seeming just as bewildered as the rest of the bridge crew.

"I believe he is," Jason replied, now remembering the open-mouthed stares Ricket received earlier from captured Craing crewmembers. The Craing priest was speaking again. Three more Craing priests, wearing cone-shaped headdresses, were huddled together kneeling with their heads bowed.

"How could this be, your Eminence?" The four Craing cone heads seemed to be at odds with one another. They continued to squabble in hushed undertones. Eventually, High Priest Overlord Lom, chastising the others, looked up and spoke again.

"We have analyzed your image, your Eminence. Clearly you have undergone the transformation of eternity. There can be no doubt; you are our Emperor Reechet of House Polk."

Jason didn't know what the hell was going on. Jason had time to catch Ricket's eye. Was it enough? Ricket stood and spoke in Terplin, the Craing native language.

"Greetings, High Priest Overlord Lom. Yes, I am the Emperor Reechet. Please, get up."

Overlord Lom got back to his feet, exclaiming, "But how is this possible? It has been nearly two hundred years since you went missing and were presumed dead?" The other priests nodded their heads in unison.

"Missing, yes, deceased, obviously not. But as your emperor, it is time for me to come home." Ricket, obviously making this stuff up on the fly, hesitated a moment and then continued, "Immediately. You will prepare for the release of your prisoners and to then leave this sector. These humans rescued me and should not be harmed."

The cone heads talked among themselves again. Then Priest Overlord Lom spoke: "Respected and honorable Emperor Reechet, there has never been a time when two emperors walked amongst the Craing simultaneously. We are at a loss and, at the very least, must seek direction from Emperor Quorp. This will take several cycles."

Just above a whisper, McBride broke the tension. "Sir, we're now ten light-minutes beyond the solar system. We'll be within weapon's range of the Craing fleet in five minutes."

"High Priest Overlord Lom," Ricket said, "I assume Emperor Quorp would be most unhappy with those responsible for putting me in harm's way. If I remember correctly, immediate separation of your heads from your necks by way of a warrior claxon's sword is protocol. Is that protocol under the direction of Emperor Quorp?"

Jason watched Ricket's performance with admiration. Playing on Craing cowardice was a good bet. Jason had witnessed it, especially with the Overlords, first hand.

"Please, let us discuss this further with our council. We can continue this conversation shortly."

"Their fleet has come to a halt, Captain," Ensign McBride reported.

"Any way to determine which vessel the admiral is being held on?" Jason asked.

Orion got up from her console and walked to the comms station on the other side of the bridge. "Actually, his NanoComs are now in range and look to be operational. Should I attempt a hail?"

"Give it a shot, Gunny," Jason said, surprised.

Several moments later the deep baritone voice of Admiral Reynolds filled the bridge.

"Go for Admiral Reynolds," the voice replied.

"Admiral, this is Captain Reynolds. It seems you're in a bit of a jam," Jason said, making light of a situation he wasn't sure he'd be able to remedy.

"Good to hear your voice. Figured it might be you. I take it you know what my status is here, yes? Tell me, what's going on with The Lilly and with Earth?"

"Both fine for the moment, sir. We've been discussing your situation with your captors. Seems they know our Science Officer. In fact, they believe he's their long lost emperor," Jason replied.

There was a momentary pause before the admiral responded. "Come to think of it, that actually makes a strange kind of sense. Whatever you plan, do not let the Craing get hold of Ricket. He knows far too much."

"I'm guessing they'll be looking for some kind of trade."

"Don't even think about doing that, Jason. Ricket is far too important——."

Jason cut him off, replying, "Agreed, Admiral. Any chance you know where you're being held? Which vessel?"

"I'm in their Fleet Command Battle Dreadnaught vessel. This ship is immense. You can't defeat it in battle. You know that, don't you? Anyway, I just had a personal visit from their High Priest. I believe I'm on the menu for tonight. Consuming their conquered is a big deal for them."

"Yes, we've had the pleasure of talking with High Priest Lom ourselves. For now, I'm going to ask you to sit tight, sir. This new development shakes things up a bit. I'm going to ask you to trust my judgment on what action we take."

"You do what you have to do. I had my chance. And we know how that turned out." Jason cut the connection and put his attention back on matters at hand.

McBride looked over to the captain. "Sir, we're within three thousand miles of the tip of the fleet. The fleet itself is widespread, over seventy thousand miles."

The XO, Lieutenant Commander Perkins, moved away from his seat at one of the consoles to sit in a chair next to Jason. "I'm sure you realize we've been provided with an excellent opportunity—one aspect of our plan we hadn't figured out yet."

Jason nodded, "Uh huh, an opportunity to get in close enough to phase-shift—I know. But it's still a double-edged sword, XO. The Lilly will be right in the middle of that hornet's nest. For much of the maneuvering about, you'll have the con. I'm counting on you, that if it comes down to it and you can't shift away, just know The Lilly cannot be taken."

"Understood," Perkins replied, and his expression acknowledged the implications.

"We're being hailed, Captain," McBride reported from the helm.

Priest Sol, now alone on the display, was back to his smiling self. "Captain, please accept my apologies for the delay. We have been in contact with Emperor Quorp. He wishes, in all haste, to have Emperor Reechet brought onto our vessel. It is for obvious reasons that we will not release our prisoners, or forestall the inevitable invasion of your planet." Jason noticed their fleet was on the move again and Craing vessels were already encircling The

Lilly.

"In a rare exhibition of kindness," Priest Sol went on, "the emperor will allow you to live, albeit subject to imprisonment, and your crew as well. Admiral Reynolds will survive the day. Emperor Reechet must be brought to our Council of Priests immediately. Any attempt to avert the capture of your ship and crew will result in its immediate destruction."

"That would result in the death of Emperor Reechet as well," Jason replied, but understood their intent.

"As mentioned earlier, there has never been a time when two emperors walked amongst the Craing simultaneously, and there never will be."

Jason watched the display. Sure enough, the massive cube-shaped Battle Dreadnaught was moving closer to The Lilly. But still not quite close enough.

"What would stop us from just self-destructing right now?"

"That would be unfortunate, but you must do what you feel best, Captain. If you wish to save yourself and your crew, you'll ready your ship to be boarded. If not...." the Craing priest, with the same patronizing smile, held out his palms and shrugged. Jason smiled at the universal gesture for oh well, you're fucked. "A transport vehicle has been dispatched. Prepare to be boarded."

Typical of their other smaller craft, the Craing transport looked like an insect, but this one more like a squat green ladybug. It was infinitesimally small compared to the mass of the Battle Dreadnaught, as the entire bridge watched it disembark and head out towards The Lilly.

"How much time do we have before that bug reaches us?" Jason asked Ensign McBride at the helm.

"About ten minutes, sir."

The wrap-around display was now segmented. Multiple feeds came in from throughout The Lilly. On the flight deck, five of the six fighters were manned and ready on the forward end of the deck. Close behind were the two large shuttles, with their rear gangway doors open.

"XO, you have the con. It's game time, everyone."

* * *

When Jason entered the flight deck he wore a hardened combat suit with a plasma pulse sidearm. At the rear of the deck, Billy had assembled fifteen separate teams. Each team consisted of ten SEALs and fifteen rhino-warriors. All were equipped with advanced plasma pulse rifles. The rhino-warriors also carried their heavy hammers. Billy ushered one of the teams onto a shuttle on the port side, a tight fit, but with some jockeying around and angry remarks from the huge rhino-warriors, they all squeezed in. Once the shuttle's rear gangway was secured, Jason helped Billy repeat the same boarding process onto the other shuttle. Billy crammed in with the others, while Jason stepped back to let the hatch close.

The Pacesetter fighter was moved away from the bulkhead and prepped for preflight. Lieutenant Craig Wilson stood directly below the fighter's cockpit. "Sir, I highly recommend you let me pilot this mission, or at least come with you. No offense, but this is your first time behind the stick," Wilson said, his frustration evident.

"Thank you, Lieutenant, but the nature of this mission is personal. If I fail, it's on my head." With that said, Jason climbed the inset footholds leading up to the cockpit. Once strapped into the seat, the effect of his HyperLearning kicked in. He sighed in relief. Jason had experienced before the staggering amount of information made available via the HyperLearning sessions. The information only became assessable when it was actually needed, or specifically retrieved. He looked at the myriad of flight instrumentation controls and virtual displays laid out before him. "No problem, I got this—I think," Jason murmured, as he attempted to bring the Pacesetter into formation with the other fighters. He completely missed the mark and the Pacesetter hovered at an off-angle. The other pilots looked over at him; all were grinning and several gave the thumbs- up sign. Jason answered an incoming hail.

"Go for Captain."

"Captain, the Craing transport has arrived and is hailing us," said the XO

Jason had to smile at the prospect of The Lilly disappearing right before their eyes. "In that case, go ahead and phase-shift."

"Phase-shift complete, we're now in the primary hold of the Dreadnaught, mid-ship."

Chapter 20

The Dreadnaught's mid-ship cargo hold was easily twice as large as the holds on the other Craing vessels. A virtual schematic representation of the massive ship now hovered in front of Jason. He pulled at the virtual corners and enlarged the center section, revealing the sites where their coordinated shifts would situate them. At this point, the two shuttle pilots and the five fighter pilots were doing the same thing. A predetermined phase-shift coordinate location for each vessel was indicated in various colors. Jason's Pacesetter phase-shift location was marked as a violet circle. The shuttles were given numerous drop locations. Once they dropped off a load of SEALs and rhino-warriors, they would return to The Lilly's flight deck for another load. As Jason studied the wide corridor with miles of cages, he couldn't help but think he'd brought Mollie and Nan right into the lion's den. Jason looked over to the other pilots. They glanced back at him, waiting for his signal. He nodded once, and one by one, they all disappeared. Then Jason phase-shifted as well.

* * *

Jason's Pacesetter phase-shifted into the mid-section of the Craing prisoners' confinement corridor. Looking out past the nose of the fighter there was the typical Craing sooty haze, a foreboding dark cloud. The open corridor he now hovered in was several hundred feet wide and miles in length. And both sides of the escalating space were lined with multiple decks—row after row of containment cages. Talk about finding a needle in a haystack, Jason thought to himself. He hailed his father.

"Go for Admiral Reynolds," came back the older man's tired voice.

"I need you to do me a favor, if you have a second?"

"I think I can work something out, what do you need, smart ass?"

"Tell me when you see me." Jason pushed the joystick and the fighter abruptly kicked forward, gained speed too quickly, and nearly veered into a side support bulkhead. He repositioned the stick and tried again, realizing he needed to work on finessing his touch. After several moments, Jason reached the end of the corridor, U-turned, and headed back the way he'd come, only now he was positioned several decks higher. In spite of the dire situation, Jason was enthralled with flying, and he knew he was hooked.

"If you're the idiot flying one of The Lilly's fighters inside this corridor, then I guess you just passed me. I'm back about one hundred yards."

Jason looped again with an ass-over-teakettle maneuver and slowed to a crawl as he passed by the cages. Up until then, he had been moving too fast to make out any details, see into the cages. Faces stared back. Some human, some bizarre-looking aliens; all appeared desperate and scared.

"Hold up there, hot shot, you're almost in front of me," his father said. Jason looked to his left and saw the large stature of his father standing at the bars of a cage. Attempting a bit of his newly-acquired finesse, he instigated a tricky horizontal lateral movement, which scooted the fighter right up to the deck's catwalk. He locked down the controls, opened the cockpit canopy, and crawled back down to the catwalk.

"I specifically told you not to bring The Lilly into harm's way," the admiral bellowed.

"Yeah, well, I was in the neighborhood. If you'd rather catch the next cab, I have other places I can be," Jason said.

"Smart ass."

Jason looked for the release lever on his father's cage door. This one was configured differently than the latches on the older Craing vessels.

"No, it's up above, see? Just pull the damn metal pole."

Jason saw what he was pointing to and gave it a tug. The metal latch mechanism at the front of the cage clanged open. Jason removed his helmet.

Now, standing face to face with his father after a fifteen years' absence, he was unsure what to do next. For some inexplicable reason his eyes welled up and a lump the size of a golf ball filled his throat. Admiral Perry Reynolds, appraising his son, slowly nodded his head and, with equally moist eyes, engulfed Jason in a long overdue hug.

"Listen, before we go, we need to release someone else and bring him with us." The admiral gestured to the nearby cage.

"What the hell are you talking about, Dad, there's no room for—"

Holding up his hand, the admiral cut him off. Then, looking toward the next cage, he gestured for Jason to look. A small boy, no, not a boy, an alien approximately Mollie's age, gazed back at Jason. Like Dira, the boy had the same violet skin and long lashes. But the similarities stopped there.

"What are you looking at?" the boy asked him, with the meanest scowl Jason had ever seen.

The admiral shrugged. "He's a little rough round the edges, but basically he's a good kid. We can't just leave him here."

"I'm not planning on leaving any of them here, but right now there's no room in the fighter." Jason saw the disappointment on the child's face.

"All right, give me a second." Jason moved to the front of the boy's cage and opened the latch. Just then, an alarm claxon sounded in the far distance. He was familiar with the sound, and how it caused an overwhelming sense of impending dread in those who heard it. "I guess they know we're here," Jason said. "OK, kid, get in the back. Dad, you're in the front."

"I don't know how to fly that thing, Jason."

"I expect it was part of your HyperLearning, but you won't need to fly it. Hop in." The admiral frowned at Jason and proceeded to climb into the front cockpit seat. "Wait, what about you? We can't leave you here, they'll kill you the second you're discovered," his father said, distress in his voice.

"Don't worry about me, I'll catch a ride." Jason replaced his helmet and accessed his comms.

"Go for Billy."

"Billy, I need a ride; can you pick me up at this location with the next shuttle load?"

"You got it, hang tight, Cap," Billy replied.

Jason closed the cockpit canopy and accessed the fighter's controls via his HUD. He gave his father a quick nod and remotely phase-shifted the Pacesetter back to The Lilly. Hopefully, no one would be standing at the drop location.

When Billy's shuttle arrived it was a mess; hundreds of energy weapon blast marks scorched her outer hull. As the ramp came down, Jason boarded the ship. He contacted the XO for their latest status.

"The fighters have begun phase-shifting to nearby Craing vessels," Perkins said. "It's a slow process. As we did with The Lilly, one by one they are targeting the Craing weapon systems from their interior holds. After that, they target their propulsion systems. So far, they've disabled ten of their nearest ships. Unfortunately, the element of surprise is gone and at this point the Craing are waiting for them when they arrive, and our fighters are taking a pounding."

"What about our Battle Dreadnaught drop teams?" Jason inquired.

"The news isn't any better there. The first two teams that tried to take the bridge have been taken out. And, in addition to their highly-effective security hover drones, it's been reported the Craing patrol their confinement decks with some kind of lizard."

"Come again?" Jason asked, not sure he heard his XO correctly.

"That's right, maybe closer to a small dinosaur, although these are blue and have hands." Jason remembered Mollie talking about these creatures at the Zoo.

"There called Serapins. They're sacred to the Craing."

"Not sure how they managed it, but they don't attack the Craing. In fact, they walk right by them. Captain, if we can't secure that bridge, our plan falls apart."

Jason thought about the Serapins and saw the logic. Having grown up with stray dogs frequenting the scrapyard, vicious towards strangers and yet like family pets toward Gus and Jason most of the time, it was a system that definitely could keep the riffraff out. Jason cut the connection.

"Billy, we need to change direction. To the Dreadnaught's bridge." Billy nodded, and several moments later the shuttle banked to the right, then rose up to the upper decks. The shuttle's back ramp lowered as they approached the new drop off, and Jason skittered down. Another team was already there, taking cover, wherever possible, from bright plasma bolts. Four Craing hover drones were guarding access to the forward fifth deck, which was the only access to the bridge. Jason stole a quick peek around a corner while the closest drone was engaged by the other team. The drones were white, cylindrical in shape, but smaller than he'd expected, at about three feet in length.

Two rhino-warriors lay dead on the catwalk as well as a SEAL. All three had taken blasts to the head. Jason snatched up the dead SEAL's plasma pulse rifle and scrambled for cover behind a bulkhead. The weapon's charge level was still at 80%. The drones not only could hover and spin in any direction, they could target and fire from their two separate mini-pulse cannons simultaneously, making it damn near impossible to get a clear shot.

Billy was on comms: "There is no way in hell we're going to take this bridge, Cap. And even if we could, the inside corridors are teaming with those raptor things."

Jason had already noticed their icons on his HUD, approaching on the other side of the bulkhead. A flurry of energy blasts erupted mere inches from Jason's head and all around his teammates. Ducking low, he witnessed several rhino-warriors go down. The catwalk shook with three thousand pounds of dead weight hitting the deck plates all at once. He shook his head. The rhino-warriors tended to attack straight on, relying on their size, brute force and bravery, which, unfortunately, were no match for the drones' powerful mini-pulse cannons. Jason hailed Lieutenant Wilson.

"Go for Wilson."

"I'm programming your clearance to fly the Pacesetter as we speak. Wilson, lock onto my coordinates and shift over here ASAP. We have a drone problem. Ensure your shields are up."

"Aye, Captain, on my way," the lieutenant replied excitedly.

Jason figured Wilson may have been sitting in the cockpit, because when he looked up the Pacesetter was already hovering nearby in the corridor and powering up its weapons.

Jason had just enough time to yell for the team to take cover before the Pacesetter's plasma gun blasts tore through much of the forward fifth deck. Like the rest of the team, Wilson's HUD indicators revealed where friendlies were positioned versus enemy drones. When the firing stopped, the hover drones were nothing more than smoldering scrap metal on the deck.

"Nice shooting, Wilson. OK, you're now on continual rover duty. Help out the various teams as needed and take out any hover security drones you come across."

With that, Wilson was gone.

"Cap, behind this bulkhead and through that access hatch is the primary conduit to the bridge," Billy said, as he helped his men to their feet and reassembled his battered team.

Jason looked at his HUD. "There are eight left: four other SEALs and four rhino-warriors. And what about those ten other life forms I'm seeing?"

"Yeah, those are the…? What did you call them?"

"Serapins," Jason replied.

"Yeah, anyway, those raptor creatures are extremely fast. And they definitely work in teams. We made the mistake of underestimating their strategic capabilities on Deck 2 and lost half our team."

Jason didn't like the thought of going up against those creatures. But one thing was certain: without taking down the Battle Dreadnaught, they wouldn't stand a chance of defeating the remaining five hundred Craing warships.

"Let's position the rhino-warriors to charge first, and we'll bring up the rear," Jason said. Then, thinking better of it, he walked to the front of the team and looked up at each of the large beasts individually.

"This is it. The fate of our two worlds rests on this one battle. Without defeating the Serapins, without taking control of this vessel's bridge, today will be lost. I've seen you in battle. You fight with honor, bravery, and you never surrender. When we blow this hatch, we will be up against ten other formidable warriors. I'm asking you to fight like you've never fought before, and help us win this day."

Jason noticed then that Traveler was among the rhino-warriors. As Jason spoke, the others became more and more fidgety, shifting their weight side-to-side, anxious for combat to begin.

"Blow the hatch," Jason commanded.

The massive eight-foot-high by ten-foot-wide hatch exploded inward, fortunately decapitating the closest of the eight awaiting raptors. The rhinos-warriors rushed forward without hesitation. Under normal conditions, a ten-foot-wide corridor would be a decent size for a confined space battle. The rhino-warriors and Serapins were close in height and mass. They went for each other. Traveler's heavy hammer was already in the air and making its downward trajectory within seconds of entering the corridor. With the combined weight of the heavy hammer and the unbridled strength behind the blow, thousands of pounds of momentum crashed down on the closest Serapin's skull, first shattering the cranial bones, then flattening the creature's brain matter to the size of a standard pancake.

Another Serapin had its wide jaws tightly secured around a rhino-warrior's forearm. Bones cracked and the arm tore away with simplistic ease. But without losing a beat, the injured rhino-warrior let loose his hammer, much in the same way Traveler had done previously. Jason, Billy, and the other SEALs had their plasma pulse rifles aimed and ready. No one fired. Maybe it was instinctual, but Jason knew they needed to let the rhino-warrior play out his battle. Win or lose, they would fight to the death.

Two Serapins were attacking a single rhino-warrior; both had their jaws around its head. The rhino fought tirelessly, but in the end, his head came off in one of their mouths. Jason heard the sound of heavy hammers striking flesh further down the corridor. Two rhino-warriors were bludgeoning the last of the Serapins. The rhino-warriors had been victorious while never using their pulse weapons, ensuring an honorable and fair fight.

Standing amongst the carnage, Jason hailed the bridge for a status report.

"Go for XO."

"What's the status of The Lilly and our fighters?"

"Two of the fighters have returned to The Lilly for repairs. They are taking a beating, Cap. The Craing are now lying in wait for them with plasma cannons. The good news is we've disabled forty-two Craing warships."

"What about The Lilly?"

"They discovered us in their hold about ten minutes ago. They brought in numerous mobile plasma cannons and even a massive rail gun, but they couldn't penetrate our shields. And in return, we turned their guns to slag. So we're

OK here for now. We've been watching your helmet cams. Looks like you're ready to breech the bridge?"

"Yeah, I'll keep you posted," Jason replied.

"Wait a minute, Captain," the XO said, excitedly. "Something's happening out there in the hold. It's being depressurized and we're hearing something. Captain, Ricket tells me those are the hold retaining clamps being released. They're going to jettison the hold..."

The XO was cut off in mid-sentence. Jason noticed on his HUD, The Lilly was no longer aboard the Battle Dreadnaught. He changed the display to an outside virtual representation of the Battle Dreadnaught and its surrounding vessels. Then he noticed the small rectangular hold floating in open space. With the exception of the forty-two disabled Craing vessels and those that did not have a clear firing solution, the entire Craing fleet opened fire on the hold. Bright bolts of energy shot from hundreds of Craing warships. In mere seconds, the hold container flashed bright white and then disintegrated.

Chapter 21

He didn't really care if he died at that point. What he did care about was saving Earth and killing as many Craing as humanly possible. For now, his focus would remain on the mission. He couldn't allow himself to linger on the horrific thoughts pulling at his subconscious. They'd still be there later, waiting for him. Jason, Billy, three SEALs, and the two rhino-warriors continued down the corridor in silence. Another large hatch blocked their advancement to the bridge.

"Let's blow the hatch," Jason commanded, and watched as two SEALs placed the explosive charges. They all egressed back down the corridor. The hatch exploded and blew inward with a thunderous shockwave. Eleven hybrid combatants were waiting by the inside entrance to the bridge. The rhino-warriors stood aside. This time the SEALs would have the honor of engaging the enemy.

To Jason, the hybrids looked as human as his own SEAL team, even wearing their own version of hardened combat suits. They were already so close that this was going to be a hand-to-hand confrontation. Then he noticed that Billy and his four SEALs had slapped a long protruding rectangular patch right below their hipbones on their hardened combat suits. A thirteen-inch Ka-Bar knife snapped forward from a hidden, quick-release mechanism. Jason followed suit and accessed his own knife.

With pulse weapons held high, it became obvious the hybrids were not expecting close-quarters fighting; they were able to get off several bursts before they had to drop their weapons altogether and defend themselves.

Both Billy and Jason engaged their respective hybrid combatants with the exact same move at the exact same time—ducking low, while simultaneously spinning 180 degrees, and bringing their Ka-Bar knives up and under the hybrid's breast plates and into their hearts. But neither hybrid went down. Fleetingly, Jason remembered hybrid General Bickerdike from the Pentagon and his two hearts. Billy must have remembered the same thing, because he and Jason double- thrusted their weapons, also at the same time.

The other two SEALs began battling hybrids before the fallen two hit the deck. A sudden jolt of pain in Jason's upper left shoulder made the use of his left arm less effective. At least with energy weapons, if you survive the hit, the wound is cauterized and you won't bleed to death. The hybrids, even with better than two to one odds, didn't have the training or skills necessary to repel the SEAL onslaught. As with Jason's shoulder, others too suffered wounds, but none were fatal.

The bridge was large, but Jason had assumed it would be much grander or more impressive in some way, especially based on the total size of the Battle Dreadnaught. Craing crewmembers were situated in ten rows at flight control and other system consoles. They stopped what they were doing. Wide-eyed, they first looked from Jason's SEAL team, to the rhino-warriors, and then toward the aft section of the bridge where their officer's section was located.

The reflection from the gold medallion across the room made it easy. Jason pulled his plasma pulse sidearm and held it at his side as he strode across the bridge. All eyes followed his progress. Jason knew his men would be taking up parameter posts around the room. And it didn't really matter where the rhino-warriors went; it was no secret they had just defeated a pack of raptors. No one was going to screw with them. The four officers watched Jason approach. Their bronze, copper, silver and gold medallions hung from thick metal chains around their necks. He raised his sidearm and pointed point blank to the forehead of the small Craing officer wearing the gold medallion.

"Do you understand what I'm saying?" The officers nodded their heads.

The Craing captain flinched when Jason reached over and snatched the medallion from around his head and placed it around his own. "Do you know what this means?" Jason asked. The small alien nodded resignedly. "Do what I ask, and you will all live." The remaining officers said nothing. "You have ten seconds to start firing on your fleet. If I don't see Craing warships blowing apart soon after that, you will all die. It's you're choice."

Jason watched the captain's expression and realized he may have misjudged him. The captain was one of the few Craing he'd come across who seemed to have a backbone. His eyes were unwavering, almost calm. But the first officer, silver medallioned, moved his eyes back and forth and he was taking short quick breaths. Jason took a step back and looked around the bridge for Traveler. He was pacing at the far end of the bridge. Jason signaled him to come forward and they spoke in low tones until the large warrior nodded his massive head and headed back down the corridor. Less than a minute later, Traveler was back dragging a Serapin carcass, leaving a smeared trail of red blood. Traveler unceremoniously dropped the carcass at the Craing captain's feet. It was the carcass Traveler had used his heavy hammer on to flatten its head.

"If you have any doubts as to what will happen to you, look on the floor in front of you," Jason said in a flat steely voice.

"I cannot do as you ask," the Craing captain said, still showing not the slightest fear.

He shot the captain where he stood, between the eyes.

"Please do not harm us," the Craing first officer said, to his fellow officers' obvious relief.

"What is your name?"

"I am First Officer Calter."

"Okay, First Officer Calter, you now have

five seconds," Jason responded, raising his gun again.

The officer yelled something in Terplin directly to the crewmembers at the closest consoles. All heads turned in his direction and there was an audible intake of breath and shock on their faces. But there was no movement. Jason walked over to the Craing sitting at the end of the console, raised his weapon and held it to his temple.

"Tell them they will follow my orders or end up on the floor with the others."

But there was no need; the crew was now busy doing what was asked of them. Several large overhead monitors displayed fleet logistics. One of the nearby Craing cruisers flashed white and disappeared.

"The rest of your fleet now considers you a combatant; I suggest you utilize this vessel's defenses to its full advantage."

The first officer barked off more orders, scurrying back and forth between consoles. He then stopped and looked at Jason. "Even a Battle Dreadnaught cannot defeat five hundred warships," he said, fear in his voice.

"Well, it's probably closer to four hundred and fifty, and if you're right, we'll find out soon enough," Jason replied.

The battle raged on in open space. The Dreadnought continued to systematically concentrate a massive amount of combined energy from hundreds of separate plasma cannons toward single targets, just as the Craing fleet had used their combined resources to destroy The Lilly. It was clear that the Battle Dreadnaught was taking a devastating pounding as well. The occasional vibration on the bridge had turned to persistent, almost earthquake level shaking, making it impossible to stand without holding on to something solid, such as a console or bulkhead. The fleet repositioned their newer destroyer-type warships, which not only had the standard complement of plasma cannon weapons, but four turret-mounted rail guns as well. The death toll grew into the multi-thousands on both sides, as the three hundred or so remaining warships barreled down on the less and less effective Battle Dreadnaught. Half of its plasma cannons had become disabled, and large chunks of its outer hull had fractured off into space, a result of the destroyer's powerful rail guns. Jason realized it wasn't just Craing being slaughtered here, which was the price of war, but thousands of innocent beings held in their confinement cages.

* * *

Eight of the fifteen drop teams eventually called in, but there was no word from the shuttles, or from the three fighters, including Williams and the Pacesetter. They had returned to The Lilly and had met their fate. Not having The Lilly to handle logistics was initially a problem, but Jason had taken on the bulk of those functions himself, to the best of his ability, and issued orders directly to team leaders as needed. Systematically, they cleared the vessel.

The security hover drones had continued to be a problem, but once the bridge was secured, they had been deactivated. Remaining roving packs of Serapins were still a problem and Jason's crew stayed on the lookout. It was clear enough: the Craing never expected any of their vessels to be vulnerable to infiltration. That alone had allowed Jason to get as far as he had. But now, without The Lilly, Jason and his team knew they were fighting in vain. Eventually, the Battle Dreadnaught would fall and the surviving Craing fleet would simply continue on toward Earth.

Pacing back and forth on the Craing bridge, Jason continued to see the writing on the wall. He needed to try something else. The Craing first officer was seated at a console several rows back. He was shaking, and tears streamed down his large triangular face. Not everyone was officer material. If you're weak, pressure will snap you like a dry twig.

"First Officer Calter, I need you to target the destroyers first, before the other warships. They're causing too much damage. Do you understand?" Jason asked. "Also, fire at three vessels at a time instead of just one."

First Officer Calter didn't move and had apparently gone into shock. Billy, frustrated, stood at Jason's side, looking down at the Craing officer.

"Seriously?" said Billy

A moment later Traveler joined them, his heavy hammer poised. Which triggered something, because the first officer was back on his feet and barking orders to the Craing bridge crew again.

That worked, to some degree. The destroyers were being eliminated three at a time. But only a third of the command ship's plasma cannons were still operational, and substantial areas of the Dreadnaught were breaking off from the ship and floating free into space.

Jason first thought it was his imagination, but he quickly realized the fleet's bombardment had substantially decreased. He no longer had the need to grab hold of anything to keep upright. Then he realized why: multiple small crafts had been deployed and were heading for the Dreadnaught.

"Boarding teams," Billy said, over their comms.

Jason simply nodded, but it didn't make any sense. Why bother? The Dreadnaught was starting to break apart, had mere moments left. Why not just finish her off? And then he had the answer: there was something or someone onboard they wanted to save.

Chapter 22

Two of the SEAL teams were brought in to hold the bridge, while Jason, Billy, and the rest of their existing teammates headed off toward something called the Craing Grand Sacellum, some kind of shrine or sanctuary. Battle Dreadnaughts came equipped with ultra-fast hover train systems that connected throughout the ship. Made sense; it would be impossible to walk the distances necessary to get anywhere.

As he stood looking out the train car's large window, with a blur of colors and shapes streaking by, Jason almost let himself crack open that door where the pain could squeeze through and overpower his consciousness with their devastating loss. The train was slowing and, according to the nervous Craing first officer, they were to get off at the first stop. Surprisingly, there were very few Craing out and about. No doubt, they were hiding within their living compartments and cabins. The train was constructed with smaller inhabitants in mind, yet they'd managed to squeeze into the compartment with less than an inch or two of headroom to spare. The two rhino-warriors were uncomfortably hunched over nearly in half, impatiently awaiting the train's destination. Soon after leaving the Dreadnaught's bridge, communications with their fellow team members became impossible.

The Craing Grand Sacellum was not dissimilar to a large church or mosque back on Earth, although the Craing were unique in how they integrated their diet and meal consumption with their religious precepts. Eating was not solely for the sake of nourishment. Apparently, the Craing required fresh meat, preferably from those most recently conquered. Where Earth's slogan was from farm to table, the Craing version was from cage to table.

The automatic doors slid open and Jason and his team exited the train car onto an open concourse. Not more than half a mile distance away, hundreds of Craing hybrids had arrived via transport ships and were now breaking into small combat units. Soon, several groups would attempt to retake their bridge; others would be headed to extinguish Jason's team.

The dreadful alarm sound was louder here. They knew they had found the right place; it was like no other they'd seen on the Dreadnaught. More like a palace than a place of worship—all gold, with tall spires and elaborately carved panels depicting scenes of Craing and the Serapin-Terplins, as well as carvings of Craing with tall, cone-shaped headdresses. Characteristic of an early 20th century factory, dark, sooty smoke billowed from stubby chimneys at each of the distant two back corners of the edifice. The thought that initially crossed Jason's mind as they made their way through the massive double doors was for such small-statured people they sure liked to build structures on a colossal scale.

The elaborate building held nothing more than a huge feeding area inside. Typical of the other Craing ships, the room stretched several hundred yards in each direction. There were countless stone, donut-like tables. At their centers, dancing amber light emanated from fiery caldrons, and, similar to other Craing vessels, the rear of the Sacellum had direct access to the confinement cages. The screeching sounds from a pair of Serapins patrolling the above catwalks echoed off the gilded paneled walls. Thinking back to the tall spires viewed from the outside, Jason knew there had to be an access point to the Grand Sacellum's upper floors.

"Here we go, Cap," Billy said on their comms. "Over here, stairs seem to lead to upper levels."

The winding staircase was a tight fit for the rhino-warriors. The second floor was a bust, so they cleared it and continued on up the winding staircase. They hit pay dirt on the third floor. This was the same backdrop Jason had noticed behind the high priest earlier on. The room was not large, almost intimate in size and circular with more carved gold panels. Ten high priests, unarmed, in ridiculous cone-shaped headdresses, were kneeling before a gold Serapin statue. It stood on a marble pedestal; its outstretched muscular arms held a large fiery caldron over its head.

Jason wasted no time and headed directly

towards the center of the group and for High Priest Overlord Lom in his green robes. With one quick movement, the priest's neck was solidly in Jason's firm grip. Slowly, Jason lifted the small Craing off his feet, forcing him to hang several feet in the air.

"You murdering cowards. I'm going to enjoy squeezing the life out of each and every one of you," Jason threatened, bringing the Craing's face close to his own and watching Lom's terrified expression as Jason tightened his grip.

"Perhaps you will listen to reason, before you snap poor Lom's fragile neck, Captain Reynolds," came another voice near by. Startled, Jason almost did exactly that. Instead, he let the high priest fall to the floor in a whimpering heap. At first, he thought he was staring into the face of Ricket, with its similar moving gears, pistons and actuators behind near transparent skin. From behind, the emperor looked nearly identical to the other priests, but under closer inspection there were clear differences. His cream-colored robes were more intricately woven; his headdress was square rather than cylindrical, and shorter.

"I am Emperor Quorp. Yes, I have undergone the transformation of eternity. This is the same process Emperor Reechet underwent over two hundred years ago. Harming us will do you no good. My lineage is long and succession is a simple matter. Understand, tens of thousands of Craing warships reach to the far corners of the galaxy. We have proven, time and time again, that we are the chosen people. Please understand there is no malice, no hatred. We respect and honor those that serve the Craing Empire," the emperor said, in a calm, deliberate voice.

Jason caught Traveler's attention. Just as he'd grabbed Lom moments before, Jason now did the same with the little emperor. All nine of the other priests inhaled in shocked unison. From previous experience, Jason knew the emperor would be nearly indestructible. With a metallic clunk, Jason slammed Quorp's triangular-shaped head down onto the statue's solid marble pedestal. Realization set in as two orange orbs looked up at Jason, first confused, then terrified. Jason barely had time to move his hands away before the rhino-warrior's heavy hammer, with thousands of pounds of pressure behind it, slammed down onto its mechanized skull. It took several blows before the emperor ceased to exist. It may not have accomplished much, but Jason, Traveler and the rest of the team nodded their heads in silent approval.

Billy bent over the crumpled emperor's body, and said, "Vete a la mierda."

They made their return to the main open area of the Grand Sacellum. Back in the main feeding area, Jason's HUD indicated that close to a hundred hybrid combatants were making their way onto the concourse outside the two enormous entrance doors. It was just a subtle nod, but Jason and his team, one by one, acknowledged each other.

Taking in the room again, Jason figured this would be as good a place as any to make their last stand. The men double-checked their weapons' charge levels. The two rhino-warriors began their characteristic shifting of weight back and forth. Jason got Traveler's attention and signaled for him to follow. At the front of the Sacellum, Jason looked around. He tried lifting up one of the large solid-rock tables closest to the door on its side. It wouldn't budge. Traveler understood and hefted a close-by table onto its side with relative ease, which in turn knocked its center caldron to the floor, sending a blaze of sparks and hot coals skittering about. The caldron's big metal grill continued to roll around, while flakes of charred meat and flesh fell out. With a loud clang the grill finally came to rest near the front doors. Nodding his appreciation, Jason signaled for the other rhino-warrior, Silent Hunter, to help flip more tables, creating a major obstruction into the room. The team repeated the process with tables at the very back of the Sacellum. Here is where they would make their last stand, Jason thought to himself. The big rock donuts would be perfect cover.

There was knocking at the front door.

"What are they going to do, ask to come in before shooting us?" Billy asked, looking over to Jason.

With a shrug Jason made his way back up to the Grand Sacellum's front doors, a difficult passage with the upturned tables and still glowing hot coals strewn about. While the remaining four SEALs took up positions behind back tables, both Traveler and Billy accompanied Jason.

According to his HUD, several hundred hybrids had taken up positions around the concourse outside. But the one standing on the other side of the door was not only being read as human, but also United Planetary Alliance personnel. Jason looked to Traveler and Billy—both gestured for him to open it. Jason cracked open the door and peered outside. Nothing could have prepared him for what he saw, not in a million years.

Chapter 23

The last time Jason saw his brother was close to seven years. That was before Brian had been reported killed in a friendly fire incident in Iraq. He'd attended his brother's full-honors military funeral—visited Brian's grave at Arlington National Cemetery on two occasions. Now his brother, if this was his brother, stood before him wearing a standard spacer's jumpsuit and looking no worse for wear.

"Hi, Jason," Brian said.

Jason didn't respond at first, only stared into his older brother's face. He felt the anger rise in him. He'd grieved for his brother. And here he was, standing in this doorway and acting as if none of that had mattered. Jason nudged the door open with his left foot, while simultaneously letting loose his right fist towards his brother's smiling face. The blow hit Brian below his eye, sending him sprawling to the ground.

"I guess I deserved that," Brian said, rubbing his cheek. "But you only get one. Next time, I'll kick your ass."

Jason assessed his brother, who was slowly getting to his feet. He'd be thirty-eight now and there were a few grey hairs at his temples. "When we were young kids, I was about six, you were eight, I stole something from your room. Something important," Jason said.

"You stole my G.I. Joe. And up until now, you'd never admitted it, you shit," Brian said, with a friendly scowl.

It was his brother Brian. But how, Jason wondered to himself? He stepped aside and let his brother pass through. Out on the concourse, a small craft sat with its gangway lowered.

They found one of the few unturned tables and sat across from each other. Jason had removed his helmet and waited for his brother to say something.

"Sorry about the whole charade, having to attend my funeral and all. I guess seeing me here, still alive, brings up a few questions."

"You think?"

"I'd always suspected something was fishy about Dad's disappearance, or so-called death. So when he contacted me, I wasn't completely surprised. Although when he told me he was fighting aliens thousands of light years from Earth, well, that did shock me. His intention was to bring you along as well. The Alliance needed officers, and Dad needed people he could trust."

"So what happened, Brian? Why the hell are you here? Why are you with the Craing?" Jason asked, clearly disappointed.

"I'm what you'd call an emissary. I negotiate with other humanoids on their behalf. But to back things up a little, I was captured by the Craing two years after I'd joined the Alliance. I'd been through HyperLearning on The Lilly, trained as a space-fighter pilot and was eventually given a small battle cruiser to command. Two months later, a Craing warship stumbled upon our small fleet and obliterated it. I spent months in one of those confinement cages. As far as I know, I was the only survivor."

Jason looked over the dancing flames of the caldron at the center of the table and raised his eyebrows. "What kept you from being barbecued like everyone else?"

"I think it was my big mouth." Brian hesitated before continuing, as if looking for just the right words to say. "Let me be perfectly clear here, right from the get-go, Jason. I'm not a traitor to the Alliance, and especially not to Earth. Dad might not see it that way, but I'll let you decide. Fair?"

Billy, standing near by, gestured to his helmet. Jason held a finger up for his brother to hold on for a second. With his helmet back on and able to see his HUD again, Jason could see that additional contacts, mostly hybrids, had taken up positions across the catwalks at their backs. They were now flanked from both sides.

"Go ahead, Brian, tell me how you're not a traitor to your planet and family."

"I'm not. In fact, just the opposite. Do you think it's an accident the Craing have stayed away from Earth these last few years? Not only did they want to infiltrate earlier, they planned to make Earth their seat of power. To them, Earth is the jewel of the galaxy. I can't tell you how many times I've manipulated them to divert their fleet elsewhere, gone so far as to instigate wars hundreds of light-years away in distant sectors."

Jason shook his head, not seeing it. "Why haven't you escaped, gone back to the Alliance or even Earth?"

"As a Craing emissary to a humanoid race on another planet, one similar to Earth, I fell in love. She was my counterpart; she was negotiating for the survival of her people. She came to realize that I was working on her behalf far more than for the Craing. Although the natural resources of her world have been plundered ruthlessly, the people there have gone untouched. I live on this planet, Jason. She's now my wife, we have two kids." Brian looked at Jason and shrugged, almost apologetically.

"And let me guess, the Craing use that as constant leverage to keep you as their emissary?" Jason asked. Brian simply shrugged again, seemingly resigned to how things were.

"So what do you want from me, Brian?"

"I want to keep you alive, Jason. I want to continue to protect Earth. And I can do that if you let me. Let me do what I'm good at. I have the emperor's ear."

"So you don't know," Jason said, more of a statement than a question.

"Know what?"

"The Craing destroyed The Lilly, with Mollie, Nan, and Dad onboard. I've lost everything I care about. What could you possibly offer me now?"

Brian's mouth fell open. It was a while

before he spoke again. "I'm so sorry, Jason, I didn't know."

"Oh, and I wouldn't put too much faith in the emperor's ear thing, The high point of my day was watching Traveler here use his heavy hammer to flatten his ugly skull."

"He's here, onboard now?"

"What's left of him," Jason said, nodding his head.

"I knew he was with the fleet, but I had no idea he was here. Jason, you have no idea what you've done. What you've done to Earth."

"I did what you should have done the first time you were in the emperor's presence," Jason replied, "and by the way, Earth's their next stop."

Brian got up and turned to leave, then turned back to his brother. "I'm sorry, truly I am. But there is nothing I'll be able to do for you now." With that, Brian turned and left through the Grand Sacellum's front doors.

How could he? Even indirectly helping the Craing was unthinkable. Jason felt sick at the thought of his brother continuing to do the Craing's bidding.

"I'm not going to sit here and wait for them to come through the front doors. What do you say we cause some trouble?" He got up, checked his weapon's charge level, and headed for the rear of the Grand Sacellum.

* * *

He counted about one hundred hybrid contacts strategically positioned on the lower level catwalks—presumably with their pulse weapon sites trained down on anything on the move into the open courtyard below—cutting off access to any of the eight lifts. At first it looked hopeless, no way out. But under closer scrutiny the lift shafts did have heavy metal-sided bulkheads, and the lifts themselves seemed to be fairly well-shielded from the hybrids.

"Traveler, Silent Hunter, we need to get onto the lifts without getting ourselves killed." He scurried over to several overturned tables. "Can you break off all but one of those table legs?" Jason asked, pointing to the solid rock, twelve-foot diameter tabletop. Traveler grunted, and the two of them put their heavy hammers to use until a single table leg protruded from the back of the table.

"Perfect, now let's do the same thing with the other table," Jason said, seeing a rough, though ludicrous, plan come together in his mind. With a rhino-warrior positioned behind each table, along with three SEALs, the warriors lifted the tables onto their rims. Using the table leg as a lever, together they began to roll the tables forward in the direction of the courtyard. With the two teams huddled behind both tables, they slowly made their way out into the open.

Plasma fire erupted from above but couldn't penetrate the solid rock tabletops. Jason was the first to trip and almost got himself killed when he momentarily fell beyond the table's protection. But once they'd all gotten into the rhythm of jumping over the table leg as it came around, things started to go a bit smoother. Staying clear of the open cutout was also tricky, and if it weren't for their hardened combat suits, several legs may have been blown off. Jason's group made it to the first lift. The second team had another few moments of rolling to do.

Jason heard Billy, who was part of the second team, spew a string of derogatory comments over the comms, something about all the crazy shit Jason comes up with. Once in front of the lift, their next problem was keeping the table upright. It took a few tries before the rhino-warriors simply spun the table in place and the leg was back at the bottom, providing enough coverage while everyone ducked into the lift. Jason turned the mechanical lever for the lift to move upward. According to his HUD, the top decks were clear of combatants. Plasma fire continued to pound the lift's heavy metal doors as they progressed past the lower decks. At Deck 8, Jason stopped the lift and opened the doors. He checked his HUD, and then peeked out. It seemed clear, but the hybrids were already clambering into the other lifts below.

"Can you disable those lifts before they reach us?" Jason asked, looking over to Traveler and Silent Hunter. Without answering, they headed off down the catwalk, heavy hammers raised high. Looking out at the wide-open corridor, Jason realized he was back where he had started. His father's cage had been somewhere close to this same spot. Dark smoke rose in the distance. Billy and the other team joined Jason on the catwalk.

Jason tried to reach the two SEAL teams holding the bridge again without any luck. Behind them were the thousands of Deck 8 confinement cages that stretched miles into the distance. He avoided looking into the cages. Mealtime preparation for the Craing had come and gone and only partial body parts remained. The catwalk deck plating shook in accordance to Traveler's and Silent Hunter's heavy hammers going to work on the lift mechanisms, bending guide rails, smashing pulleys, and dislodging cables. At least for the time being, they wouldn't be dodging plasma pulses. Their relief was short-lived though. Three Serapins were headed their way from the other end of the catwalk. Their approach should have been indicated earlier; something was wrong with his HUD.

According to his readings, the rapidly approaching icons were just the tip of the iceberg; at least ten more were headed their way. The catwalk was wide enough for Jason, Billy and the other four men to stand side-by-side. With weapons raised, they waited for the raptor-like beasts to come close enough to target accurately. At fifty yards, they opened up on them. Short bursts had little or no effect; only combined sustained plasma blasts from multiple weapons had any real effect. The fallen Serapins were quickly trampled. At ten yards out, Jason's team walked backwards as they fired. Three Serapins lay dead on the catwalk—ten remained.

At this near-distance, the beasts pace had slowed some. Smoldering black burn marks covered their bodies. Ever determined, they trudged forward, their large jaws snapping with anticipation. At five yards, Jason and the others dropped their rifles and accessed their Ka-Bars. Mallory, the SEAL to Jason's left, was the first to die with most of his upper torso disappearing into a Serapin's mouth. As its jaws gnashed and tore at the still-kicking SEAL, Jason brought his Ka-Bar down onto the Serapin's skull, killing it instantly. With hands slick with blood, Jason found it nearly impossible to get a solid grip on the hilt of his knife. Jason and Billy continued to fight on, side by side, just as they had done countless times before. But now, exhaustion had set in. Jason realized this would be their final battle.

Together they would die here fighting the Serapin. As the realization set in, he was perfectly fine with that. That is, until both he and Billy were picked up and thrown several yards backward. Hammers raised, and this time hand-held plasma weapons firing, Traveler and Silent Hunter engaged the Serapins. Another SEAL had gone down in the meantime. Billy, still sitting on his ass, looked over to Jason.

"So we do all the work and they barge in

and take all the credit. I see how it works." In the end, the Serapins would be defeated, but not before Silent Hunter lost most of his horn and Traveler an ear.

"Billy, have you been able to contact the bridge teams—or any of the teams, for that matter?" Jason asked

"Not since the train. HUD's acting weird too," Billy said. He'd removed his helmet and wiped the sweat from his face. "What's our next move, Cap?"

Jason took in the scene around him. They'd all taken off their helmets and were leaning up against the confinement cages behind them. The two rhino-warriors, Petty Officer Rizzo, Billy, and Jason stared across several hundred yards to other decks and identical confinement cages. There had been constant movement over there, just two levels down, but no one noticed.

Perhaps it was exhaustion, but when Petty Officer Rizzo's shoulder gushed red in a bright flash, and plasma bolts erupted all around them, there was no place to hide or run to, or anything to take cover behind. If it hadn't been for their hardened combat suits, they would have been killed in seconds.

Jason and the others scrambled to replace their helmets and reach for their side arms. Their plasma rifles were back down the catwalk where they'd dropped them. The assault was nothing short of a long distance firing squad. The two rhino-warriors were back on their feet.

"We will face this last battle with honor,

not on our ass," Traveler bellowed, while firing his hand-held plasma weapon across the corridor. Jason, Billy, and injured Rizzo got to their feet and stood with the rhino-warriors, firing until their weapons grew hot in their hands. Increasing black scorch marks erupted on the front of their suits. Jason took a direct hit to his helmet—a horizontal crack splintered across his visor. Rizzo went down first, followed shortly afterwards by Billy. And then there was nothing but black.

Chapter 24

The Lilly had shifted back, and was now positioned right in front of them. Billy stirred, looked up, and grumbled in Spanish, "¿Qué coño?"

Jason sat down next to his friend, took off his ruined helmet, and watched as the flight deck doors began to open. The Lilly's forward and aft pulse cannon snapped into place and quickly dispatched a maelstrom of plasma fire onto the Craing and Craing hybrids on the opposite lower decks. Within seconds, the guns were secured back inside The Lilly's hull. Only now would he let his thoughts go there, to the realization of what he'd almost lost, and now, inexplicably, had regained. His thoughts turned to Mollie, Nan, and his father. And then to Dira.

* * *

As soon as Jason was back onboard, he ordered The Lilly to shift further down the corridor, closer to the Dreadnaught's bridge, and pick up the remaining SEAL teams and rhino-warriors. Their fighters and two shuttles were now onboard as well. Billy and Rizzo were rushed to Medical. Traveler and Silent Hunter were too large for the MediPods, but preferred, anyway, to return to their natural habitat in the Zoo, where they could have their wounds attended to by their own kind.

Jason wanted The Lilly away from this damn Dreadnaught as soon as possible. Although tempted to stop off and see Mollie and Nan, there was still a formidable battle ahead. He went directly to the bridge, half expecting to see the admiral sitting in the command chair, but he was not on the bridge. Taking his seat, Jason studied the virtual representation of the Craing fleet; he realized it was substantially reduced in size—much smaller than it had been.

"Status report," Jason requested, looking over to his XO. "How the hell did you survive the destruction of that hold?"

"Welcome back, Captain," Lieutenant Commander Perkins replied. "When the hold was jettisoned we immediately phase-shifted— fortunately, we'd previously set the emergency default coordinates for the three mile limitation."

"Where did you go?"

"It was an arbitrary shift and we ended up on top of another Craing Cruiser. We basically cut her in half. We'd sustained damage prior to phase-shifting, and we were dead in space. All systems were offline: gravity generators, environmental, drives, helm control, everything. Ricket went to work getting the AI online first; then, one by one, we brought the other systems back online. We phase-shifted several more times into the holds of several more Craing ships. That's when we scanned the Dreadnaught for your position and shifted back."

"Well, not a second too soon. Thank you for saving our bacon. So how many Craing vessels remain?"

"About two hundred and fifty. The Battle Dreadnaught and the rest of its fleet went after one another for quite sometime. We assumed that was your doing. We thoroughly enjoyed the show."

Jason looked around the bridge. McBride was at the helm, but Orion and Ricket were not at their stations. Perkins must have read his expression. "Ricket and Gunny have something they want to show you up on sub-Deck 4B."

Jason took note of the time on the bridge clock. "We'll need to maintain control of this Dreadnaught for a minimum of twelve more hours. I want you to rotate a combination of SEAL and rhino-warrior teams on patrol, and any area near their bridge. Also, let's maintain aerial sorties up and down the main corridor. Hang here for the time being with our shields up. Put a plasma bolt into anything that moves," Jason said as he headed out of the bridge.

On the way, he stopped off at Medical just as Billy was climbing out of a MediPod. Jason surmised Rizzo was still in another MediPod; his injuries had been critical. Billy looked up as Jason entered.

"Have a nice nap?" Jason asked, smiling. But before Billy could answer, Dira entered from the adjoining room. Startled, her surprised, wide-eyed expression quickly turned to one of relief, and something else?

"Captain, good to see you're back," she said. He felt the warmth of her hand on his arm, her eyes momentarily locked on his, and then she brushed past to remove a small bandage from Billy's forehead. He'd never noticed her eyes were violet-blue with small violet and amber speckles.

"Thank you. How's Rizzo doing? Will he make it?"

"He'll be fine; needs to take it easy for a while. And you should too," she said to Billy as he got up out of his MediPod. Smirking, Billy eyed the two of them, and then stood up. Jason scowled and said, "What?"

"Nothing, I didn't say anything."

* * *

He'd reached sub-Deck 4B with its large school bus-sized phase synthesizer unit. Standing at a nearby display, Ricket and Orion were in the midst of a heated discussion that was cut short with Jason's arrival.

"Welcome back, Captain," Orion said with a smile. Ricket simply nodded his head, the bill of his Dodger's cap waving up and down.

"Gunny!" Jason acknowledged her, "and Ricket, or do you prefer Emperor?" he asked with a chuckle. "What's all the commotion about in here?"

Orion and Ricket looked at one another. "Well, are you going to tell him or should I?" Orion asked. Ricket walked over to an output bin-hopper at the side of the phase synthesizer, picked up several items, and returned.

"Captain, here is the integrated fusion power plant we recently incorporated into our fighters, allowing them to phase-shift as The Lilly does." Ricket handed Jason a metallic cylindrical object about the size of a standard shoebox. Jason flipped the object over in his hands several times. Very similar to the devices he'd seen in old Gus's tool shed.

"Heavy for its size," he said. Ricket took back the device and handed Jason a different one about the size of a standard compact disk, although several inches thick.

Ricket said, "And this one is our latest version. Almost equal-power distribution and a fraction of the size and weight." Orion and Ricket didn't say anything else, just stared back at him, waiting for Jason to connect the dots. Then he had it.

"By any chance, is this small enough to fit within the substructure of a missile?" They both nodded.

"How long would it take to integrate this, along with the phase-shift circuitry, to where it's operational?"

"That's what we were discussing when you arrived. The missile has to stop firing its thruster just prior to hitting a ship's shields, then phase-shift to a designated target, and detonate."

"Yeah? So what's the problem? Can we do that?" Jason asked, excited.

"We think so. We've come up with a

prototype that we need to test," Orion said, looking down at Ricket and shrugging.

"If it works, how long before you can integrate it into the JIT munitions, like any other missile?"

"It would be instantaneous. In fact, they are already constructed by the multiverse," Ricket said. Just then explosions reverberated in the distance. Jason steadied himself as The Lilly shook violently.

* * *

Ricket needed another hour to fine-tune his design before it would be ready to test. Jason walked through the final DeckPort to Level Four and headed for the officer's cabins, stopping in front of Nan and Mollie's cabin. Seconds later, the hatch disappeared. Admiral Perry Reynolds, with Mollie up on his shoulders, was there to greet him.

"Look who we have here," Admiral Reynolds said.

"Dad!" Mollie's smile lit up and then turned to a scowl. "Did you know we were almost killed? Set me down, Grandpa, I've got a bone to pick with the Captain here." Jason put on as serious a face as he could muster up, and crashed down on a nearby couch.

"Why do you keep running off? You know the lights went out and we started floating around." Mollie was providing visuals with her story, holding her arms out straight and moving in slow motion.

"Well, someone had to go and fight the Serapins."

"You fought Serapins, like the ones in the Zoo?"

"The ones in the Zoo are kittens compared to the ones I fought."

"Holy crap! Okay, I guess you're forgiven."

"Watch your mouth, Mollie," came a voice from the back bedroom.

Jason looked over to his father. His hair had been gelled and spiked. "Looks like Mollie has you ready to join a boy band."

"What's a boy band?" his father asked from the other end of the couch.

"We have an emergency officers' meeting in one hour. We're getting ready to finish off the rest of the Craing fleet. Want to join us?"

"Two days ago I wouldn't have thought that possible. Now, I'm not so sure. I wouldn't miss it," his father said, while Mollie proceeded to apply a generous amount of lipstick to the admiral's lips. Feeling the ship shake again, and hearing the distant explosions, Jason wondered if they were simply ignoring the Craing missile strikes, or had just gotten used to them. The Dreadnaught was immense, but sooner or later, the inner compartments would breech.

Not sure if he'd have energy enough to stand up, Jason slowly got to his feet. He went back down the hallway to where he'd heard her voice earlier. Nan was sitting on her bed, a paperback in front of her nose. "Are you hiding back here?" he asked.

"I don't know which one is more juvenile, the eight-year-old or the sixty-year-old," she said, lowering her book. She caught Jason's eyes lingering again, this time on her chest. She didn't scold him. Instead, she placed the paperback down on to the bed, rose up on her knees and gestured for him to move closer. She kissed him long and tender, like he hadn't been kissed for a long time. When she pulled away, she continued to look into his eyes. "Welcome home, sailor." Nan fell back down on the bed smiling, and reached for her paperback.

Chapter 25

One more attendee had joined the emergency officers' meeting so everyone had to cram together around the conference table. Jason insisted Admiral Reynolds take the head of the table. The plan was simple: find a way to defeat the Craing fleet, at least those 250 Craing warships surrounding the crippled Battle Dreadnaught.

"Okay everyone, we'll have to keep this meeting short. Soon we'll be engaging the enemy one more time. As the admiral will attest to, the Craing shields are virtually impenetrable. Their fleets have gone unchallenged for hundreds of years. What we accomplished yesterday was a first. Two hundred and eighty Craing vessels have been destroyed. Their emperor has been killed. They are in disarray, so we need to act quickly and decisively."

"Why not continue doing what worked previously?" the admiral asked.

"Unfortunately, we won't be able to use the same tactics that have gotten us this far. The Dreadnaught is basically drifting dead in space with no weapons to speak of. Phase-shifting in and out of holds of their warships is no longer a viable solution. They are expecting something along those lines again, and after what happened to The Lilly yesterday, I don't want to chance it."

The admiral asked, confused, "What other options do we have? You can't possibly think we can go toe to toe with that fleet? They'll destroy The Lilly within minutes, then continue on to take their revenge on Earth."

"We have a few ideas—Ricket and Orion will run us though the technical aspects."

* * *

"I still don't see how you're going to avoid what happened yesterday. Two hundred and fifty warships targeted, it's ludicrous," the admiral said, sitting by Jason's side at the back of the bridge.

"I agree, that would be ludicrous on our part," Jason replied. "Watch the display. You'll see that we're only engaging fifty to seventy Craing vessels at any one time."

"Gunny, prepare all tubes for fusion-tipped missile loads. XO, have our fighters powered up and ready to go on the flight deck. Prepare to phase-shift to open space to specified coordinates. Remember, I want our ass right up against the hull of this Dreadnaught. Shift," Jason commanded.

The Lilly shuddered and materialized within five hundred feet of the external hull of the cube-shaped Battle Dreadnaught. All eyes were on the overhead virtual display.

"Well, son of a bitch!" the admiral exclaimed. "You're using the Dreadnaught as a shield—most of the Craing warships can't even see us. Not to mention get a clear firing solution."

Jason kept his attention on the display. "Gunny, I want their drives and shield-generators targeted first, weapons are secondary."

"One moment, Captain, The Lilly's still acquiring targets," the Gunny said, excitedly.

"Captain, were taking fire from twenty vessels, thirty, forty... Shields down to 95%."

"Targeting complete, Captain," Orion yelled.

"Fire all tubes," Jason ordered, stealing a look at Ricket. Everything came down to whether or not his missile loads worked.

"First round missiles away, JIT reloads in progress. Second round missiles away, reloading, and third round missiles away."

The admiral was on his feet now, standing at Jason's side. Three formations of bright yellow icons moved out from The Lilly. Individual missiles separated to follow their own targeting vectors. The closest Craing warship was a destroyer; two missiles were closing in on their target.

"Shields down to 90%, sir," the XO reported.

"Missiles within ten miles of target," said the XO. Then the two yellow icons disappeared off the display. "Both missiles have been destroyed, captain." The next vessel, a battle cruiser, also destroyed the incoming missiles.

"Crap!" yelled the admiral.

"Shields down to—"

Jason cut off the XO. "Just let me know

when they're down to 80%."

"Gunny, can you shift those missiles any earlier—they're targeting them faster than we anticipated." Orion looked over to Ricket, who jumped off his chair and was at her station, fingers moving, entering commands at lighting speed. When finished, he turned and nodded toward Jason.

"Our remaining missile formations were all destroyed. Let's try this again, Gunny. Three more sets with adjusted shift parameters; fire when ready," Jason commanded.

"First round, second round, third round missiles all away, Captain."

"Helm, go ahead and phase-shift us to our second coordinates. Gunny, acquire the new targets."

The latest round of missiles moved toward their assigned targets. This time they disappeared from the display substantially earlier. Jason expected to hear they'd been destroyed, but no one spoke.

"Direct hits, sir. Two battle cruisers and one destroyer. They're dead in the water."

Jason felt the weight of his father's hand on his shoulder as they both watched the display. The remaining missiles shifted and too found their targets. "Forty-five warships have been disabled, sir. We'll need to phase-shift back there again for the remaining five." The admiral was pumping his fist in the air now. "Yes!"

"We're not home free yet, Pops," Jason said, but found it hard to keep the smile off his face. "XO, go ahead and phase-shift our active fighters into the holds of those disabled ships. We need their weapons systems taken out."

"Sir, shields just dropped to 70%."

"Next batch of missiles are away, sir. And there's ten percent more Craing vessels on this side. We need four sets."

As before, the missile formations headed off in groups, but quickly broke off according to their individual targeting parameters. One by one the missiles vanished from the display. The bridge went quiet in anticipation.

"All sixty-two Craing warships have been disabled, sir."

Perkins looked over his shoulder toward Jason. "Shields substantially down, sir, 40%."

"Gunny, can Lilly preconfigure the targeting for both the third and fourth shifts ahead of time?"

"Already ahead of you, Cap, but their ships are changing positions. They've figured out what we're doing. But Lilly's tracking them, we're good."

"Helm, make the third shift," Jason commanded again. The next volley of missiles were immediately deployed, again with four batches. "And now make the fourth shift, Helm. Gunny, same thing. Deploy your missiles."

Jason noticed Perkins was getting fidgety in his seat. "Shields down to twenty percent, Captain. And forward shields could go down any time."

"Helm, put us back inside the Dreadnaught.

Phase-shift us out of here."

"Power reserves are gone, we can't shift for at least five more minutes, sir."

"Shields will be down in two," Perkins barked back.

The last of the remaining yellow missile icons disappeared. All sixty vessels were disabled from the third shift and another seventy from the fourth. The Craing fleet had been nearly decimated.

"Status report, Gunny?"

"Only five warships remain from the original shift," replied Orion. "They are quickly moving to intercept."

Perkins was fidgeting again. "Shields are gone, sir. All power reserves are depleted. Weapons are down too, no power reserves; we're switching to backup power but that's barely enough to keep our environmental systems going."

"What about the fighters?"

"Maybe, but they're all requesting help from us. The Craing were waiting for them. We can shift them to the approaching vessels, but they'll encounter the same resistance."

Watching the display, Jason saw the five warships move into position. The Lilly was dead in space. They couldn't phase-shift away, and their weapons were inactive.

"They're engaging, sir, concentrated plasma fire at our drives," the XO said. Jason had no more rabbits to pull out of his hat. He wished he'd had more time with Mollie. The admiral retook his seat. He too was aware of what must be done.

"Ricket, we need to self-destruct The Lilly. Prepare for—"

"Captain!" Perkins was up on his feet. "One of the Craing warships just disintegrated."

The bridge crew looked back up towards the display.

"Status—anyone!"

Orion rechecked her console. Her confusion turned to astonishment and then she looked up. "Captain, The Surprise, The Trickster, The Last Chance, and The Gordita just cleared the solar system and are engaging the Craing warships. Seems they caught them by surprise." Plasma blasts erupted from both sides.

"Captain, our rail guns just came back online," Orion reported. "Request permission to use PQR ordnances on the Craing vessels."

Jason looked over to Orion with the hint of a smile. "The same ones that obliterated that solid granite ridge?"

"The very same, sir."

"Permission granted, Gunny."

To be continued…

Thank you for reading Scrapyard Ship. If you enjoyed this book and would like to see the series continue, please leave a review on Amazon.com.

To be notified of the soon to be released next Scrapyard Ship book (Hab 12), contact: markwaynemcginnis@gmail.com, Subject Line: Mailing List.

Acknowledgments

First of all, I'd like to thank my wife, Kim, for providing the loving and supportive space for me to write this book. There were plenty of other things that I could have—and probably should have—been working on. Both my mother (Lura Lee Genz) and sister (Lura Fischer) were instrumental in this book being published. In fact, the seeds of an idea for this book came about while having lunch with my sister, Lura, and it was her support and motivation that helped to get the ball rolling for me. Thank you to my amazing editors, Lura Lee Genz and Rachel Weaver—the many hours invested are so appreciated. I'd also like to thank Eric Sundius for his expert technical information regarding the Pentagon and the Joint Chiefs of Staff. Gratitude goes out to several best selling authors who were giving of their time and advice, including H. Paul Honsinger and B. V. Larson—both continue to be an inspiration to me. Thank you, Drusilla Tieben; your support has meant a lot to me. I'd also like to thank the many others who supported, contributed, and reviewed this book, including James Fischer and Sue Parr.

About the Author

Mark Wayne McGinnis grew up on both coasts; first, in Westchester County, New York, and then in Westlake Village, California. Currently, Mark and his wife, Kim, live near Boulder, Colorado with their two dogs, Zoey and Rika. When Mark isn't writing, he is a marketing entrepreneur and film editor.

9630544R00186

Made in the USA
San Bernardino, CA
22 March 2014